THE DÉBUTANTE'S SECRET

THE QUILTING CIRCLE SERIES

The Widow's Plight
Book One

The Daughter's Predicament
Book Two

The Damsel's Intent
Book Three

The Débutante's Secret
Book Four

THE DÉBUTANTE'S SECRET

The Quilting Circle Series

By Mary Davis

Dedication

And if one prevail against him, two shall withstand him;
and a threefold cord is not quickly broken.
Ecclesiastes 4:12

Dedicated to my aged, black Norwegian Forest cat, Buffy.

Acknowledgments

A special thanks to Miralee Ferrell for believing in this series and being a wonderful editor, and to all the staff at Mountain Brook Ink for making this series great. Thanks to Lynnette Bonner for another beautiful cover, and to Sarah Joy Freese and WordServe Literary Agency. I'm so thankful to work with each of you!

One

Central Washington State, Spring 1894

GENEVIÈVE MARSEILLE PEERED THROUGH THE GRIMY train window. This couldn't be right. This couldn't be Kamola, her destination. Though bigger than most of the frontier towns the train had passed through, it wasn't nearly as large as she had imagined or hoped. And nothing like her beloved Paris.

Several dusty cowboy-looking men mingled on the platform. Or were they outlaws? She blinked and blinked again. Was that an *Indian*? She knew the West was lawless and wild, but this was worse than she'd imagined.

An unkempt old cowboy on the platform turned to her window, smiled with dirty teeth, and winked at her.

She inhaled sharply and jerked away from the glass. Her breaths came in short gasps. She had been fortunate enough to have procured a private sleeping compartment. Scarcely enough room for one to turn around in, but better than being forced to mingle with all the other passengers. She didn't do well in crowds of strangers for long periods.

At the knock, she turned around.

Julius, a black porter, slid open the door, his salt and pepper hair preceding his broad smile. "Miss Marseille, your trunk has been deposited on the platform with your other luggage, and arrangements have been made to have them delivered to the White Hotel. Are you ready to disembark?"

Geneviève shook her head and lowered herself to the bench. "I do not think I can do this."

The kindly porter, who had been a help and comfort to her during her trip, stepped inside but only barely. He understood propriety. "Sure you can, Miss Marseille.

You've been around the world, and now you've traveled clean across this country all by yourself."

"But the people look...scary." That sounded silly, but they did. She had no experience outside of polite society, who were cultured and well educated. "I do not know how to talk to such individuals."

"They's just like you and me. You talk to me just fine. You just don't know them yet. I've traveled from one side of this country to the other many times as a train porter, and you know what I noticed?"

Geneviève shook her head. "What?"

"People is pretty much the same everywhere. And a lot of them are scared, just like you, when they get to a new place."

"You think so?"

"I know so. You come for a purpose. It'd be a shame to not see it through."

She *had* come for a purpose. To prove her brother wrong and to put an end to that charlatan woman who would try to steal any of her family's money. She drew in a deep breath and stood. "You are right, Julius. I can do this." But her insides weren't convinced yet.

"There you go, Miss Marseille. I know'd you could do it."

What would she do without this porter?

Grand-mère would have a fit at Geneviève for being so familiar with a servant. Maybe she was right, but the man had been indispensable. Everything about Geneviève's trip would have given *Grand-mère* the vapors. Traveling alone. Her destination. Her purpose in coming. But if she'd told anyone her plans or brought even a lady's maid, someone would have stopped her. Geneviève had to talk her brother out of his absurd plan.

Julius stepped out of the compartment doorway and aside in the corridor.

She retrieved her reticule and looped the drawstring handles over her gloved wrist. "I wish you could come with me."

He smiled. "You be just fine."

"*Merci beaucoup.*" She straightened her shoulders and headed toward the exit as she lifted a silent prayer, one more in a string of many throughout this trip. Rallying her courage, she descended the stairs, ignored the cold April wind nipping at her cheeks, and strode with confidence along the platform. Her progress halted abruptly.

Something had caught hold of her slipper. She glanced behind her. Her heel wedged in a knothole and wouldn't pull free. Tugging only managed to release her foot from her shoe. She hopped in a circle to view the trouble.

A ruffian in a brown leather vest and brown hat, not a gentleman's hat or attire, descended on her position. *Oh, dear.* Would she die here and now? What should she do? Run with only one shoe? Scream? Instead, she held her breath. She never should have come.

When he scooped her into his arms, a squeak escaped her. How dare this man take such liberties, and without even asking? Was he kidnapping her? Would anyone stop him? No one seemed to take notice or care. Would they if she screamed? Is this how men thought they should get a wife out in the untamed West? Well, she wasn't going without a fuss.

Before she could do or say anything, he deposited her on a wooden bench and retrieved her wayward slipper. Upon returning, he knelt in front of her and pointed toward her foot. "May I, ma'am?"

The cowboy had kind brown eyes and an engaging smile. Without thinking about proper etiquette, she poked her stockinged foot out from under her skirt.

And like Cinderella in the fairy tale, he slipped her shoe back on. It was no glass slipper and this ruffian was no Prince Charming, but still... "*Merci beaucoup, Monsieur*—I mean thank you, sir."

He tipped his hat. "My pleasure, ma'am. Deputy Montana at your service."

"Deputy?" Her gaze homed in on his tin star. "Why you are not a ruffian at all. You are in law enforcement."

He chuckled, deep and warm. "You thought me a ruffian? Much obliged."

Julius hurried over. "You all right, Miss Marseille?"

She kept her gaze on the deputy. "I will be fine, Julius. *Merci.*"

The porter nodded and returned to the train.

The deputy nodded to the porter as well, then turned back to her. "I can tell you are new in town. May I escort you to the White Hotel?"

"How do you know where I am staying?"

"Being decked out as you are, I wouldn't imagine you'd be staying in one of the less reputable establishments. That doesn't mean you aren't staying with family, friends, or acquaintances, but if you were, someone would have come to meet you at the train station. Therefore, the most obvious choice is the White Hotel. Personally, I'd choose Aunt Henny's instead."

"I do not believe it would be appropriate for me to stay with your aunt."

"She's not my aunt. She's no one's aunt. She's just Aunt Henny to everyone."

What a strange notion. "I do have a reservation at the White Hotel, and my luggage will be delivered there. I would appreciate an escort."

He poked out his elbow. "I'm at your service, Miss Marseille."

Did he expect her to take hold of him? "I appreciate your offer, but a lady does not accept a gentleman's arm whom she is not related to or acquainted with for some time. It would be highly inappropriate. People would think me a woman of loose morals."

Deputy Montana rubbed his hand across his jaw. "Why's that? I've already held you in my arms."

Geneviève sputtered. "That was not by choice. A lady does not go around holding on to any man who asks her to."

"I guess out here, those kinds of rules got dumped alongside the trail, out of necessity. You let me know what your fancy rules are, and I'll abide by them."

The man didn't seem put-off or offended or judgmental. Merely accepting. She expected such courteous behavior from well-bred men of her station but had experienced the opposite from people of a lower station. Quite refreshing.

Montana reached the end of the platform and descended the steps. He turned and held out his hand. "In case you need to steady yourself. I'll leave that to you."

He should cut this fancy lady free. She would realize soon enough he wasn't worth her time. People of her station generally didn't socialize with a lowly person like himself. But something about her made him want to walk her to the hotel. Once there, it would likely be the last he'd see of her. Something in her shocked expression when he'd scooped her into his arms. He hadn't thought at all, saw her in need and acted. He'd expected to get slapped—and hard—once he set her on the bench, but he hadn't. Then the lilting tone of her French accent had done the rest.

Might as well enjoy her company for the few minutes he had it.

She placed her gloved hand lightly on his as she glided down the steps. How did refined ladies look so graceful when taking stairs? He just tromped up and down them.

Her butterfly touch sent a warm shiver skittering to his core. Her outfit had so many parts, it was hard to tell where one thing ended and the next started. The long skirt went clear to the ground but didn't quite touch it. The shorter skirt—if that's what it was—hung over that. A jacket with sleeves so wide, she would need to turn sideways to get through a doorway. Her shirt peeked out in a wad of white ruffles. Not to mention other drapey and hanging things, tassels and fringe and such, here and there. To top it all off, a hat sat atop her blond hair at an angle that should cause it to tumble off, but it didn't, and a feather, the same color as her dress, shot out from it. Her attire should be a confusing mess, but it all worked together to frame this beauty perfectly. No sooner had her feet landed on the ground than she broke the contact.

What could he do to get her to touch him again like that? Maybe there would be a puddle or two to dodge between here and the hotel. Unfortunately, the weather had been dry as of late.

On the street side of the train station, Miss Marseille glanced about. "Do you have a conveyance here at the depot?"

"Conveyance?"

"A means of transportation."

"Just Cletus." He moseyed over to his horse.

She stroked Cletus's jowl. "He is a fine steed."

"I can boost you into the saddle if you like."

She stared wide-eyed at him. "Pardon? That is not a sidesaddle. It is wholly inappropriate for a lady."

He'd seen plenty of ladies out West riding astride. He supposed her extra fancy getup wouldn't allow for it. "The hotel's not far. I could go to the livery and get a buggy, but we could walk to the hotel quicker'n that would take."

She remained silent a moment, presumably contemplating her options. "Very well, proceed. I could do with a bit of exercise after being cramped on a train for a week."

He checked to see no wagons were barreling down the middle of the road and motioned. "It's safe to cross."

She seemed to be carefully tiptoeing to the other side.

He'd never noticed how many droppings were in the street before. Had he, he would have chosen a less troublesome place to cross. He pointed. "Careful. There's one over there."

"*Merci.*"

Montana breathed easier once on the opposite boardwalk. "What brings you to Kamola?"

"My brother is here in town."

"Then why didn't he come for you at the train station?" Montana might not be fancy bred, but he knew enough to meet a female relation. Wasn't right to leave her to find her own way.

"My visit is impromptu."

"You should have told him so he could meet you. What if some scoundrel had happened upon you?"

"Like someone lifting me off my feet on the train platform?"

"I'm a ruffian and a scoundrel now?" Though not in the true sense of the words. Bad people preyed on women alone. "Promise me you'll contact your brother right away and let him know you're in town."

"I will. He is staying at the hotel, which you said was not far."

"It's up yonder."

"Mr. Montana, your American dictionary defines *not far* differently than mine. That distance has come and gone." She waved her gloved hand in the air to emphasize her point.

One side of his mouth hitched up. "I could carry you if you're too tired." He had offered to put her atop his horse or get a buggy. Both of which she had rejected.

"I will manage." She stepped off one boardwalk and onto the next.

He did the same. "You can call me just Montana."

"No one is *just* their name. Everyone has some sort of a title."

"Most call me plain Montana. I like it that way."

"Well, you must have a title."

"Why?"

"Using one's title shows a sign of respect and honor to a person."

"Is this another one of your fancy rules?"

She gave a nod and held out one hand palm up. "So, either mister"—she held out her other hand—"or deputy."

"I'm no mister."

"Then Deputy Montana it is."

It didn't matter what she called him. Once he saw her to the hotel, she wouldn't be calling him anything. She would go her way, and he his. "Here it is." He pulled open the hotel's front door and watched to see if her voluminous sleeves touched the doorframe.

She turned slightly toward him. *"Merci."* At the same moment she spoke, her leading shoulder cleared the entrance, a shift and a step, and she was inside.

Impressive. She made the action appear natural and unintentional. He suspected it was a well-practiced maneuver in such a getup.

He followed and went with her to the desk. "Howdy, Grant. Miss Marseille would like a room."

"Hello, Montana. Marseille? I believe we have a reservation under that name." Grant shuffled a couple of papers. "Here it is. Geneviève Marseille?"

"*Oui.*"

A pretty name for a pretty lady.

"We've another guest by the name of Marseille."

"That would be my brother. Is he in his room?"

"No. He's been out all day. Would you like me to let him know you're here when he comes in?"

"*Oui.* I mean yes. Wait. Do not tell him."

Montana's hackles raised. She better not wander off alone. She needed a man seeing to her safety.

She continued. "Reserve a table for us in your dining room. Tell him he has a supper reservation with a young lady. I want to surprise him."

Montana could live with that.

"I'll see the arrangements are made." Grant spun the registry to face her. "Do you have luggage?"

"*Oui.* The train depot will be sending it along." She signed the book.

"Very good. I'll have it sent to your room straight away." Grant handed her key across the desk to an employee waiting there. "I've put you in the room next to your brother."

"Perfect." Miss Marseille faced Montana. "Thank you for your assistance. Until we meet again, *Deputy* Montana." She headed toward the staircase.

Would they meet again? Not likely. Merely something people said to make a good-bye not so final.

Montana turned to Grant behind the desk. "If for any reason she's not able to meet with her brother this evening, let me know."

"I will."

Montana shifted his gaze to the stairs again.

The lovely French lady glided up as though she were an apparition. At the landing halfway, she turned and gifted him with a smile, before continuing her ascent.

Then she disappeared.

Well...that was it. The last he'd see of her. He should head back to the sheriff's office. Instead, he stood there like a dolt.

Henny rose from the chair in the White Hotel dining room. Saul Hammond handed her modest hat to her. She pinned it atop her head. A lot of ladies left their hats on during meals eaten out, but she preferred not to. "Thank you, Saul. Luncheon was delicious. You spoil me."

He smiled. "You deserve to be spoiled. You work hard, running your boarding house."

His lingering gaze unnerved Henny. He oughtn't look at her in such a way. And she oughtn't have such flutterings in her middle in response. He was a few years older than her fifty-one years, and he made her feel special and quite young again. Nothing could come of their friendship, not that she thought Saul would ever pursue anything more.

She pulled her shawl tight around her shoulders. "Shall we go. All that work at my boarding house won't take care of itself."

"I wish we could lollygag all day, but I also have chores at home." He poked out his elbow.

Henny took his offered arm.

In the lobby, one of the town's deputies stood, staring at the empty staircase.

"Deputy Montana?"

Seemingly startled, he turned. "Huh? Oh. Howdy, Aunt Henny. Mr. Hammond."

"Good afternoon. You seem distracted. Have you followed a miscreant into the hotel?"

"What? No. No miscreant." A flush colored his neck.

Saul chuckled. "Let's leave the poor boy in peace." He guided Henny outside.

Once past the threshold, she caught a glimpse of a man dashing around the corner. Something familiar about the figure pricked at her. Could he be the same man she'd seen several times, watching her last fall? When he'd no longer appeared from time to time, she'd assumed him to be a figment of her imagination. If this were the same man, she had a lot of questions for him. Why had he watched her before? Was he watching her again? If so, why had he stopped several months ago?

"Henny? Have you heard a word I've said?"

She shifted her attention to Saul and pointed. "Did you see him?"

Saul glanced about. "Who?"

"A man. Remember how I kept seeing a man last fall?"

He nodded.

"I'd thought he could be watching Nicole and the boys, but they have all moved out to Shane Keegan's ranch now. Do you think that man could be trying to find them again?" She would rather the stranger was after her. Those children had experienced enough trouble in their lives. "I think I saw him again, just now."

Deputy Montana exited and stopped short. "Is anything wrong?"

"Yes." She turned to him. "Remember last fall when I came into the sheriff's office and told you about a man I'd seen several times?"

He nodded.

"I saw him a moment ago."

The deputy surveyed the surroundings. "Where?"

"He ducked around the corner." She pointed. "But I doubt it would do any good to go after him. Whenever I tried, he disappeared as though he never existed."

"I'll take a gander anyway and let Sheriff Rix know."

"Thank you. I'd appreciate it."

With a nod, Deputy Montana strode off to do his duty.

Saul patted Henny's hand still clutching his arm. "My son and his deputies will get to the bottom of this. The man can't hide around corners forever."

She hadn't realized she'd had such a grip on him and loosened her hold. "I feel better knowing Edric will be apprised. I don't want Nicole and her cousins to have any trouble."

"And what about you, Henny? What if he was watching *you* and not them?"

"Why would a young man have any interest in an old lady like me?"

"You are *not* an old lady, and you're quite interesting. At least to me."

The fluttering inside her danced around again. She would love to linger in the joy of the feeling but needed to get control of it—and quickly. A romance at this point in her life wasn't an option. She wished it were.

Two

Genevième trailed up the stairs behind the young man with a shock of brown hair. Once on the second floor, she willed the hotel page to hurry to her room.

He opened the door and handed over the key. "Is there anything else I can do for you?"

"No, *merci*." She gave him a tip and gripped the edge of the door as though to close it.

He held the money out on his open palm. "This isn't necessary. We don't tip in this country."

Why did so many Americans think tipping was somehow wrong? She had been taught it showed good breeding. She held out her hands as though she didn't understand and rattled off string after string of nonsensical French words to get him out of her room. She inched the door toward its frame.

Before it shut, he said, "When your luggage arrives from the train station, I'll bring it to you straight away."

"*Merci*." She smiled sweetly before the latch caught. Finally. She rushed to the balcony doors, opened them, and peered at the street below, one way and then the other, trying to catch one last glimpse of the handsome deputy. Where was he? Had she missed him?

When she had climbed the stairs, she'd paused on the landing to see how close he was to the exit to gauge the amount of time she had. She'd never been so bold. Deputy Montana had been watching her. *He* had been bold as well. How thrilling.

Finally, he appeared below. Once across the street, he turned and scanned the building. She should go inside before he caught sight of her. Or she could look elsewhere. Let him see her, but not let him know she saw him. She did neither. Transfixed on the deputy, she waited for his gaze to find her. When it did, her stomach fluttered. He smiled and tipped his hat. She gave him a nod in return. Bold, indeed.

Grand-mère would have a fit if she witnessed Geneviève's forward behavior. But *Grand- mère* wasn't here to disapprove, so Geneviève was free to do as she pleased for a change. He walked backward for a few steps then spun around to the direction he was headed. She watched the kind deputy as he strolled out of sight.

That had been something so simple, yet so pleasing. What harm had been in it? None.

She returned inside her room. Now, what? She hadn't a clue how to occupy herself without her usual needlepoint or stationery to write on. Her whole life she'd had people telling her what to do, where to go, and what to say. She couldn't recall making one decision on her own. How did one make a decision? What must one consider?

Actually, she'd made the decision to look for the handsome deputy out her hotel window. Which meant, she was capable. She'd also decided to make this trip. Or more accurately, her brother had made this decision for her by coming to this frontier town to seek out that horrible woman. He'd given Geneviève no choice but to follow him so she could talk him out of this foolishness.

She wished her trunk and cases were here so she could select a dress to wear to supper. Because she didn't plan to stay for more than a day or two, only long enough to talk her brother into returning back East, she hadn't brought a full wardrobe suitable for any and all occasions. She mentally pictured the contents of her luggage. She had an additional traveling suit, a morning dress, two afternoon dresses, a garden dress, and two evening dresses as well as the appropriate hat and accessories to go with each. She'd had to sacrifice bringing a lavish evening gown as she doubted she would have the opportunity to go to an elegant evening function with so short a trip. After seeing this town, the chances of a formal event were as plausible as the moon actually being made of cheese.

She wished Silvie, her lady's maid, were here to help her. In order to sneak out, she hadn't been able to bring

Silvie who was loyal to the ones who paid her wages. Even enlisting the help of the one stable hand had been risky.

Of her two evening dresses, she could wear the pink silk taffeta with gorgeous French lace around the bottom of the modestly puffed sleeves, beautiful detailing on the bodice, and a slight train—or her blue striped satin with fully puffed sleeves, no train, and large accent black bows from the sleeves and bodice to the waist and skirt. She loved puffed sleeves. The puffier the better. The contrast between the blue and the black was stunning, and the color brought out her eyes. It would suit for this evening.

And if she should happen to see Deputy Montana, he wouldn't be able to help but notice her.

Twenty minutes later, Deputy Montana stood in the sheriff's office by the window with a cup of coffee in hand. The supposed stranger had disappeared. Being that it was Aunt Henny, he believed she'd seen this man last fall and then again today. Anyone else, and he would wonder if the man was even real. Likely not a local, but he was crafty to avoid detection.

He let the image of Miss Marseille sashay through his thoughts. *Lord, I wouldn't mind seeing the pretty lady again.* Most wealthy people he'd met acted as though they were better than others because of their money, but not this French socialite. She seemed to have had a connection with the black porter who'd asked after her welfare on the train platform.

Beanpole strolled down the street, leading a mule pulling a two wheeled cart. A notion popped into his head. That would be perfect. *Thank You, Lord.* He dashed outside. "Hey, Bean."

The fifteen-year-old boy turned. "Yeah, Montana?" The lad's father ran the livery.

Montana trotted down the steps. "How much you charge for the use of your cart?"

Bean's eyebrows shot up. "I'm always in for earning a little money. Whatcha need?"

"To collect some luggage from the train station and deliver it to the White Hotel." Then he would get to see the pretty French lady again.

"Doesn't the train station or hotel take care of that sort of thing?"

Yes, they did, but if he was fortunate, he'd get to her baggage before the hotel collected it. "I'm doing someone a favor."

The boy turned the cart around. "Let's go."

At the train station, Bean helped Montana load a sizable trunk and three large suitcases onto the cart. "Is this luggage for two or three families?"

One would think, but as far as Montana knew, this was all for Miss Marseille. "It belongs to a fancy lady. They tend to have those dresses with all those parts that poof out all over. It's probably not so many clothes as you or I might fit in all these." But didn't ladies like her tend to change cloths more than once between sunrise and sunset? What for, he wasn't sure. He wore the same thing day after day, except Sundays when he wore his go-to-church clothes, which were pretty much a newer version of his everyday clothes. Took the thinking out of getting dressed in the morning.

"What's a person need so many clothes fer?"

"When you see a pretty lady walking down the street in one of those frilly dresses, don't you think she looks nice?"

Bean shrugged one shoulder. "I don't know. Can't go fishing in it or ride a horse or play baseball or do anything much that's fun."

"Just you wait a few years, and you'll think ladies in fancy dresses are real fine."

"I think all the clothes I'd ever own in my life until the day I die wouldn't fill half of what this lady has here."

Montana chuckled. The boy was right.

At the hotel, Bean tethered the mule to the hitching rail.

"Let's carry in the trunk first." Montana took one handle and slid the trunk to the edge of the cart. "Get the other end."

The boy grabbed the handle and hoisted it. Beanpole mirrored his name in appearance, being thin and wiry, but he held his side without visible difficulty. "You're going to let me see what this lady, who needs all these clothes, looks like, aren't you?"

"We'll see. I don't know if the hotel will allow us to go to her room. By the way, a lady doesn't *need* all these cloths to be beautiful, she'd be lovely in any old calico just as easily."

Montana pushed his back into the door, crossing over the threshold, and held it with one hand while Bean maneuvered his end of the trunk through the opening. They set it near the desk. "Bean, go fetch the other suitcases while I speak with Mr. Dawson."

Bean hurried outside.

Montana turned to the desk clerk. "Howdy, Grant."

"Howdy." Grant eyed the trunk. "Let me guess. Miss Marseille's luggage?"

"Yep. There are three more suitcases."

"We sent our porter over to the train station to gather her luggage as well as that of two other guests'."

Good thing Montana had come across Bean when he did. "We can take them to her room, being your porter is out and all."

Clunking sounds at the door garnered both men's attention. Montana and Grant rushed over to help Bean with the other three suitcases. The boy had piled them on the walk out front. Each man took one case and set them with the trunk.

Montana pointed to the stairs. "Shall Bean and I carry them up?"

"That would be helpful, but they can sit there until our porter returns."

He didn't want to abandon this mission of seeing the pretty French lady again just yet. "Why make the lady wait?"

Grant gave a knowing smile. "She's in room 23 on the second floor."

Bean gaped at the staircase. "We have to haul all this stuff up all those stairs?"

"You don't have to. I can take it myself, but I'm sure the pretty lady would appreciate your help." If the boy wanted to see her for himself, he'd have to pitch in.

Bean heaved a sigh. "All right. What shall we take first?"

"The trunk." Montana gripped one handle while Bean took the other. "You go first." That would rest most of the weight on Montana as they climbed.

Up a half of a flight on the landing, Bean paused. "If rich people had to carry their own luggage, they'd bring a lot less."

"I can take it myself if it's too much for you."

"No. I can do it." Bean put his feet back into motion.

On the second floor, Montana led the way and halted in front of room 23. He raised his hand to knock but stopped and turned to Bean. "Don't say anything embarrassing or rude."

The boy rolled his eyes. "I won't."

Montana knocked. "We've brought your luggage, Miss Marseille."

Lithe footsteps approached the door, and the barrier opened. Yep. Miss Marseille was as pretty as he remembered.

She smiled. "Oh, my. Deputy Montana."

"Yes, ma'am." He motioned toward the trunk. "Where would you like this?"

"This is unexpected." She stepped aside. "Put it over by the bureau. Could you stand it on end so it opens properly? *Merci.*"

The boy set his end down, and Montana lifted his. Most trunks he knew, laid flat and the top opened. This was some fancy trunk. He faced the lovely French lady. "Miss Marseille, this is Beanpole."

She held out her lace-gloved hand. *"Enchanté, Monsieur* Beanpole."

Bean didn't say anything.

She gave a little laugh and retrieved her hand.

Montana turned to the boy whose mouth hung open. He put the back of his hand under Bean's chin and closed his mouth. "Pardon him." There wasn't really an excuse he could give for the boy so offered none, but he understood how the lad felt. She was definitely something to behold. "We'll go fetch your other bags and be right back." He gripped a wad of shirt material at Bean's shoulder and led the boy out.

Once at the top of the stairs, he released the lad. "I'd ask what got into you, but I know. A pretty lady will make a fellow stupid every time."

Bean finally found his voice. "I never seen anyone like her before."

Montana understood. "Don't be thinking all there is to a lady is what's on the outside. What counts is what's inside, deep down."

"So, you think Miss Marseille is good deep down?"

"I couldn't say one way or another. I don't know the lady well enough to make that call." But he hoped so.

"She must be. She looks like an angel."

In the lobby once again, Montana hoisted the two largest cases, leaving the other large case and the carpet bag for Bean.

At room 23 once more, the door stood open. "Here is the rest of your luggage. Where would you like them?"

"Put that one on the luggage stand, that one on the bench at the end of the bed, and the last one and the carpet bag on the bed."

Montana and Bean did as instructed.

"*Merci*, Deputy Montana. *Merci, Monsieur* Beanpole."

The boy found his voice this time, sort of. "Huh?"

Her tittering laugh tickled Montana's insides.

"I said thank you, Mr. Beanpole."

"Oh. You're welcome, miss! Any time."

She handed them each a tip.

"Golly. Thanks!" Bean said.

Montana extended his hand. "I can't accept this. I was merely doing my duty."

"I'm sure delivering luggage is not in your list of deputy duties."

It wasn't, but he'd *wanted* to deliver her luggage. "I wouldn't feel right." He set the money on top of her upended trunk.

Bean glanced between Montana and Miss Marseille. "Do I have to give mine back too?"

Miss Marseille spoke quickly. "No. You keep it. You worked hard for that."

Montana wouldn't argue with the lady nor tell her he'd already paid the boy. "We'll let you be. Have a fine day." He tipped his hat and backed toward the door.

"Deputy Montana, I have need of a lady's maid. Can you recommend someone?"

Montana rubbed his chin. "What does a lady's maid do?"

"Helps me with things. Unpacking, my wardrobe, and the sort. I'll only need her for a couple of days."

"Hmm. I'm not sure. I think I know who to ask." He closed the door as he left.

He sent Bean on his way, hurried over to Aunt Henny's, leapt onto the porch, and knocked.

Aunt Henny opened the door. "Deputy Montana, I wasn't expecting you. Did you locate that man?"

He scoured his brain. Yeah, that's right, the man she'd seen. "No, ma'am, but I'll keep looking. We'll find him."

"Then what can I do for you?"

"I need a lady's maid."

The older woman's eyes widened. "You what?"

"Oh, no. Not for me. A French lady came to town and needs one. She's staying at the hotel. I figured you might know who to ask."

"Why don't you ask your sister?"

His twin sister had come to live with him a little over two weeks ago because of some trouble at home. "She doesn't know anything about being a lady's maid. This French lady is real fancy."

"Felicity is a smart young woman. She will learn quickly what needs to be done. I'm sure she would appreciate the opportunity to earn a little money."

"But who will cook for me?"

Aunt Henny gave him a withering stare. "What did you do before she came?"

"Ah, Aunt Henny. I don't like cooking. I'll have to start eating at the hotel and the cafés in town most nights again. That gets expensive." On the favorable side, he might see Miss Marseille there.

"How long is the woman going to be in town?"

"A couple of days."

"I think you'll survive that long." As usual, Aunt Henny was right.

Montana headed to his cabin and walked inside. "Felicity?"

No answer.

Where could his sister be? Hopefully not getting into more trouble.

He headed to the barn. It wasn't much of a structure. More like an overgrown shed, big enough to house his horse and some hay for the winter. "Felicity, you in here?"

She stepped out of the single horse stall. "Right here. What are you doing home this time of day?"

"There's a visitor in town who needs a lady's maid."

His twin stared at him. "So?"

"Aunt Henny thought you might be able to do it for a little money."

"What do I know about being a hoity-toity lady's maid? Those kind of people with *lady's maids* look down on people like us."

"Aunt Henny thinks you could do it, and the woman will only be in town for a couple of days."

She drew in a deep breath and released it. "All right. I'll give it a try. But if she says mean and rude things about people like us, I won't be polite back."

"Thank you. I think you should wear your church dress."

Felicity rolled her eyes and planted her fists on her hips. "I do know better than to wear work-around-the-cabin clothes."

With his sister helping Miss Marseille, he might have a chance to see the French lady occasionally.

Three

Geneviève had all her suitcases open as well as her trunk. If the deputy was unable to find her a suitable lady's maid, she might have to remain in her traveling suit to go to supper, a grievous social faux pas. She should have brought Silvie, her own maid, but she'd feared if any of the staff knew what she had been planning, they would stop her.

Could she get the blue dress on without help?

At the knock on the door, she startled, then opened it. Her insides twirled at seeing the handsome deputy. "Deputy Montana. I am so glad you have returned."

"Me too." He stared for a moment.

The young woman with him stuck out her hand. "I'm his sister Felicity." Her simple peach calico dress fit her well enough, and her braided hair hung down her back.

Geneviève held out her hand. "*Enchanté*, Miss Montana."

"Oh, our last name isn't Montana. It's Gladwell."

Geneviève shifted her gaze from the sister to the brother. "Montana is your given name?"

"No. Not really. People just call me Montana."

"I see. I should call you *Monsieur* Gladwell."

The deputy sighed. "Please don't. I thought we agreed upon Deputy Montana."

For some reason he didn't care for his last name and had changed his first name. Why? Maybe she could get the answer out of the sister. "*Mademoiselle* Gladwell, you are a lady's maid, yes?"

"No, but I'm a fast learner if you tell me what I need to do."

Not ideal but workable. Better than dressing herself. "I can do that."

"And please call me Felicity."

Geneviève tilted her head. "Why do you Americans have issue with the use of your surname?" The young woman's brother had the same proclivity.

"It sounds too pretentious. If you can't call me Felicity, then the deal is off."

Stubborn as well. "Let us see how you carry out the tasks tonight and decide from there."

Felicity turned to Deputy Montana. "Brother dear, I'm sure you are needed at work. I'll see you later."

"When should I return to take you home?"

Both brother and sister looked to Geneviève.

"Let's say nine o'clock."

Felicity pushed her brother toward the door. "I'll meet you in the lobby at nine."

The deputy left.

This arrangement with his sister helping would likely afford Geneviève the opportunity to see the handsome deputy. Maybe.

She spun around. "Your main job will be to help me get dressed and undressed. I am dining with my brother this evening, and I will be wearing the blue gown."

Felicity fingered the dress. "Oh my, that's beautiful."

"*Merci.* Anything you do not know, ask. I can explain it to you. I would rather you ask than do it incorrectly."

"I'm here to help you and to learn."

"*Magnifiqué.*" Geneviève crossed to the bed. "First, I need my clothes moved from the traveling cases to the bureau and the dresses and suits need to be hung up."

"I can do that." Felicity got busy.

"I am fatigued from my trip. I am going to lie down for a little while." Geneviève stretched out on the bed and closed her eyes. "Rouse me in thirty minutes."

"I will."

It would be nice having a lady's maid who wasn't really a lady's maid. This young woman wouldn't be judging her every move and scolding her for doing something a little wrong. She likely wouldn't even know if Geneviève did something socially inappropriate. Not a slight faux pas nor a major one.

Geneviève felt less than invigorated after her rest. She would have preferred to have slept until morning, but that would never do. She needed to meet Pierre for supper. If it went well, she could be on a train returning to Virginia tomorrow or the next day. Felicity had done a fine job of unpacking—and had done it quietly. This girl would work out fine.

She indicated the blue dress. "I will be wearing that one to supper."

Felicity helped her into it and fastened it in the back. "This is a beautiful dress."

Geneviève studied herself in the floor mirror. "Beautiful, *oui*, but is it appropriate for a critical supper with my brother? I have an important issue to discuss with him. I think the puffy sleeves might be too much." But she loved that the blue dress brought out the color of her eyes. She had not thought out her wardrobe choices well enough. Her lady's maid at home had always managed to have the perfect clothes for every occasion. Silvie would have known better what to pack for such a trip. What else had Geneviève erroneously brought along? She needed Pierre to take her seriously.

Felicity fingered Geneviève's other traveling suit. "This looks as though it would be good for a serious conversation."

The girl knew nothing about fashion. "Possibly, but since this is an evening affair, it would not be appropriate." Geneviève wished Silvie were here. She would know which to choose. "The pink one with the lace and train is my other option."

"My, that's beautiful too."

"Hold it up for me."

Felicity did.

"Bring it over here to the mirror."

Felicity did and stood next to her so both dresses reflected in the looking glass. After a moment, she slid the pink dress in front of Geneviève so it appeared as though she might be wearing it, though the blue sleeves puffed out beyond it. She moved it away and then in front of Geneviève again. Silvie would not have done that. She would have known which dress to wear from the start. No discussion needed. She'd never realized how important of a role her maid had played. "I think the pink one might be better."

Geneviève shifted her gaze from one dress to the other. "But the blue brings out my eyes."

"True, but your brother probably doesn't care about the color of your eyes and has seen them your whole life. The pink, though elegant and feminine, says 'I'm worth listening to'."

A smile tugged at Geneviève's mouth. "I believe you are right." The girl had an eye. "Help me change."

Once in the pink dress, she sat at the vanity. "Can you do my hair?"

"Do? You mean brush it?"

"Fashion it into an appropriate upsweep for evening."

Felicity stared for a moment. "It looks pretty the way it is."

Maybe so, but this evening required a different style. "The hair is pulled to the back of my head. It needs to be more up." She touched her crown. "With curls hanging down."

"I can try."

Geneviève coached the girl through the process. She hadn't realized how much she had taken in over the years of watching Silvie tending to her hair. The girl did fine. Not as good as Silvie, but who in this frontier town would know the difference? She felt positively scandalous.

Geneviève mentally prepared herself for her encounter with her brother. "Felicity, would you go down to the front desk and ask the gentleman there if Pierre Marseille is in the dining room? If not, wait until he is seated in there then come inform me. I want to arrive after him."

"Why is that?"

"A lady should never be left waiting. One waits for a lady."

Felicity scrunched her eyebrows. "But you will be waiting here. Isn't that the same?"

"You are perceptive. *He* will not know I was waiting."

Felicity shrugged. "I'll be back in a moment." She left.

Geneviève liked having the girl around. Refreshing.

Felicity returned shortly. "Grant, at the front desk, said he's seated in the dining room. Said he's been there for ten minutes. Apparently anxious to find out the identity of the mystery lady who invited him to supper."

"Thank you. I will head down." She opened the door and hesitated. "You did a fine job of putting my things away. Would you please make some small changes? You would have no way to know this, but in the bureau, I prefer to have the articles of clothing arranged from top to bottom as they would be on the body. Chemises in the top drawer, then corsets, slips laid flat—not folded—and pantaloons in the bottom." *Was* it the way she preferred? Or the way Silvie had always arranged things? "I will return in plenty of time for you to help me change and meet your brother in the lobby around nine." She stepped into the hall and closed the door behind her.

She placed her hand on her stomach before continuing. How would Pierre react to her presence? He could either be pleased to see her or furious she'd traveled all this way alone. If this weren't so important, she would not meet with him. Instead, she would head straight to the train station and leave. She drew in a slow breath and continued on her way.

She stopped at the front desk. "Mr. Dawson, is it not?"

"Yes, ma'am. What can I do for you?"

"My lady's maid is upstairs. Would you see to it a supper tray is sent to her?"

"I can do that. What would you have me to order for her?" He pulled out a pad of paper and poised a pencil over it. "We have steak, baked chicken, and pork roast this evening."

"Steak isn't straightforward as people prefer theirs prepared different ways. Would you see she receives a portion of both chicken and pork so she has a choice? And charge it to my room, number 23. *Merci*." She could delay no longer and headed toward the dining rom.

Pierre noticed her the moment she stepped into the doorway. He had almost appeared nervous until he saw her. "Vivi! I can't believe you came." He stood.

Geneviève loved her brother's nickname for her. She spoke in French. "You are the only one who calls me Vivi. I love it." She greeted her brother with a kiss near one cheek then the other and again to the first.

He spoke in French as well. "Where is *Grand-mère*?" He glanced about.

"Probably on her way back from Boston by now."

"She let you come alone?" He held out her chair.

"Let?" She sat. "She'll find out soon enough."

He retook his seat. "You left without her permission? Does *Grand-père* know?"

"They never would have approved this trip. It's not as though *you* asked for their blessing to come. Besides *Grand-mère* is the one who deals with me most."

"But I am a man."

"And I am a grown woman." But her speech was all bluster. She had been terrified the whole trip and now took comfort in having her brother close. He had always looked out for her.

The waitress stopped at their table. "What would you like to eat?"

Geneviève spoke in English before Pierre did. "I will have the pork roast."

"You haven't even read the menu." Pierre picked up the paper in front of him.

"I inquired at the front desk on my way down."

He shifted his gaze to the waitress. "I'll have a steak, medium-well done."

The waitress collected their menus and left.

Pierre leaned forward and resumed in French. "I take it you are staying at this hotel."

Not as though she'd had much choice. "I understand this is the most reputable place in town. I am next to you in room 23."

"Splendid, but there are a few other nice places, a couple of worthwhile boarding houses, and a Mr. Atwood is building a hotel. The town is big enough to need a second one. I'm thinking of investing."

"Investing?" This couldn't be good. So far, her brother seemed pleased she was here. Would it last? "I will not beat on one side of the bush and then the other. I have come to take you home."

Pierre chuckled. "Why else would you have come?"

"This idea of yours is ridiculous."

"It is not. I found a woman I think is related to Anne Henderson. She might be her sister, which would make her our aunt."

"Now you are talking foolish. Even if what you say is true, it doesn't matter. She will only incite trouble for us. She will try to take *Père's* money. You cannot trust anything she says."

He placed his hand on hers. "She won't. Even if she tried, I wouldn't let her."

"Please stop this and come home."

"I cannot. You know I am teaching at the Washington State Normal School."

"You are too good to be a professor. You could quit. You do not need the money." She knew her argument was weak, but she didn't know what else to say to change his mind.

"Not yet. I need to learn all I can. *Père* said to find Anne Henderson. I think this woman might know her."

"You are a fool, *frère.*"

"I'm merely a son trying to find out as much about my late mother as possible. Don't you want to know too?"

"No." Their mother had abandoned them and died. What more did she need to know? "You are stubborn like *Grand-mère.*"

He smiled and patted her hand. "*Merci* for coming. It's good to have you here."

"And you are soft-hearted like *Père.*" She would not capitulate. She could be stubborn too. This woman would be nothing but trouble. Geneviève could feel it to her core.

Deputy Cord slapped Montana on the back. "Let's go have a late supper at the White Hotel before you're off duty and the town becomes my responsibility. And before the saloon hooligans get rowdy."

A part of Montana leapt to agree to the idea, but another part cautioned him. What if Miss Marseille thought he was following her? "Supper sounds good. Are you sure you want to eat at the hotel?"

"I have a hankering for one of their steaks. Thick and juicy."

Montana needed to be there at the end of the day anyway to take his sister home, so he went.

Though most of the supper crowd had gone, the pretty French lady remained. She'd changed into a dress with smaller sleeve tops, allowing her easier access through doorways. So that was one of the things to come out of the trunk and suitcases they had hauled up the stairs.

He didn't recognize the gentleman she sat with. But why should he? He'd never met her brother. As he passed her table, he tipped his hat. "Miss Marseille." As he continued on, he heard, "Why is a deputy greeting you?"

Though too far away to hear her answer, he knew the tale. He sat across from Cord.

Cord leaned forward and batted his eyes. *"Miss Marseille."*

Montana grumbled. "Stop it."

"She's a pretty little thing. New in town?"

"Yes. I helped her find the hotel when she got off the train this afternoon."

"And?"

"And what?"

"There's more to this story."

The waitress approached. "Two steaks?" She pointed her pencil at each of them. "One rare and one medium?"

Cord smiled at her. "Are we that predictable, Doris?"

"You are two single men with heathy appetites."

Montana didn't feel like steak. "I'll have the pork roast." He noticed the same on Miss Marseille's plate. There had still been a portion on her plate. It would make him almost feel as though he were eating with her.

"Got it. One pork roast and one steak, rare." She left.

Cord pinned him with a stare. "You helped her find the hotel and then what?"

"Nothing."

"That's not what Beanpole was bragging about."

The kid had a big mouth.

"Bean and I collected her luggage from the train station and delivered it to the hotel." He might as well tell him the rest. He'd likely hear about it before morning anyway. At the very least, Cord would wonder why Montana hung around the hotel after they finished supper. Cord would assume it would be to see Miss Marseille. It wasn't. He needed to wait for his sister. If Miss Marseille happened to stroll by, so be it. "She needed a lady's maid, so I brought Felicity."

Cord smiled wide. "Too bad you'll probably run into the pretty lady, with your sister helping her. You are a sly one."

That was the hope. "Aunt Henny suggested Felicity."

"You didn't have to take her up on it." Cord leaned forward. "Remind me what experience your sister has being a fancy lady's maid."

This was destined to be a very long meal.

After supper and far more ribbing from Cord, Montana sat in the hotel lobby, waiting for his sister.

Shortly after Miss Marseille and her brother went upstairs, Mr. Marseille came down again.

Montana stood when the man stopped in front of him.

"Are you waiting in hopes my sister will come to the lobby?"

Not exactly, but Montana wouldn't mind if he saw her. "No. I'm waiting for *my* sister."

Mr. Marseille studied him a moment. "What is your business with my sister?"

"Nothing. I merely helped her find the hotel."

"And now you have your sister watching her."

"What? No. Miss Marseille asked for a lady's maid."

"And you figured yours could let you know the whereabouts of mine?"

"No. Aunt Henny said she might be able to do the job."

The man's expression and stance changed. "*Your* aunt knows about lady's maids?"

"Well—yeah—no—I don't know. She suggested Felicity. There aren't really many lady's maids in town. Any that are here are already employed by the wealthy."

Mr. Marseille continued to study Montana. "Tell me about your aunt."

Montana hadn't expected a question that wasn't in regard to his sister. "She's not *my* aunt. Not really anyone's aunt. She's sort of an aunt to everyone."

"Where did she come from?"

Montana shrugged. "Don't know."

"Hmm. I'll speak to my sister and determine if this arrangement will continue."

"I would expect nothing less." Montana didn't like this man's scrutiny but understood. "I would do the same for my sister."

"Very well." Mr. Marseille left, returning from where he'd come.

At half past nine, Felicity strolled down the stairs. "Thank you for waiting. Miss Marseille said to apologize for keeping me late."

"That's all right." The possibility of seeing the pretty French lady made any inconvenience worth it. And having her brother not outright send him away was a good sign. "Let's get home." Out front, he swung up into the saddle and helped his twin onto the back of his horse. "Come on, boy. Let's go home."

Cletus nickered, and Felicity rested her hands on Montana's waist.

He wouldn't mind if it were a beautiful French lady sitting behind him. "How did you like working for Miss Marseille?"

"She was nice. Real nice. She wants me here at seven in the morning."

"So, what exactly does a lady's maid do?"

"I unpacked her clothes and helped her dress and the like. She has particular ways she wants things done but was kind about how she told me to fix things. Did you know that rich people have different clothes and hair styles for different times of day? One can't wear a morning dress for afternoon tea, and a traveling suit isn't fitting to wear to supper."

He was glad she was nice. "Did she pay you for today? Or is she going to pay you at the end of your service?"

"She gave me three dollars!"

"Is that for several days?"

"No, only for today. She said if I could be available—at her beck and call, as she put it—all day tomorrow and each day she's here, she'll pay me five dollars a day."

Generous of her.

He liked the pretty French lady better and better, and with his sister working for her, he would likely get to see her from time to time. That was if her brother allowed this arrangement to continue. Montana chose to believe the man to be reasonable. A woman like Miss Marseille couldn't be without a lady's maid.

Yep, this arrangement would work out fine, very fine.

Four

THE NEXT MORNING, HENNY SAT WRAPPED in a quilt on her porch in one of her four rocking chairs. She moved the chair back and forth in stilted motions. It would be soothing if she weren't so agitated.

Saul Hammond sauntered through her gate and along her walk. "What are you doing out here? It may be April but it's chilly today."

Clouds hung heavy in the sky, and the dampness in the air made the cold go clear through a person.

"I'm waiting."

"For what?" Saul cocked an eyebrow.

"That man to show himself. This time I'll be ready for him." No one else had seen him except for his disappearing form around a corner, which could be anyone. People were beginning to think her daft and that she was imagining things. She wondered as well.

"What makes you think he'll come today?"

"It's only a matter of time. He's been here more than any other place. I'm sure he'll return, and I'm going to catch him."

Saul held out his hand and helped her to her feet. "It's too cold to be sitting out here. You'll get sick. Come."

The chill had begun to seep into her joints and make the leg she'd broken last summer ache, so Saul didn't have to waste a lot of breath to convince her. She allowed him to usher her inside.

"Sit here." He led her into the parlor. "I'll make you a cup of hot tea."

"I'm not an invalid, Saul."

"I know." He covered her with the afghan from the back of the settee. "But you are going to sit there without arguing and let me get you something hot to drink."

Henny huffed. "The coffee is still on the stove."

Saul smiled triumphantly and strode across the room.

"I prefer mine with sugar and milk, which I have. It's in the cold pantry." Henny pushed aside the curtain and peered out the window. Where was he? The one time she was prepared and had a witness close at hand, and the stranger didn't show up.

Saul returned with two mugs of coffee held by their handles in one hand and her small, china milk and sugar set palmed in his other. He set the cups on the serving table, causing the spoons in them to clank. "One lump or two?"

"Two and a generous splash of milk."

While he prepared her coffee, she peeked out the window again.

"Anyone out there?"

Henny heaved a sigh. "No." She took the offered cup. "I know you and everyone else wonder if I'm touched in the head. I'm beginning to wonder myself."

"If you believe you've seen this man, then I believe you."

Not actually comforting. "You believe that *I believe* I've seen him, but you don't necessarily believe he truly exists. I can't say I blame you. If I were someone else hearing my story of a mysterious disappearing man whom no one had seen, I'd wonder if I was hallucinating."

"I, for one, sincerely hope you do see him again so I can get a good look at him, and ask him what he wants. Maybe I should come over more often. We could drive around town and see if we can find him."

Now that *was* comforting. Saul was a dear. If the stranger would only make an appearance so her friend could see she didn't need to be committed to an asylum.

The same day, Geneviève sat in her brother's office at the normal school in town, visions of the handsome deputy dancing in her head. No good could come from thinking of him so much. To distract herself, she stood and perused the small, sparse office. Nothing in this room fit Pierre's personality.

Though she knew he had classes to teach, she never pictured him in the classroom but rather in his office. He'd taken a job as a visiting professor. The normal school had been short-handed since one of their professors had quit suddenly last fall and left town in a hurry. Apparently, whispers of scandal followed him.

Geneviève had come to talk some sense into her brother, but now found herself in an empty office. She had given Felicity the morning off while she visited with Pierre. She shouldn't have turned her new lady's maid loose so quickly, not. She hadn't considered the ramifications of her actions. *Grand-mère* never would have made this kind of error.

Strolling out to the receptionist, she engaged a young man in his early twenties. "I released my carriage with my lady's maid. I wish to leave now. How would I send for a Hansom Cab?"

"Handsome?"

"A carriage for hire to take one places."

"We don't have anything like that here in Kamola. There are a few industrious fellows who park along the street to take the professors, deans, important people, and such to places they need to go."

"Perfect. Where would I find one of these industrious fellows?"

"Go down the long hall to the right, all the way to the end, and out those doors. If there are any available, they will be waiting on the street there."

"*Merci.* I would like to leave a message for Professor Marseille."

The man handed her paper and pen. She wrote her note, folded it, and handed it to him. "You will see he gets this the minute he returns to his office."

"Yes, ma'am. I'll put it in his message slot so he'll see it as soon as he returns." He slipped it into a niche behind him.

"*Merci.*" Geneviève strolled out of the building as the man had instructed. A single small carriage stood waiting. Was this one of the industrious fellows? She glided over to it. Though the young man standing next to it wasn't wearing a uniform nor a suit, he appeared clean. *"Excusez-moi.* Is your carriage for hire?"

The driver stepped forward, snapping to attention. "Yes, ma'am. I can take you anywhere you need to go. If you have money."

"Of course. Please take me to the White Hotel."

He opened the door and held out his hand to assist her.

After stepping in, Geneviève sat, and soon the carriage was on its way. Down the road, she glanced through the window and saw Deputy Montana outside the sheriff's office. A thrill went through her at the sight of him. She was in the west now and could apparently do as she pleased. Her attraction to Deputy Montana was overriding her good breeding, which would never allow her to stop at a man's work who wasn't her intended. Battling her upbringing, she knocked on the roof of the cab. "Please stop."

The carriage came to a halt. "Is anything wrong?"

"No. Please pull over to the sheriff's office." She would never be able to act on this impulse at home. It made her a little giddy. This freedom was fun.

After pulling the carriage to the side of the street, the driver climbed down and opened the carriage door for her.

Deputy Montana's eyes widened, and he rushed over. "Miss Marseille, it's good to see you."

Now, she had two gentlemen offering her assistance. To not offend either, she put one gloved hand in each of theirs. *"Merci. Merci."*

The driver released her first.

The deputy didn't relinquish her hand. "What brings you here?"

Oh, dear. She couldn't say the real reason—him. "I wanted to let you know your sister is doing a fine job as my lady's maid."

"I'm glad to hear..." He opened his mouth as though to say more.

But a man came out of the building and clapped him on the shoulder. "Who's your lady friend?"

Deputy Montana backhanded the new arrival in the chest. "Behave."

"Always." He doffed his hat. "Deputy Sammy Beckwith at your service."

"Sammy, meet Miss Marseille."

"*Enchanté.*" Geneviève dipped her head. "Pleased to make your acquaintance."

"The pleasure is all mine." Deputy Beckwith elbowed Deputy Montana. "She's easy on the eyes and exotic to boot. No wonder you're always making excuses to get over to the hotel."

Deputy Montana clenched his jaw and the muscle there twitched. "Don't you have some place to be? Work you need to do?"

"I do." Deputy Beckwith bowed. "I hope we meet again." He replaced his hat and sauntered away, whistling.

Deputy Montana cocked his thumb in the direction of the retreating man. "I'm sorry about him."

"Are all men out West so brazen? Or merely the deputies?"

He tilted his head as if to say, *Touché.* "I'm afraid we haven't made a very favorable impression on you."

Had Deputy Montana not been present, the other deputy's forwardness would have frightened her. She wasn't used to directly relating to people without *Grand-mère* as a buffer. Only certain people got by her. Approved people. How would Geneviève know whom she could trust? She trusted *this* deputy. "*Some* people have made a better impression than others."

"Some?" He quirked an eyebrow.

He had certainly made an impression.

"*Oui.* When I stepped off the train and found myself in distress, a kind gentleman helped me."

He half smiled. "As I recall, you had a horrified expression as though you thought I might carry you off and called me a ruffian."

"*Moi?*" She touched her fingertips to her upper chest. That had been exactly what she'd thought. "I seem to recall you *did* carry me off."

"Only to the bench so you didn't topple over, balancing on one foot."

She very well may have toppled without his quick thinking. "It all turned out well. I much appreciated your assistance."

"Say, tomorrow is my day off." He hesitated, slipping his hands into his back pockets. "Maybe I could show you around town or something, unless you have plans with your brother."

The idea of spending time with him appealed to her more than she would have imagined. More than she should allow. "My brother will be busy most of the day at the normal school. He is a visiting professor. What did you have planned for your day off?"

"I was gonna go fishing, but I'd rather spend time with you, if you'll let me."

"I do not wish to spoil your plans. Take me fishing."

He rubbed the nape of his neck and appeared a little out of sorts. "You want to go fishing?"

"*Oui.*"

"You ever been fishing before?"

"I have." *Grand-père* had chartered a fishing boat for a day trip.

"Well, I guess if you want to. I normally leave at dawn, but I could leave a little later if that would suit you better."

She hid a smile. He hadn't expected her to agree to go. She had caught him off guard. Good. Best to keep a man guessing. "I will make sure I get plenty of rest. I will let Felicity know to come early to help me dress."

"Is there some kind of etiquette about us being off alone? Would that be bad?" He hurried on. "Nothing would happen between us. I promise."

She thrilled at making her own plans for a clandestine rendezvous. "You are correct. It would not be right. Felicity will come and be our chaperone."

"Then I'll see you tomorrow."

"Until tomorrow. I must go now." Geneviève returned to her hired carriage with a lightness she hadn't known before.

The driver helped her in and drove her to the hotel.

She paid the man handsomely for waiting so patiently while she spoke with Deputy Montana.

Inside, Felicity sat in a lobby chair. She stood upon seeing Geneviève. "I came early in case you needed me."

"It is providence. Let us go to my room. I need you to tell me what to wear tomorrow." Geneviève continued to the staircase and headed up without checking to see if her lady's maid was in pursuit. She would be. By the time she reached her room, Felicity was at her side.

"I don't know if I'm qualified to help you make the right choice. I don't exactly understand the need to wear different clothes for different times of day."

"You are the only person who can help me. I am going fishing with Deputy Montana tomorrow. Should I wear my morning dress or my walking suit?" Geneviève pointed to each. "Which would be appropriate?"

Felicity scrunched her face. "Fishing? With my brother?"

"*Oui.* You will come as chaperone."

The girl stood with her lips parted.

"Since we are leaving so early, I could wear my blue morning dress. What do you think would be best?"

"No. None of them." Though Felicity shook her head, the motion seemed to be more out of confusion. "Have you ever been fishing?"

"My *grand-père* rented a fishing boat for a day trip when I was seventeen."

Her lady's maid squinted. "How many fish did you catch?"

"I did not catch any. The men did the fishing."

She raised her eyebrows as though understanding something. "What did you do while they fished?"

"*Grand-mère* and I sat below deck, had tea, and played dominos."

Felicity closed her eyes and shook her head again. "I'll tell my brother you changed your mind and won't be going with him."

"Why would you do that?"

"Taking a boat trip and drinking tea is nothing like fishing in a lake or stream. You have to bait your own hook and clean the fish you catch."

"I am ready to learn." This was something her grandparents would not approve of for her, so Geneviève must do it while she had the chance. "First, I need to know what to wear."

Felicity waved her hand toward Geneviève's wardrobe. "You have *nothing* that would work. All your clothes are too nice."

"So, what do I need? Something similar to what you are wearing?"

The young woman smoothed her hands down her skirt, frowning. "No. This is even too nice. This is my church dress. I figured my regular everyday work clothes wouldn't be good enough for this position with you."

True. Geneviève's normal lady's maid did have finer clothes. "Pardon. I did not mean to insult your wardrobe."

"You didn't. Not really. I know my clothes are practical, and I like them that way."

That had been kind of Felicity.

She held out her arms. "So, I need to get an outfit suitable for fishing. Where do I get one?"

"You want to buy something today?" Felicity's eyes widened.

"*Oui.* We are going tomorrow, so it must be today."

Her lady's maid stared at her a moment. "Well...there are a few places. Waldon's Mercantile would have a few readymade items. Carole makes and sells clothes from her home. She has a few garments already constructed. And Celeste Dumont's dressmaker shop, but I think hers will all be too nice. Like what you already have."

"Her name sounds French."

"It is."

"I want to go to her shop, but perhaps not today. Let us go to the other two places you mentioned." Geneviève headed out the door. At the front desk, she spoke to the clerk. "Mr. Dawson, would it be possible for you to send for a hired carriage for us?" She knew better than to ask for a Hansom Cab again.

"I can. When do you want it?"

"Right now."

"Oh. It will take a bit. If you want to wait in your room, I'll send word when it arrives."

Felicity inclined her head. "We could wait in the dining room and eat. Unless you don't plan to eat dinner."

"This is a good idea." Geneviève turned from her lady's maid to the clerk. "We will be in the dining room." She had never eaten a meal with Silvie, but this was the west and she felt Felicity was also her friend. Or at least becoming one.

After eating, she sat in the carriage with Felicity who gave directions to the driver to the mercantile. Geneviève paid him to wait for them.

Inside the establishment, Felicity greeted the clerk with a wave and guided Geneviève to a small selection of clothing. "So, these are mostly skirts and blouses. Here is a lovely yellow dress that might fit you." She stood behind the mannequin and held out the skirt portion.

Geneviève could tell her lady's maid favored the dress. She fluttered her hand near her face. "Yellow washes out my complexion."

The female clerk came over. "Hello, Felicity."

"Hello, Franny. This is Miss Marseille. She needs something to go *fishing* in."

The shop girl raised her eyebrows. "Welcome."

"*Enchanté.*"

The young woman stared at her.

"*Excusez-moi.* Pleased to meet you."

"You're French, aren't you?"

"I am."

"I can tell by the way you're dressed that our clothes probably won't be to your liking."

"The problem *is* the way I am dressed. Felicity tells me this is not good for fishing."

"She's right, but... Fishing?"

"*Oui.* Do you have something suitable?"

"For ladies, we only have skirts and blouses and the one yellow dress Felicity already showed you. We have skirts in black, brown, navy, and hunter. We have white blouses, beige, light blue, and light green, to go with the skirts."

"I will see the blue ones."

The clerk removed a navy skirt and held a blue blouse above it. "This would suit your eye color nicely."

The skirt was a solid color with no adornments whatsoever. The blouse, as well, had little to catch the eye, or a gentleman's attention, except pin tucks down the front. "It is so plain."

Franny returned the blouse to the rack and held out a blue floral print.

Better. "Maybe. Do you have any skirts with more to them?"

The young lady set the blue outfit aside but didn't return it to the rack and removed a brown and black plaid skirt with a beige blouse. "I'm afraid we don't have a great selection. The yellow calico dress is about as decorative as we have."

"I will take this skirt and floral blouse for myself and the yellow dress, as well as a hunter green skirt and green blouse for my lady's maid."

"Your what?"

Felicity pointed to herself. "I'm her lady's maid while she's in town." She shifted her attention to Geneviève. "You don't have to buy me clothes."

"As my lady's maid, it will be your uniform of sorts." At home, her maids all dressed in black skirts with white blouses, but she thought Felicity would prefer the green, and *Grand-mère* wasn't here to disapprove.

Franny wrapped everything in brown paper, and Geneviève was surprised at how little they cost.

In the carriage once again, Geneviève said, "Now we shall go to the house you mentioned with the dressmaker shop."

"Why? You already bought something."

"I do not know if I want to wear that."

"Then why did you buy it?"

"In case I do not find anything else." And if she were to have the opportunity to spend time with the deputy again, she would be prepared. When the time came for her to leave, she would give all the clothes to Felicity, as *Grand-mère* would only have Silvie toss them out at home.

Carole's Creations dressmaker shop was indeed housed in someone's residence, painted in sunshine yellow with robin's egg blue trim. Carole had more style options to choose from.

A royal blue gingham dress called to Geneviève. "I like this one." The color would bring out her eyes.

Carole smiled "Excellent choice."

Felicity shook her head. "It's taffeta. You don't want to wear that fishing."

The shopkeeper's eyes widened. "You're going fishing?"

"I am. I like this one." It was so different from what she normally wore. "I will take it." She perused several more and bought a blue and green calico dress in a Felicity-approved cotton. She also bought a two-toned green striped blouse for Felicity as an alternate to the plain one to go with her skirt.

This had been fun shopping with a friend—even if the young woman was her employee. She felt more like a friend.

Now she would be ready for most anything. Even fishing with a handsome deputy.

In the day's waning light, Montana stood on the White Hotel's boardwalk, leaning against a post. He would have waited inside for his sister if he thought there was any chance of catching a final glimpse of the pretty French lady. Since he wouldn't, he preferred the fresh air. The evening was cooling off nicely. Soon the nights would become too warm to sleep well.

Finally, Felicity exited with three parcels wrapped in brown-paper in her arms. She extended them toward him.

He automatically took them. "What are all these?"

She indicated the bottom package. "This one has a skirt and blouse." She touched the middle one. "A second blouse to go with the skirt." Her hand ran slowly across the top one. "You remember that pretty yellow dress in the window of Waldon's Mercantile? That's in here."

"Is Miss Marseille having you do some mending for her or something?"

Felicity shook her head. "These are all mine."

"You spent your money on clothes you don't need?"

"Who's to say I don't need them?"

He quirked an eyebrow. His twin had never been the extravagant type before.

"Miss Marseille thinks I do."

That nettled him.

"A gentlewoman has more fashion needs than a man."

Was the French socialite a bad influence on his sister?

Felicity tapped his shoulder. "Don't look so vexed. The skirt and blouses are my work clothes. She says her regular lady's maid wears a uniform. So that is mine."

"And the yellow one?"

"That's just because."

He wasn't sure what to think. "Am I to understand that she pays you a wage and then expects you to spend it all on clothes?" He detested the idea of anyone taking advantage of his sister. Worse yet for it to be Miss Marseille. He kind of liked her.

"Of course not. She bought these for me in addition to my wages." She patted her skirt where a pocket lay tucked between the folds.

He softened immediately. That was kind of her, but was it wise? "Don't be getting too big for your britches."

"Brother dear, if you haven't noticed, I don't wear britches anymore. I haven't since we were ten."

"I've noticed." He grimaced. "And so have a dozen or more men in town."

Her mouth formed an O. "Who?"

"No one you'd be interested in." He didn't need his sister running around with the wrong sort.

"I'll be the judge of that."

"Ne'er-do-wells the lot of them." Some had spent a night or two in a cell to sleep off their indulgences.

She heaved a sigh. "Too bad."

He tilted his head toward his horse and crinkled the packages in his arms. "If I tie these on the back, you'll have to walk." He didn't plan to be chivalrous. It had been too long of a day.

"I'll hold them." She snatched them back from him. "Go on. Get on Cletus."

He mounted his horse and removed his foot from the stirrup closest to his sister. "Hand me the packages."

She gave them to him. Gripping his bent arm, she stepped into the stirrup and swung up behind the saddle.

He tried to picture the fair Miss Marseille climbing onto a horse as his sister had. Couldn't do it. She was too delicate for such an action. Had she ever ridden? Probably not. She must have been horrified when he'd offered to put her on Cletus at the train station.

With outstretched arms, Felicity wiggled her fingers.

Reaching around, he handed her the parcels.

Cletus plodded forward without any encouragement. He must want to get home as much as Montana did.

Maybe he would invite Miss Marseille to go horseback riding next. He could teach her. If she happened to tumble into his arms while trying to get up into a saddle, so much the better.

Five

Montana hitched his small buckboard and loaded it with two blankets and a quilt, the food Felicity had packed, as well as a few other nonsense things his sister had insisted he needed. Since when had going fishing become so much trouble and fuss. He usually jumped on his horse with his fishing pole and rode out.

Felicity held her index finger to his face. "No comment about her dress *or* her hat, and no laughing at her."

"I would never laugh at her." Did his sister think him a dolt? "I don't see why we can't ride horses. It would be easier to get where we're going."

His sister planted her hands on her hips. "Can you picture Miss Marseille in a saddle on a horse?"

He thought a moment, raised one eyebrow, and shook his head. "Nope. The buckboard it is."

"While we're on the subject, did you ask her if she'd fished before?"

"I did, and she said she had." Which had surprised him. "Why?"

His twin's lips moved as though she were going to speak, but no words came out at first. "Let's just say her experience fishing is a little different from yours and mine."

"How different? Fishing is fishing. There aren't other ways to do it."

She gave him a knowing smile. "You'll have to ask her about the details of her experience."

At the hotel, he waited in the lobby. Dawn had come and gone. How long did it take to get dressed? It was doubtful any fish would be biting this late in the day. Predawn was best. He'd hoped to have trout for dinner and supper. A change from beans, rabbit stew, or what he got at the hotel restaurant. He would focus on the upside of today's outing, getting to spend the day with Miss Marseille. If he told her they would fish until they each caught three or more, this event could last all day.

Finally, the pair of women descended the staircase.

What was Miss Marseille wearing? Her blue and white checkered dress shimmered and made a swishing sound as she moved. What did she have on top of her head? Flowers, lace, and ribbon sat around the wide brim of her hat with a large feather plume jutting out the top. A long length of netting streamed down the back of it.

Hadn't Felicity told her what she should wear? Her dress might get ruined. That must have been why his sister had insisted upon bringing several blankets for the ground.

He approached and spoke cautiously. "This is a fetching dress. Did you want to wear something else?"

"Why? Do you not like this?" She seemed hurt.

"No. I like it very much. I would hate for it to get dirtied."

She waved a hand in front her. "It will be fine. It was not expensive."

It appeared very expensive. He glanced at his sister who shrugged and rolled her eyes. If Felicity couldn't talk this lady into wearing something more suitable, then he didn't have much hope to succeed either. "The rig is outside." He understood why his sister said riding horses would be out of the question.

In front of the hotel, she stopped at the wagon and glanced up and down the street. "Where is the carriage?"

He hoped he hadn't made a mistake by inviting her to go fishing. "We're taking the wagon." He motioned toward the conveyance.

"Oh." Her voice came out small and unsure.

Was she doomed to have a terrible day?

He couldn't allow that to happen. "It'll get us where we need to go. Climb aboard."

Miss Marseille glanced about. "Where are the steps?"

"You have to use the wagon wheel."

"I what?"

"Grab the seat and use the spokes like steps." He darted a glance to his sister who bit her lips as though struggling to contain her mirth. He wanted to grab the pretty French lady and boost her up, but he also didn't want to insult her by breaking one of her rules she was so fond of. "Miss Marseille, will you allow me to assist you?"

Felicity covered an escaped snicker with a series of coughs. "Excuse me. I must have a tickle in my throat."

"Deputy Montana, I would be most pleased for your assistance." She held out a gloved hand cocked at the wrist.

He hadn't said *how* he would help her and tapped her hand. "Take this hand and grip the foot board." He tapped her other one. "Grip the seat with this one."

She took hold where he indicated. "I do not see how this is going to help."

It would help. He tapped her right foot with his fingers and then to a horizontal spoke. "Put that foot there."

She did, and he noticed her fine leather ankle boots. How did she expect to traipse through the wilderness in those? Answer...she didn't. Had she really ever gone fishing? Didn't matter. She'd agreed to spend time with him, and he intended to take advantage of it.

"When I say now, push off the ground with your other foot, and I'll see you make it all the way up."

"You will what? How?"

No sense explaining it further and giving her a chance to change her mind. "Now."

"Oh." She made a movement as though she were pushing.

He gripped her waist and lifted her. She couldn't weigh more than a sack or two of grain.

She let out a string of what appeared to be startled words in French.

He held her aloft long enough for her to get both feet over the edge and onto the floorboard.

She wavered slightly as she got her balance and quickly sat.

To avoid the scalding glare he expected, he shifted his attention to his sister. "Come on, and I'll help you."

She gave him a wink. "I'll sit back here." She clambered onto the rear wagon wheel, swung her leg over the edge, and settled on the blankets.

Even if the pretty lady gave Montana an earful, he looked forward to having her next to him. He climbed aboard.

Miss Marseille fussed with her skirt as though she needed to get the folds precisely right. "I have never ridden in a wagon before."

He'd guessed as much. "It is a bit different from a buggy or carriage. We don't have to go fishing. We could do something else." He didn't want her to be miserable all day. He merely wanted to spend time with her if she'd let him.

She turned her blue eyes on him. "No. I want to fish."

"If you're sure."

"I am."

Montana snapped the reins and sent the horse into motion. The buckboard jerked forward.

Miss Marseille gripped the side of the seat. "This will be fun. Is the boat far?"

He swung his gaze to her. "Boat?"

Felicity did laugh now.

"Don't worry. We'll sit on the shore. No fear of getting wet."

"We are not taking a boat? Then how does one fish?"

"Drop our lines in the water." Now, he was curious. Felicity had told him Miss Marseille's experience was different. Maybe the French *did* fish in a vastly different way. "You said you've done this before. How did you do it then?"

"My *père* took us on a day trip on a boat. The men stayed above with poles while my *grand-mère* and I sat down below."

"So, you never actually fished."

"I suppose not."

"Maybe we shouldn't go then."

"Please. I want to. Teach me." She gazed at him with her blue eyes and batted her lashes.

He knew the eyelash thing was a ploy, but he didn't care. "Then we'll go fishing." He needed to readjust his plan. His three favorite spots were out of the question. They would be too hard for her to get to. He could take her to the pond, but the chances of catching anything there were nil. There was that sandy stretch on the river where the water ran deep. A patch of grass, a log and a rock to sit on, and a chance at catching something. Perfect.

Geneviève rocked on the wooden wagon seat for over an hour. The only saving grace of the discomfort was sitting right next to the handsome deputy, closer than *Grand-mère* would ever approve of. She wore her new blue taffeta gingham dress. Felicity had tried to convince her to wear the blue and green calico one, even outright refusing to assist her to dress if she didn't. Geneviève could be stubborn too and proceeded to dress herself—very clumsily, until Felicity gave in and helped.

Her backside ached. She would likely be black and blue. Had she known the seat would be so hard, she would have brought a cushion. No, then the deputy would think her weak, and because of that thought alone, she kept quiet. Besides, the deputy had said she looked fetching.

He finally pulled the wagon to a stop and helped her down.

The sound of rushing water both soothed and terrified her.

Deputy Montana unhitched Cletus and staked his horse out on a lead rope, then he collected the picnic basket, fishing poles, and gear. "I'll go down first and make sure it's passable. Then I'll return for the two of you."

"Is it dangerous?" Geneviève knew she must sound like a ninny.

"Naw. It's a little steep in places, but not at all bad. I'll keep you safe."

How could four words make her feel safe? Maybe it was the confidence in which he spoke them.

"I'll be right back." He took off down the slope.

"He makes it seem so easy."

Felicity shook her head. "Don't let his agile footing fool you. It can be tricky. When he guides you down, follow his instruction and you'll be fine."

"I think I understand why you encouraged me to wear the green and blue calico dress."

"Your dress is fine."

That may be, but the other would have been more fitting. Why had she been so insistent upon going fishing? She had foolishly wanted to do something outside of her normal activities. Doing something from Deputy Montana's day-to-day world had seemed like a good way to get to know him better. A picnic or going to the theater might have been better suggestions. Did Kamola even have a theater? Anything of culture? It didn't matter now. Her insistence had brought her here, so she would try it. If the trek down to the river didn't kill her.

After setting his burdens down, he scrambled up the slope. "I'll go ahead of you. If you start to lose your balance, use me to steady yourself."

She stepped to the edge where the ground sloped down. Grass, dirt, rocks, and tree roots encumbered what appeared to be an uneven serpentine path. "I do not know. It looks steep."

Her lady's maid stepped forward. "How about if I go first so you can see how to do it?"

"All right."

Felicity moved toward the path.

"I'll go first." The deputy stepped in front of his sister. "This will show Miss Marseille how to use me for balance."

Felicity nodded.

Deputy Montana moved forward a few steps, turned sideways, and held out his hand.

The young woman made circles with her finger. "Turn around. I have a better idea." He obeyed, and she put her hand on his shoulder.

The deputy moved forward, and her lady's maid followed easily. She was as sure footed as her brother. At the bottom, she released her brother and turned. "See? It's easy."

It hadn't looked so easy.

Deputy Montana climbed to the top again. "Your turn."

"I do not know if I can do it."

He held out his hand and spoke with quiet assurance. "I know you can."

How could he have confidence in her when she didn't have it in herself? But his belief in her made her want to try. She placed her hand in his.

At the beginning of the down slope, he turned and waited for her to put her hand on his shoulder.

She took a deep breath and put her hand lightly where he indicated. He took a stride forward, and she took two unsure steps. One stride for him, and two for her.

Where the path became steeper, Geneviève's dubious footing gave way. She tried to lock her elbow to steady herself, but it buckled instead. The earth beneath her feet propelled her forward, and she crashed into the deputy's back.

His feet slid slightly on the loose ground, but he remained upright and solid. He reached his hand up and put it on hers. "You're fine. I've got you."

She felt like such a fool. *Oh, please. I want to go fishing.* Felicity had made it down without trouble and could have done so without help.

"Let me know when you're ready."

He was being so kind and patient with her. Truthfully, she didn't want to move at all. She wanted to stay against his strong form, allowing him to support her. She pushed away a few inches. "I am ready." But she wasn't.

He took one tentative step, she took three shuffled ones.

One.

Three.

One.

Three.

One.

Three.

Until he stopped and turned, holding out his hand. "You made it."

Glancing about, she realized her destination, the bottom of the slope, sat beneath her feet. Gazing up at the path, she couldn't believe her accomplishment in traversing it. The return climb would be a challenge, but she'd achieved a feat she hadn't thought possible. "I cannot believe it." Excited, she whipped her head around, got lightheaded, and lost her balance. Her arms shot out to steady herself.

If not for Deputy Montana's strong arms latching around her waist, she would have found herself on the ground. His face lingered mere inches from hers. His brown eyes gazing into hers. "Are you all right?"

"*Oui.* I think so." Her heartbeat rivaled the speed of a racing train. What if he could feel it with her pressed against him? She liked being in his embrace, but she shouldn't be there, and pushed away. "*Oui*, I am fine. *Merci.*"

More than fine. If Felicity were not with them, she would be tempted to swoon in his arms. Now, she understood *Grand-mère's* insistence on a chaperone.

And why some couples arranged to sneak off alone for a moment or two. Not that she and the deputy were anything close to a couple, but she did understand.

Montana spread the quilt on the log near the bank. "You can sit here."

As Miss Marseille sat, her movement reminded him of an apple blossom drifting to the ground. Lithe and graceful.

His sister held out her hands. "Aren't you going to spread a blanket for me?"

Montana tossed her a blanket.

She harrumphed as she caught it. "Some gentleman you are."

"I figured since you could climb into the buckboard on your own and are a self-sufficient woman, you wouldn't want me to insult you by fussing over you."

He handed Geneviève a fishing pole.

She held it out as though he'd given her a snake.

Felicity grabbed her pole, moved a few feet down the bank, and sat on the still folded blanket.

Montana shifted his attention to the pretty French lady. He offered her a tin can of worms. "You need to bait the hook."

"What?" Then came a string of French words while she swished the pole about. "This is yours."

He pointed to the third pole. "Mine's over there." He plucked a worm from the can for her.

"Brother," Felicity called from her post, "are you sure you want to make her do that? Be a gentleman."

His twin had a point. Fishing wasn't supposed to be this much work. It was supposed to be fun and relaxing, but he was spending time with Miss Marseille, so any trouble was well worth it.

He ran his hand down the line past the cork until he found the hook, then he secured the worm in place. The cork helped keep the line from getting caught on the bottom or around rocks. When he shifted his gaze to the French lady, her eyes were squeezed tight. Felicity had been right. "It's fine now."

Miss Marseille opened her eyes and grimaced at the dangling worm.

"Now, swing the pole over your shoulder and cast your line into the water."

She gingerly moved the tip of the pole back and then forward. It plunked into an inch of water at the very edge of the river.

"You need to give it more oomph. Really throw it."

Miss Marseille tilted her head to look at him. "I do not want to hurt the worm."

Out of the corner of his eye, he caught his sister shaking her head. She was probably silently laughing as well.

He sat on Miss Marseille's left and reached around her and gripped the handle of the pole with both hands over hers. Too bad she wore gloves. His heart slammed against his ribcage at her nearness. She smelled of sweet perfume. Could he help her as easily without reaching his arms around her? Yep. Was he taking advantage of the situation? Yep. Was he going to feel guilty about this? Nope. If she told him to get away, he'd skedaddle immediately. But she didn't. Instead, she gave him an almost smile as though she might fancy him close to her. "Now, swing it over your shoulder. Relax your arms and let me move them."

She did and cast the line out into the slow-moving water. Kind of a pitiful cast, but it was in the water, nonetheless. The cork bobbed.

Her mouth pulled into a smile now. "Am I fishing?"

"Yes, ma'am." He retracted his arms but remained close at her side. Just in case she needed him. "Hold the tip down so the line can travel with the current. Make sure to have a tight grip so when you catch a fish, it doesn't pull the pole from your hands." Not that he expected any of them to catch anything.

She held the pole toward him. "I do not know what to do. You take it."

He put out his palm. "You're doing fine. Let it rest in the water for a few minutes." He stood to prepare his own.

"Where are you going?"

"To get mine. Don't worry." He retrieved his and baited it.

"Oh, no!" Miss Marseille squealed and then spoke rapidly in French.

Montana spun around to see what the fuss was about.

Miss Marseille's pole bent and bobbed. "What is happening?"

"I believe you've caught a fish." He dropped his pole in the dirt and settled behind her.

"Please take it."

Instead, he reached around her and wrapped his hands around her gloved ones again. "We're going to lift it out of the water and throw it onto the ground."

"I do not know how."

"I'm here to help." He raised the pole. A medium-small fish wriggled from the end. He swung the pole around and banked the fish which flopped on the dry ground.

"I caught a fish! Yes?"

The high pitch of Miss Marseille's delight hurt his ears, but he didn't mind. She'd caught a fish, which made her happy. "You certainly did."

Within an hour, Felicity had caught two fish and Montana had caught two as well. Miss Marseille was content with her one and refused to participate any further, preferring to watch.

Montana gathered wood to build a fire so Miss Marseille could experience her trout the way it was meant to be eaten, floured and fried in a pan with bacon fat over an open fire. His mouth watered in anticipation.

Miss Marseille stood near him and watched his every move, making him nervous. Would she think he was doing something wrong? Or criticize?

"What are you doing with those dried out leaves?"

"They will help start the fire." He arranged tiny twigs then small sticks and bigger ones within reach of the fire ring.

Miss Marseille indicated his piles. "Why have you separated the wood into sizes?"

"The smaller ones will light first and then I'll add bigger and bigger pieces."

"I see."

Did she truly?

He removed his flint kit from his pocket and used it to light the leaves. He blew on it until the flames caught and added the larger and larger combustibles.

"I have never seen anyone begin a fire." Miss Marseille retrieved a stick. "May I add one?"

"Sure."

She placed it on the small blaze much the way he had done. She was an observant learner.

Once the blaze had caught, he climbed the bank to the wagon and brought down the cooking supplies. No sense hauling it all down if they hadn't caught anything. He was pleasantly surprised they had. Felicity broke out the other food and cooking gear she'd packed.

Montana hefted the bucket with the day's catch in it. "The rule is, each person has to clean their own fish if they want to eat."

Standing behind Miss Marseille, Felicity shook her head. "Oh, brother, don't."

"Since this is your first one, I'll clean it for you." His twin didn't seriously think he would make the pretty French lady clean her own trout, did she?

Felicity nodded then donned a mischievous smile while batting her eyelashes. "Mine too?"

He was in a good mood and feeling generous. "Yours too, but you get to cook."

"Deal." His sister was far superior to him with a frying pan, so it wasn't exactly a fair trade. He was getting the better end of the bargain.

Miss Marseille's eyes glimmered with excitement. "If cleaning a fish is part of the experience, I want to clean my own."

Taken aback, Montana stared for a moment. "I don't think you do."

"Is it not like washing one's hands but on the fish?"

Montana shook his head. "There is more to it than that."

With a mischievous glint in her eyes, Felicity positioned her hands as though she held a trout in one hand and a knife in the other. "You take the knife and stick—"

"Let's just say you have to get the innards out." Montana couldn't believe his sister was about to describe the process. Or maybe she wouldn't have. Hard to tell with her. "It's rather messy."

Miss Marseille blinked at him, then a glimmer of understanding washed color from her face. "I will help Felicity cook."

"She would like that. Wouldn't you, Sis?"

Felicity was fussy about others getting their hands in her preparations. She had her own ways of doing things and others could frustrate her.

Much like Montana with his horse tack.

"I would love to have your help." His sister's tone hinted otherwise.

Geneviève couldn't believe she'd caught a fish and helped prepare it. She never would have imagined she could do those kinds of things. *Grand-mère* forbade her from entering the kitchen and learning to cook, as such duties were beneath her station. Geneviève had found the process quite rewarding, but she wouldn't want to do it all the time. She had to admit, though it smelled delicious, the cooked trout didn't look appealing, but she would try a small nibble.

Deputy Montana moved the quilt from where she'd fished to a log closer to the fire, folding it into a makeshift cushion. Geneviève lowered herself onto it, feeling like a fairy queen lounging beside a babbling brook. He handed her a tin plate with a cooked fish. She studied it a moment before grasping the utensils. She gingerly poked the flesh with the fork and hovered the knife over it.

"Wait. Not like that. Montana, help her." Felicity waved her hand toward the deputy.

The deputy sat next to Geneviève on the log. "It has bones. You remove them this way." He lifted the tail, poked the tines of the fork through the skin, and gently pulled the meat from the spindly skeleton. After doing one side, he held the utensil out to her. "You try the other side."

She didn't want to. The bones had always been removed from the fish prepared for her, so she never thought about fish having bones. "That is all right. You do it."

He touched her hand with the utensil handle. "It's part of the experience."

She took the fork. "I do not want to touch it with my fingers."

He gave her a gentle smile. "I'll hold the tail."

Grateful, she jabbed at the flesh. It didn't come off as readily as it had for him. How had he made it appear so easy? "I am not good at this. You do it."

Instead of taking the fork, he wrapped his large, strong hand around hers and guided her in flaking the meat from the skeleton.

"I did it!" She smiled at him. "Not exactly. You did it with my hand as an obstruction."

He gazed at her while still holding her hand.

Her insides fluttered. His nearness and touch pleased her. She should retrieve her hand but didn't want to. *Grand-mère* would be mortified.

He withdrew his touch and cleared his throat. "You'll want to try a bite while it's hot."

She shifted her gaze to the plate on her lap with the unappealing mangled mess. She'd never eaten food which hadn't come from an interior kitchen prepared by a staff of highly paid professionals. She gingerly poked it with her fork.

Felicity cleared her throat this time. "You don't have to eat it if you don't want to."

Geneviève had forgotten the young woman was still present. "No, I want to try it." She poked at the meat again.

Her lady's maid gestured toward her plate. "Make sure you don't get any of the skin."

She slowly lifted a small flake of trout to her mouth and scraped it off with her teeth. It sat on her tongue a minute. Flavorful. How unexpected. She hadn't experienced anything like that before, in spite of having had trout in restaurants on more than one occasion. Those had been seasoned and drenched in one sort of sauce or another. So, this was how trout actually tasted. She gazed at him. "This is good. Very good."

He smiled, and her heart danced.

She took another bite. "Very good."

Six

MONTANA SPOTTED TROUBLE THE MOMENT HE entered the hotel lobby. Appearing to have settled in, Miss Marseille's brother sat in a chair with papers in his lap. This couldn't be good. The man's head rose as they walked in. He tucked his work into his satchel and stood. Yep. He'd been waiting for them. With a quick assessment of his actions, Montana realized he should have spoken to her brother before taking Miss Marseille fishing. Too late now.

Miss Marseille greeted her brother with three kisses, alternating between his cheeks. "Pierre, good afternoon. Are you through with classes for the day?"

"I am. Why don't you go change for supper? I am sure you'll want to tidy up after your outing."

"I do." Miss Marseille returned to Montana where he stood a few feet away. "*Merci* for taking me fishing."

Montana tipped his head. "My pleasure, ma'am. How do I say you're welcome in French?"

"*De rien.*"

He hoped he didn't make a mess of it. "*De rien.*"

"Very good." She studied him a moment longer with a sweet smile. "We must do something again."

"I'd like that."

"I would as well." She turned with a swish. "Come, Felicity. I will need much help."

Montana watched the ladies climb the staircase as did Mr. Marseille. Montana contemplated slipping away while the other man's attention was elsewhere but thought better of it. Though he couldn't put his finger on it, he sensed the professor wanted to speak to him, or at the very least dismiss him with a warning.

The ladies turned the corner of the staircase and floated out of sight.

Mr. Marseille swung around. "Mr. Montana, won't you join me for a slice of pie and coffee?" The man hadn't seemed surprised by Montana still being there.

Even so, the cordial invitation *had* surprised Montana. "Sure." He followed the professor into the dining room and sat across the table from him.

Noreen, the server, approached right away. "Howdy, Montana. Howdy, Professor Marseille. What can I get you gentlemen?"

The professor gave the order. "Two slices of apple pie and two coffees."

Montana wanted to beg off the pie but thought it better not to upset the man who undoubtedly wished to talk about today's outing with his sister. Was it best to let the professor start the conversation? Or should he?

The well-dressed Frenchman studied him, a lowly deputy. "Mr. Montana, you took my sister fishing."

"I did. Montana's not my family's name. Please just call me Montana." Would he be as stubborn as his sister?

"Right. Your surname is *Gladwell*."

The man said it as though Montana was trying to hide something. "It is." He wasn't and didn't think explaining his name choice was appropriate at the moment. A lot of people went by nicknames. The man had obviously done some checking around about him to learn his surname.

"What made you decide to take my sister fishing?" For some reason, the professor's accent wasn't as heavy as Miss Marseille's.

"It was her idea."

"I doubt that."

It was hard to believe even for Montana. "She asked what I usually did on my day off. I told her fishing, and she asked to go. I probably should have asked your permission first, but it just sort of happened."

The professor raised his eyebrows.

"I know it's incredible, but I don't believe she had any idea what fishing entailed. She was a good sport about it and caught the first fish."

His demeanor changed to slightly amused. "I would have enjoyed seeing that. As a young girl she used to be game to try any new thing our father suggested. On his urging, she climbed a tree—it wasn't very big, but she thought it was quite an accomplishment. She can tie a dozen or more sailor's knots and even petted a toad our father caught."

Montana couldn't picture that.

"As she got older, our grandmother put an end to that and discouraged such behavior. She needed to conduct herself as a proper lady."

Montana found it hard to believe Miss Marseille would be game for anything more adventurous than the fishing trip they'd taken. "Your grandma can rest easy. Miss Marseille behaved every bit the lady. She did nothing to tarnish her good name."

The professor gave a disbelieving look. "Going fishing, in the manner you Americans do, is tarnish enough for our grandmother."

What a shame she was so limited in what activities she was allowed to participate in. Did she enjoy such a restrictive life? He knew his twin wouldn't. Felicity would get jittery, for certain.

Just what was the good professor's point in this little meal? He hadn't been contrary nor told Montana to go away, but he also hadn't been welcoming.

"You are probably wondering why I asked you to have coffee and pie."

Could the man read minds? "It crossed my thoughts."

"You seem like a decent fellow. A good deputy would need to be...but you must know our grandparents will never approve of you for Geneviève. They have very strict ideas of whom they deem appropriate for her. I am sorry to say you do not meet their requirements."

Montana noticed the professor didn't include himself in that disapproval. "Are you warning me to go away and not see your sister again?" Though he'd expected as much, he wanted to continue to see Miss Marseille, if she would let him.

"Of late, I have not been successful in convincing her of much she does not have a mind to do. This is not a side she shows often. I want you to be aware of where you stand with her regardless of what she says or how pleased she seems to be in your company." He moved his lips around as though contemplating his next words. "To be honest, I have my doubts. It is possible she is using you to rile me into returning with her back East. I am not saying she is, but I am not saying she is not."

Miss Marseille didn't want to stay? Of course not. Kamola wasn't her kind of town.

"I do not want you to have unrealistic expectations. My sister can be a complex woman."

Montana understood that. His own sister could be complex. Why wasn't the man discouraging him from spending time with Miss Marseille? "So you think she could be using me to irritate you into leaving town, and you are using me to distract your sister from begging you to return East. Is that about right?"

The professor gave a knowing look. "You are preceptive. The second part, yes. As to the first part, my sister's motives I can only guess at. When I speculate at such things, I am often incorrect."

Montana wasn't sure if he should be irritated that this man was using him or honored to be brought into his confidence. Either way, the man didn't seem to be set on keeping him away from his sister. "I appreciate you warning me." Was Miss Marseille merely toying with him? A plaything?

If he wanted the intriguing French lady to remain in town, it was in his best interest to side with her brother. But was that wise when there was no future in spending time with her? Knowing he might be nothing more than a distraction to her, he would make sure his feelings didn't go beyond a pleasant time with the lady.

After freshening up and changing into an appropriate evening dress, Geneviève went downstairs with Felicity. "Has your brother left?" Other than the desk clerk, the lobby was empty. No deputy in sight.

"Looks like it."

How disappointing, even though she had spent most of the day with him. Perhaps Pierre had sent him away. "You may go."

"When would you like me to return?"

Geneviève opened her reticule and retrieved Felicity's wages for the day. "You are free until the morning."

Her lady's maid accepted the money. "What about changing out of your dress?"

"I believe this gown will be manageable." Geneviève felt a little guilty for occupying so much of the young woman's time. She must have other things she had already planned that Geneviève had disrupted.

"If you're sure."

"I am. *Au revoir.*" Geneviève returned to her room. What should she do until supper with her brother?

Even though she'd recently parted from them, she missed the deputy and his sister. They lived such enviable lives, simple and without restrictions. So different from her own upbringing. They placed no stringent expectations on her. Most everything she did or said seemed fine.

Very few of her activities of late would be acceptable to her grandparents, starting with sneaking out and traveling across the country. *Alone.* Her grandparents meant well and did have her best interests at heart, as well as gave her most everything a person could want. Still, that wasn't enough. She had never known that something was missing from her life—the ability to make her own choices.

She gazed out the window. Where was Deputy Montana right now? What was he doing?

Whatever he wanted—he and his sister were free to do as they pleased.

She turned to face *her* room. She, too, could do whatever she wanted. Within reason. What would *Grand-mère* tell her not to do? Not to muss her gown. Studying the bed, she smiled. No, she couldn't go so far as to lie down in her gown. It would get wrinkled. Even so, she was exhausted from the strenuous day. She carefully reclined on her back, adjusting her gown to not bunch up. No need to go so far as to cause unnecessary wrinkles. What an odd sensation. She couldn't remember ever lying down after getting dressed for supper. Resting her hands at her sides, she closed her eyes.

Sometime later, a knock roused her. "Vivi?"

Pierre.

Refreshed, Geneviève stood and crossed the room, smoothing her gown as she went. It didn't look so bad. She opened the door, and Pierre escorted her downstairs, allowing her to go first.

"Your lady's maid isn't very proficient."

"Why do you say that? Felicity might not be traditionally trained, but she is doing surprisingly well." She was truly fond of the young woman.

"She tied your bow crooked."

Geneviève reached both hands behind her and tugged at the fabric. "How is that?" She didn't want to admit she'd been lying down in her gown.

"Let me." He pulled on the bow. "It might not pass *Grand-mère's* inspection, but it will suffice."

Once seated in the dining room with their meals ordered, she couldn't wait to tell her brother all about her adventure. "I caught a fish today. *Then* I helped cook it and ate it."

Her brother's eyes widened. "You've had an exciting day."

"Deputy Montana and his sister took me fishing along the river."

"I'm well aware. He said it was your idea."

"*Oui.* It was so different from when *Grand-père* and *Père* took us fishing on that boat. Well, maybe not so much for you. I had no idea what it entailed."

"What would *Grand-père* say about your outing?"

"I'm sure *Grand-mère* would have much to say, but we aren't going to tell her, are we?"

He shook his head. "I should be upset he took you out into the wilderness—you weren't bred for that—but I'm pleased you had a good time."

She lightly touched his hand resting on the table. "He was a perfect gentleman."

"I bet he was."

"Don't be disagreeable. The outing was all very respectable. My lady's maid was in attendance as chaperone."

He leaned slightly forward. "Would it do any good to tell you to stay away from him?"

"Why? We aren't doing any harm."

"Nothing can come of it."

He was right, nothing could develop from her budding friendship with the deputy. Nevertheless, indignation at being treated like an infant rose to her heated cheeks. "Since when do you tell me what to do? *Grand-mère, Oui. Grand-père, Oui.* Even *Père*. But not you."

"None of them are here. You're toying with this man's affections. That's not you."

She wasn't toying with him. She honestly liked Deputy Montana. True, her grandparents would never approve of him, but as Pierre said, they weren't here. They had made all her decisions, except the ones regarding this trip. She had been the one who decided to come, and she'd made all her own decisions today. Decided to go fishing. Decided to actually fish—with much encouragement. Decided to allow the deputy to sit so close to her. "You're merely not used to me making decisions for myself. I'll be careful."

"There is a reason our grandparents and our father make your decisions. You don't know what is best for you."

"What if I do?" She wasn't a child, after all. "What if I don't like the decisions others make for me?"

"Even so, you must trust we are looking out for you and only want what is best for you."

She believed that, but she also liked making her own decisions, even these small ones. She wanted to do it at least for a little while. "If you want me to stop seeing Deputy Montana, then let us *both* return to our grandparents' home back East."

"As I suspected. You are using him to force my hand. I'm not leaving. Not when I'm so close. There are answers here in Kamola. I can feel it."

Her brother's determination surprisingly pleased her—in staying, not his search for so-called answers about their *mère*. She wanted to stay as well. "Then it is settled. We both remain or we both depart." That made her staying seem like it was his doing. *Grand-mère* couldn't fault her for that.

"You be careful, and always have his sister along."

"I know to have a chaperone. Deputy Montana does as well. He was the one who mentioned it first. You have nothing to worry about."

"We'll see."

Her brother would come to realize the deputy was trustworthy. "Does the Washington State Normal School have a theater?"

"Why?"

"I wish to introduce Deputy Montana to the culture I enjoy. Return the favor for his willingness to show me part of his world."

"I doubt if he'll go."

"He will if I ask him."

"Yes, but will he enjoy it?"

"I enjoyed fishing, didn't I? And he seemed to relish my presence." She mostly enjoyed watching the deputy.

He sighed as though relinquishing the fight. "The students are putting on *A Midsummer Night's Dream*. There is a Saturday matinee. You may go with him, but nothing after dark."

"That is only the day after tomorrow. What if his engagement calendar is already full?"

"You've convinced me he'll undoubtedly make himself available to you. He is smitten, after all."

What a pleasant thought.

Seven

HENNY HAD MIXED FEELINGS ABOUT HOSTING the quilting circle. She had wanted to search the town for the mystery man. He had returned, and she would find him this time. However, it would be good to visit with her friends. Some, like Agnes Martin and Dorthea Albert, had been her friends since she arrived in town twenty years ago. She could hunt for the stranger tomorrow.

When the first of the ladies knocked, Henny was pleased to open the door to Lily Hammond. "Come in."

She did and removed her cloak. "Why is it so cold?"

"April can be like that sometimes, balmy one day and like winter the next. It'll warm up soon and stay that way. Then we'll be wishing for this cooler weather. Especially you with a baby on the way. How much longer do you have?"

Lily's midsection was swollen with child. "Three and a half months. The little one is due early August."

"The time will fly by." Henny led Lily into the parlor. "You're a bit early. The other ladies won't be here for at least a half an hour."

"I know. You can blame Edric. And his father. Those two were clucking like a pair of old hens last night."

They must have been at it again this morning to send Lily out of the house prematurely. "About what?"

Lily bit her bottom lip and took a slow breath. "You."

"Me?"

"They were going on about that man you keep seeing and wondering why no one else seems to see him."

"I've asked myself the same thing. I have to wonder if when I've seen him, those aren't the only times he's been watching me. I tried to convince myself he might have been looking for Nicole and her cousins, but certainly by now he knows they aren't here. I can't imagine why he would be interested in them. Which means, it's me. But again, I can't imagine why."

"Have you told any of the quilting ladies about him?"

"Only Agnes."

"I think we should inform the others. Get everyone involved in keeping an eye out for him. Maybe one of the others has seen him too and doesn't know it."

She had a point. More eyes meant more chances to catch this man.

"I wish someone else had gotten a good look at him." Then Henny would be reassured she wasn't imagining things. "Be honest with me. Do Edric and Saul think I'm touched in the head for believing in a phantom?"

"They're divided."

She wasn't sure she wanted the answer but needed to know. "Who thinks I'm crazy and who believes me?" Which one did she hope believed her?

"Both."

"How can that be? They either believe me or they don't."

"They both believe *you* believe this man has been watching you. They do believe he exists. They just aren't sure if he's actually following you or if you are misinterpreting what you're seeing."

"What do you believe?"

"That if we get the quilting ladies on this, we can locate this man more quickly and find out, once and for all, if he is indeed following you or if there is some other explanation for his actions."

"So, you believe he exists?"

"Well, I don't believe you're seeing ghosts."

Henny missed having the young mother and her boy living in her home. Unsure how she should proceed, she hesitated. "I don't want to worry anyone unnecessarily."

Lily put her hand on Henny's arm. "If you choose not to tell them, I won't say anything either."

Henny appreciated that. "Sometimes, I'm positive I see him, and others, I wonder if I imagined him. Since no one else has seen him or knows what he looks like, how can anyone help search for him?"

"What guidance have you felt from the Lord?"

A topic as puzzling as the disappearing man. "I sense the man's important in some way. I'm not sure if it's to me or someone close to me. Whether he is someone good or a threat. But I *need* to find him to figure it out. I'm probably making too much of a fuss. If I could confront him and get answers once and for all, I could put this behind me and forget about him."

"I believe you, as do Saul and Edric."

"Correction. They believe *I believe* I've been seeing this man. If only someone else had laid eyes on him."

Forty minutes later, all eleven ladies were present, mingling and chatting merrily. They all seemed so carefree at the moment. Lives which had been turbulent over the past year had settled into a peaceful normalcy of daily living. All was well in the quilting circle.

Telling them had seemed like a good idea, but now it seemed silly to involve anyone else. She didn't want to spoil their pleasant moods because of something that might or might not be true. Was she turning into an oversuspicious old woman?

As Henny's friends took their usual seats in the circle, Lily's words repeated in her head. *I'll keep my eyes open for anyone suspicious.* Her friends were indeed the answer.

Henny cleared her throat to catch everyone's attention. "Ladies, I have a bit of an unusual request."

Lily gave her an encouraging nod.

"A few of you know about the stranger I've been noticing about town." She made eye contact with Lily, Nicole, and Agnes as the ones in the know. "I first became aware of the outsider last fall around the time Nicole and her cousins came into my life. I thought he could be interested in them, but I'm not so sure now. He disappeared after a few weeks, and I hadn't thought much about him since. I figured my seeing him was happenstance. Then a few days ago, there he was. No one else ever sees the man. When he notices that I'm aware of him, he quickly darts away. If someone does spot the stranger, it's only his coattails as he slips around the corner."

"That's all I saw." Nicole lifted her hand. "I wish I'd gotten a good look."

Dorthea put a hand to her throat. "Henny, I had no idea."

Worried expressions settled on the faces around the room.

Neva leaned in. "What are you going to do?"

"This is a matter best handled by the sheriff." Marguerite Atwood set her jaw.

Henny nodded. "I've spoken with Edric and Deputy Montana. They are aware of the situation. Until I can give a better description, or someone can find out who he is, they can't do much."

"Does he seem menacing?" Trudy nibbled her bottom lip.

"Not in the least." Henny didn't want to scare the other women. "I have a request."

"Anything," echoed from the ladies around the circle.

"Would each of you keep an eye out for this man who might be near my house or—I don't know—watching me?"

The women eagerly agreed.

"It's a good thing you have those two professors living here," Agnes said. "That man will think twice before approaching your home."

Henny didn't think it would be wise to tell her friends that her boarding house was the place she had noticed the man most. He knew where she lived.

Agnes spoke. "Give us as much of a description as you can."

"Brown hair, average height and build, dresses very nice, like a gentleman from back East."

"That's not much to go on, but if any of us spots *anyone* lingering or idle, we'll make note of it."

"And get a good description."

"We could follow him." Several agreed.

That would be too much. "Oh, don't do that. Edric would have my head."

"We could follow at a distance to find out where he goes."

"We'll find this man, Henny. Don't you worry."

If even one of these women saw this man, she could corroborate Henny's experience.

She drew comfort from her friends' eagerness to help watch out for her safety or at least her sanity. Not one of them questioned the existence of this stranger, but that didn't mean no one was thinking it.

Nothing more precious or valuable than steadfast friends.

Montana tipped back in the chair until the top of it rested against the wall. Sheriff Rix had sentenced him to wait for a prisoner to be transferred here until a marshal could collect him tomorrow and take him on the train to Seattle. If he was stuck in the office, he might as well relax. He rested his boots on the desk and laced his hands behind his head.

He would take this opportunity to daydream about a certain blonde lady. Not much chance of seeing her today.

No sooner had he allowed his eyes to close when light footsteps walked onto the boardwalk. He lowered his boots to the floor as the door opened.

Felicity and Miss Marseille?

What a pleasant surprise. He shot to his feet and reached to tip his hat, but it wasn't there. It mocked him from the nail in the wall where he'd perched it earlier. He gave her a nod instead. "Good morning, Miss Marseille." He nodded to his sister as well. "Good morning, Felicity."

His twin smirked, no doubt at his new-found cordiality toward her.

She could make any face she wanted as long as she didn't call him out with any embarrassing remarks. He couldn't help it if the alluring French lady made him say things and behave in ways he normally wouldn't. Not that he was ever a miscreant, he simply didn't want Miss Marseille to think him a complete dolt. He hadn't had the refined learning she'd had. "What can I do for you lovely ladies on this fine day?" There he went again, acting all mannerly and genteel.

Miss Marseille glanced around. "I wished to see a sheriff's office."

He doubted that, since it was dingy, dusty, and didn't smell the greatest. It was nothing special. "Well, this is it. It's not much. Two cells, a desk, a couple of chairs, and a file cabinet."

"I had expected it to be... How do you say? More scary."

"Not much scary here, though we are expecting a prisoner soon."

Her eyes lit up. "How exciting."

"Not really. Is there anything I can do for you?"

She smiled demurely at him. "My brother says Washington State Normal School is performing *A Midsummer Night's Dream*. They have a matinee show tomorrow."

He almost reached up to scratch his head. "Are they, now?" Why was she telling him?

"Have you heard of it?"

"Isn't that one of those Shakespeare plays?" Difficult and unintelligible.

"*Oui.* It is an enchanting tale of romance. Have you seen it performed before?"

Miss Marseille obviously enjoyed high-class pastimes.

Should he be honest? "I...never did like those kinds of fancy diversions. The way the words are strung together is hard to understand."

Her beautiful smile turned to a pouty frown. "They are so poetic."

He had lost ground with her now. "I don't really comprehend poetry either."

"You might if you try. I could help you understand the story."

Did he want to try? It seemed like an impossible task. "I don't know if that would help."

Felicity huffed. "Take a hint, brother. Ask her to the play."

Montana glanced from Miss Marseille to his sister and back. How could he have been so dull-witted? He'd been too focused on himself and his aversion to culture. She had taken a stab at fishing and done well. "Miss Marseille, would you like to attend the play?"

She tilted her head with a playful grin. "With you?"

Hadn't that been what she'd been hinting at? Felicity had seemed to think so. "I would be honored if you did." He was happy Miss Marseille seemed to like his company even if she was using him to irritate her brother. He even wouldn't mind enduring Shakespeare to spend a little time with her, but he would absolutely guard his heart. No falling for this enchanting filly.

Miss Marseille gifted him with her sweet French smile. "I would be most pleased to attend with you."

He breathed a sigh of relief. He'd thought for one terrifying moment, Felicity had gotten it wrong and he'd made a fool of himself.

Outside the sheriff's office, Geneviève surveyed the street. "We should have ordered a carriage."

"Why?"

Felicity had talked her into forgoing the use of a conveyance of any kind. Geneviève had never needed to walk much. *Grand-mère* taught her that a person of her station needn't travel by foot to get places, so she shouldn't. "To go shopping for a gown."

"You bought dresses two days ago."

Geneviève pushed open her parasol. "I need one for the theater."

Her lady's maid gave her a wide-eyed look. "I'm sure one of the dresses you brought with you will work fine."

"Fine? A lady should never be merely *fine*. She should be *exceptional* and take every opportunity at her disposal to buy new things."

Felicity tilted her head. "Why?"

Geneviève opened her mouth and gave her grandmother's answer. "It is what ladies do." How else was she to fill her time? "I want to meet the French seamstress. Where can we hire a carriage?"

Her lady's maid shrugged and stepped off the boardwalk. "It's not too far."

Geneviève fell into step beside her. "Where will we put the packages? We cannot carry so much."

"We can ask the dress shop to deliver them to the hotel."

"Splendid idea. I am sure they would do that." Geneviève kind of enjoyed this walking around. It made her feel independent. "Which way?"

After traversing the distance, which was a lot farther than Geneviève had expected, they arrived at the shop. Like her brother, *not far* was a greater distance to Geneviève. Her feet hurt. The shoes which matched her mint green and beige dress were not meant for such strenuous activity.

When her lady's maid opened the door, a bell jingled overhead. Fine fabrics and constructed gowns and garments occupied a lot of the space.

A woman who appeared to be around thirty, approached. "Good morning, ladies. I am *Mademoiselle* Celeste Dumont. What may I help you with today?"

The woman had a lovely French lilt to her voice. Geneviève took advantage of that and spoke in her native language. "*Enchanté. Je suis Mademoiselle* Geneviève Marseille."

The proprietress's eyes widened, and she replied in kind. "You are French."

"*Oui.*" Geneviève drank in the sound of her mother tongue. She hadn't realized how much she had missed it.

Felicity motioned toward an area where several clothed mannequins stood. "I'm going to look at the dresses while you two talk."

Geneviève nodded to her lady's maid and resumed her conversation with the dressmaker. They spoke of Paris, the South of France, the French Riviera, the Louvre Museum, as well as other European affairs. Then the conversation moved to fashion. "I need a gown to go to the theater tomorrow at the normal school in town. It will be an afternoon performance, so I'll need appropriate attire for that time of day."

The proprietress moved toward the gown Felicity was eyeing and switched to English. "Your companion has good discernment. This cream and blue one would be lovely for your outing."

Though beautiful, it wasn't quite her style. "Do you have something with larger sleeves?" She pointed to the puffed sleeves she wore.

"I do. Right this way." *Mademoiselle* Dumont moved to the rear of the shop to an area where a mannequin wore a beautiful coral gossamer gown.

"This is stunning." The color and fabric would certainly please Deputy Montana.

"*Oui.* If you don't mind, may I suggest something a little less voluminous. People out here in the West do not have the same views as people back East or in Europe about such details of fashion. They find them excessive and pretentious."

Geneviève fingered the fabric. She adored this gown and could picture herself wearing it as she walked on the deputy's arm.

Felicity cleared her throat. "I think you should listen to her. Montana doesn't understand your big-sleeved dresses. Besides if your dress is smaller at the top, he would be able to sit a little closer to you." She wiggled her eyebrows.

What a tantalizing thought. "Very well. What do you suggest, *Mademoiselle* Dumont?"

The seamstress moved over to a red and white gown. "This would be suitable for an afternoon outing yet still very stylish."

A wonderful piece. A red tailcoat trimmed in gold over a white silk shirtwaist, a gold underskirt with a white overlay in the front with red pin stripes. The gold underskirt ruffled in the back to form a bustle of sorts. Fluffy red tassels and embroidery adorned the front overlay panel. "I love it." She turned to her lady's maid. "What color of suit will your brother be wearing?"

The girl's expression turned dumbfounded.

"I don't want my dress to clash with his attire."

"Um. He'll be wearing his Sunday clothes, so I guess black."

"Perfect." Geneviève shifted her attention back to the proprietress. "May I try it on?"

"*Mais oui.* We must fit it to you."

"Also, the blue and cream one for my companion."

Felicity's eyes widened. "What? I don't need another dress."

"You do if I say you do. Come."

With the help of one of the proprietress's employees, Geneviève changed into the red, white, and gold dress. With minor alterations, it would fit perfectly.

The blue and cream dress fit Felicity almost as well. "I don't want you to purchase this for me. I will be fine in the yellow dress you already bought me."

"That isn't suitable to attend the theater in. Why are you resistant to me buying this for you?"

"Because I feel as though I'm taking advantage of your generosity and kindness. Also, I'll likely never wear it again, so it would be a waste of your money."

How could she convince Felicity to accept it?

"Besides, Montana would be upset if I allowed you to buy something so expensive for me."

Geneviève didn't want the deputy to be cross with her. "Very well. You can wear one of the gowns I brought with me. Would that suit?"

"I guess so."

Geneviève purchased two other outfits, a dress and a walking suit, both with the smaller sleeves. She hoped Deputy Montana approved of them. Then she recalled the dressmaker's and Felicity's comments. Was she excessive and pretentious? She had only ever done what her grandparents told her to do. Buying new clothes for every occasion and function was part of her schooling. She would have to think and pray about how she wanted to be in the future. She certainly didn't want people to think of her as excessive or pretentious.

Eight

On Saturday morning, Henny swung on her pink shawl. The late April air still held a bit of a chill even with the sun shining. She looked forward to warmer weather but dreaded the scorching summer heat.

Her two boarders had eaten breakfast, so she wouldn't need to attend to anything until supper. She planned to hitch her buggy and drive around town until she found the stranger. In the process, she would do a little shopping.

First, she would peer out the window on the front door in case the man had decided to lurk outside this morning as he'd done before. She crept to the window and slowly drew the lace curtain aside.

A male face stared back at her.

Startled, she sucked in a breath and yanked open the door. "Saul Hammond, you gave me a fright!"

He lowered his hand which had been poised to knock and smiled. "Good morning to you too."

That had been rude. Where were her manners? "I'm sorry. Good morning." She wouldn't be able to go on her hunt now.

He pointed to her shawl. "I see I'm just in time."

"In time for what?" She couldn't recall having made plans with him.

"To take you in search of that man who has been watching you. I brought my buggy." He waved his hand in the air to indicate the street behind him where his rig sat.

"How...? Why...? What are you up to, Saul Hammond?"

"I've come to help you. I figured you would be heading out in search of that man."

How reassuring to have someone believe in her.

"I want to find him as much as you do. If there is someone skulking about, your safety could be at risk."

There it was, the undecided "if". "If? I thought you believed me."

His expression turned sheepish. "I do."

Planting her fists on her hips, Henny tilted her head.

He held out his hands. "Even you have to admit it's a little strange no one else has seen him after all this time."

He was right, and she'd questioned herself numerous times. "Nicole saw him."

"She caught sight of *someone* disappearing around a corner. Could have been anyone."

All true and things she'd told herself. "So why bother to help me if you don't believe me?"

"Because if there is even the slightest chance this man exists—and there is more than a slight chance—I want him found so my sheriff son can question him."

Saul was sweet for caring so much even if he only partially believed her.

"What are you waiting for? Let's go." She pulled the door closed behind her. "You don't mind if I do a little shopping while we're out, do you?"

"I have a few things to get myself."

Henny wasn't sure if he actually did, or if he only said that to make her feel better about occupying his time. She waited at the buggy for Saul to give her assistance, as that was the courteous thing to do.

He didn't disappoint and offered his hand. She put hers in his to step into the buggy.

He climbed in the other side. "Do you want to get your shopping done first? Or search first?"

"Definitely search." If they found him, she didn't want her purchases to sit in the buggy. And if a fruitless hunt took too long, she could put off shopping until Monday.

"Where shall we begin?" He put the rig into motion.

Where indeed? "Maybe head down the main street and see where it takes us."

"All righty then. I like the sound of that."

Henny's thoughts jumped tracks from the stranger to Saul's words. What had he meant by he *liked the sound of that*? She would contemplate it later. She had a man to find.

As the buggy approached the business section of town, Saul studied one side of the street then the other. "What sort of fellow should I be looking for?"

The kind that was too cowardly to speak to a middle-aged lady. "He seemed to be in his mid-to-upper twenties, well groomed, possibly five-ten or so. Brown hair and a dark brown homburg hat."

Saul swung his gaze toward her. "What kind of noggin warmer is that? Like a derby?"

"Yes, but it has a crease down the center of the crown."

"So, like a Stetson."

"Not really." How could she explain the distinctions between different hat styles? "It's somewhere between the two."

"Got it. I'll keep a lookout for a man in a homburg hat."

Henny couldn't tell if he was humoring her, or if he actually believed her and would be actively searching. Either way, she appreciated his company.

Saul pointed. "What about that man in front of the Godfrey Saloon?"

Henny's pulse quickened. Could it be him after all this time? She released her captive breath. "Too stocky."

After a few more false sightings and several streets scoured, Henny heaved a sigh. "This doesn't seem to be accomplishing anything. We might as well go to Waldon's Mercantile to take care of our shopping duties."

He turned the buggy. "I'm sorry we didn't find him." He sounded sincere.

"Thank you. I appreciate your willingness to help." Henny was sorry as well. She'd hoped to put this nonsense to rest, once and for all.

"Any time. I would do about anything to help you."

Again, his words sounded like more than friendship.

A man down the street grabbed her attention. "Stop!"

Saul hauled back on the reins. "What is it?"

"I think I saw him. Down that street." She pointed.

Saul maneuvered the buggy in the direction indicated. "Where?"

"He went into one of these buildings. Down a bit farther." She waggled her hand in the air as though shooing a raccoon out of her yard. "There! That one!"

With a tug on the reins, the buggy stopped in front of the land office. Saul set the brake. "Let me come around and give you a hand."

Henny could get down on her own but waited for him anyway. She took his offered hand, which sent a tingle up her arm.

Inside the land office, Mr. Jenkins sat behind his desk. Across from him, a brown-haired man, with his homburg in his lap, occupied the chair.

Upon seeing Henny, the stranger stood.

The land surveyor was a heartbeat or two behind him. "Aunt Henny. Mr. Hammond. I will be with you both after I finish with this gentleman."

Henny studied the customer. Was it him? She didn't think so. His hair was too dark and his jaw too narrow. "Silly me. I thought I saw a friend enter here. My old eyes must be playing tricks. We're sorry to have bothered you." She turned toward the door.

Outside, Saul helped her into the buggy. "Was it him?"

"No." Disappointing.

"Are you sure?"

"Fairly sure. That man's face is shaped wrong." At least she was fairly sure his face wasn't quite right. Something inside her told her this wasn't the same man.

He patted her hand. "I'm sorry."

Once on their way to the mercantile again, Henny studied every man they passed. Her mystery stranger wasn't among them. Maybe he'd left town again as he had before. Or maybe she had imagined him. This could push her toward an asylum.

Lord, help me forget all about this person until I see him again. When or if that happens. She needed peace of mind.

After shopping, Saul carried her purchases, as well as his own, outside to the buggy.

A glimpse of movement grabbed Henny's attention, and she swung in that direction. "There he is." She headed off.

"Where? Henny, wait!"

It didn't take long for Saul to catch up to her. "Where did he go?"

"He went around that corner." The man's usual escape.

Rounding the corner, Henny halted. The well-dressed gentleman stood with another man in scruffy attire. They both stared at her with wide eyes. The untidy one hurried off. The dapper gentleman glared at her then walked off after the other.

"Not him?" Saul asked.

Henny shook her head. "Am I doing nothing more than chasing shadows?"

Her friend shook his head now.

"You would tell me if you thought I was, wouldn't you?"

"Of course."

"Promise."

Saul patted her arm. "Promise. It doesn't hurt to look for the man."

No, it didn't. Unless she became obsessed. Which she wasn't.

Yet.

Henny hung her head. "You must think me a first-rate fool."

Saul rested a hand on her shoulder. "I think no such thing."

"Then touched in the head."

"I think there is someone you keep seeing, and we are going to find him. Maybe not today, but we *will* find him. Then we'll learn what he's up to or whether this has all been coincidence."

Henny wasn't so sure anymore. Maybe she had been seeing both of those men at different times and confusing them as the same person, sort of a combination of the two. Nonetheless, she appreciated Saul's encouragement. What would she do without him?

On Saturday, Montana stopped in front of the sheriff's home and climbed out of the buggy he'd rented. Miss Marseille couldn't arrive to the theater in a buckboard.

When he'd asked his boss what he should wear this afternoon, Sheriff Rix told him to come by his house. His new wife knew about culture things and could tell him for sure.

He'd wanted Felicity to help him, but she had to go so early to assist the pretty French lady get even prettier. Mrs. Hammond knew because she came from money even though she didn't act snobby. Montana was nothing more than a simple farm boy.

He'd never been to a play before. Well, that wasn't exactly true. As a child he'd watched silly school productions and the Bible nativity story acted out—even participated in a few—but nothing so formal as what the Washington State Normal School would put on. Never had an interest. He had one now.

He'd taken a bath, shaved, donned his best Sunday attire, and oiled his mane until every last stubborn hair stayed put. Felicity had laughed at him. He couldn't blame her when he hardly looked like himself. He couldn't remember ever being dressed like a dandy before, but he didn't want to embarrass the society beauty by being seen with a bumpkin.

At the door, he knocked and soon stood in the sheriff's living room with his boss and his boss's wife. Their three children sat snugged together on the settee, watching the spectacle he created by being there.

Mrs. Hammond's midsection bulged with the sheriff's next child. "Deputy Montana, I've never seen you look more handsome."

That was encouraging. "Then I'm dressed well enough for going to a play?"

She gave him a gentle smile. "I'm afraid not. Do you, per chance, have a suit coat in your buggy?"

He shook his head. "I don't even own one. Never needed to. Do I need one?"

"The theater usually requires one." She glanced at her husband. "I doubt yours would fit him."

"Pa has one. He wouldn't mind if the boy borrowed it. I'll get it." The sheriff headed up the stairs. He returned a few moments later with a black coat.

Montana's skin prickled at the sight, reminding him of a funeral. Corpses wore such things. "Do I have to wear that?"

His boss held it out. "If you don't want to embarrass the lady."

Never. He slipped the coat on. Not as bad as he'd imagined.

Sheriff Rix held out a narrow black tie and a braided cord to his wife. "Which one should he wear?"

"The leather cord."

When the sheriff slung the cord in Montana's direction, Montana caught it. "Put that around your neck."

Montana swallowed hard. He'd done his best his whole life to avoid a noose. "Do I have to?" The coat was bad enough.

Mrs. Hammond took the cord. "Yes, you do. It's not a snake. It won't bite."

He wasn't so sure about that. "I would rather tangle with an angry snake."

Sheriff Rix snickered. "Two things I know for certain. Don't go anywhere near a mama bear with her cubs and don't mess with a woman who is expecting. You've got both here, boy."

Mrs. Hammond looped the cord around Montana's neck and tied it in a bow. "Now you look dashing as well as handsome."

Montana swallowed hard again. He felt ridiculous in this getup with everyone staring at him. He'd thought he could get away with his Sunday shirt, trousers, and vest. Apparently, his idea of being dressed up wasn't near as fancy as he had thought. However, Miss Marseille was worth it after her being such a good sport with the fishing, even if there was no future for the two of them. He owed her that.

His boss smirked at him from the corner.

Ignoring her husband, Mrs. Hammond studied Montana and adjusted the suit coat.

Montana disliked all this attention. "Do you know about the play the normal school is putting on, *A Midsummer Night's Dream?*"

She smiled. "It's a wonderful play, one of Shakespeare's best. You'll love it."

Doubtful. "What's it about?" He knew a little from what Miss Marseille had said but wanted more details. That way he wouldn't feel as intimidated or so much like a dolt. Who was he kidding? He would feel like a dolt either way, just a little less so if he knew more. He prayed he didn't make a fool of himself.

"It's a romance and a comedy about the follies of love. Oberon is the king of the fairies, and Titania is his queen."

Montana widened his eyes. "Fairies? You're pulling my reins, right?"

The sheriff chuckled.

Mrs. Hammond turned to her husband. "It wouldn't hurt you to go see it."

The sheriff's two little girls, eight and six, clapped their hands and scooted off the settee. The oldest, Estella, clasped one of her father's hands. "Can we go, Papa? I want to see the fairies."

The younger one, Nancy, took the sheriff's other hand. "Me too, Papa. I want to go." She blinked her eyes rapidly.

Was the little poppet trying to bat her eyelashes? Look out gentlemen, in another ten years she would be stealing hearts.

"Um...um..." Sheriff Rix stammered.

This time, his wife let out a soft laugh. She returned her attention to Montana. "The principal players are four young people who are pretty much pining after the one they can't or shouldn't have. Hermia, Lysander, Demetrius, and Helena. Both Demetrius and Lysander love Hermia. Hermia loves Lysander in return, but Hermia's father has ordered her to marry Demetrius or be put to death."

"That's ridiculous." If his sister were given the choice between a forced marriage or death, she would put the noose around her own neck.

"That was the law and the father's right." Mrs. Hammond continued relaying the tale. "Helena loves Demetrius, but he doesn't love her. Oberon—the king of the fairies—felt sorry for Helena and tasked his page, Puck, to put a love spell on Demetrius to have him fall in love with Helena. Puck mistakenly puts the spell on Lysander who falls in love with Helena. The king fixes it by putting the spell on Demetrius. Then both men, who had loved Hermia, now love Helena."

Montana tried to keep all the people straight in his head, but found it near impossible.

She went on to explain a feud between the king of the fairies and his queen over a native servant boy. The king put a love spell on the queen causing her to fall in love with a mortal man bearing a donkey head.

In the end, all the spells were lifted except the one on Demetrius to be in love with Helena. In the morning, everyone believed the whole night to be nothing more than a dream and seemed happy in the end.

He would never keep it all straight. Even as he stood there, the details were fading into the dust.

The elder Mr. Hammond, Saul, came in through the kitchen. "What have we got here?"

The sheriff's wife explained the situation. She stood in front of Montana, fiddling with the leather cord tie.

The two spectating men tried to smother their laughs.

She wagged a finger at her husband. "Stop your snickering. He looks quite handsome. Miss Marseille will be proud to have him as her escort."

Montana appreciated Mrs. Hammond's help. He felt better about his appearance having her approval. He pulled at his collar. "Does it have to be so tight?"

She swatted his hand. "It's not tight. There is plenty of room between the fabric and your skin."

Saul grinned. "It's cuz you aren't used to having something close to your neck. No man likes a rope around his neck."

Montana swallowed hard. It felt as he imagined a noose would be like.

Saul and Sheriff Rix guffawed now.

Mrs. Hammond waved her arm in the air. "All right, you two. That's enough. The children are behaving better than you. Out. Both of you."

"We'll be good," Sheriff Rix said.

"Too late for contrition." Mrs. Hammond put her hands on her hips. "Go."

The sheriff and his father slunk out of the room along with the two youngest children. The older girl, all of eight, remained and gazed at Montana. Hopefully, the child wasn't moonstruck over him. His collar seemed to tighten. "I best be going."

With Mrs. Hammond's consent, he skedaddled out the front door, not wanting to run into either of the Mr. Hammonds.

Montana stopped his rented buggy in front of the White Hotel behind a fancy carriage. Inside the lobby, Mr. Marseille waited, dressed far fancier than Montana. Where was he headed? "Good afternoon, Mr. Marseille." Montana extended his hand.

The professor shook it. "Good afternoon, deputy."

Was the man trying to be casual by using deputy? Or reminding Montana of his place?

Mr. Marseille inclined his head toward the staircase. "The ladies should be down soon. I have rented a carriage to take us to the play."

So that was who the fancy conveyance belonged to. "Take us? Are you going as well?"

"I am. Do not worry, I won't be a bother."

Just having the man along as a chaperone would be a bother. Uncomfortable to say the least. Montana was glad now that Mrs. Hammond had insisted on the suit coat. "Excuse me a moment."

Montana crossed to the registration desk. "William, would you have someone return the buggy I rented to Amos at the livery? It's out front. Here is payment for the trouble." He slid a coin across the desk.

William took it. "I'll have that taken care of for you."

Montana returned to the professor and stood uncomfortably near him. What should he say? Anything? Nothing would probably be best. The professor didn't offer any conversation either but seemed more at ease with the silence.

Before long, Felicity descended the staircase. Where had she gotten that blue dress? Had she let Miss Marseille buy her more clothes?

When she reached the bottom, she raised her hand and halted his question. "Miss Marseille is letting me borrow one of her gowns."

The professor took one of her hands and bowed over it. *"Enchanté."*

Montana wanted to tell him to not touch his sister but became distracted by Felicity pointing toward the staircase.

Miss Marseille glided down, stealing all the air from his lungs. At the bottom, she gazed at him and her eyes brightened. "You look devastatingly handsome."

He straightened, not minding his attire so much.

"You are more beautiful than ever. I didn't think that was possible."

Gifting him with a smile, she tugged at the top of her gold-satin, above-the-elbow gloves. "Shall we go?"

Montana remembered to breathe again and held the door open for both ladies as well as for the professor. Mr. Marseille gave him a nod as he passed through. Was the man acknowledging Montana's courtesy or that of a servant? It was hard to tell with the man.

Mr. Marseille assisted both ladies into the carriage then glanced at the buggy Montana had rented, then at Montana, before disappearing into the carriage.

The professor must have figured out Montana had rented the buggy—unsuitable transportation for four people but would have been fine for three. Had he known, he could have rented something larger. He climbed into the carriage. He slipped into the empty place next to Miss Marseille. The pair of seats faced each other. Though he'd hoped to sit next to her, he hadn't realized that would put Mr. Marseille with Felicity. He wasn't sure he was comfortable with this arrangement.

A short ride later, Montana sat nervously in the normal school's small theater—at least that's the way Miss

Marseille had referred to it. It seemed large to him. He pulled at his collar.

Originally, he had assumed it would be only him, Miss Marseille, and his sister, but Miss Marseille had invited her professor brother along to *even up the numbers*. Why did there need to be an even number of men and women? Society people had some strange rules. Professor Marseille would no doubt keep a close eye on Montana. Why else would he have agreed to come?

Montana had set out to understand and pay close attention to the play. Not merely know what the play was about but what was going on as it was being acted out on the stage. But then Miss Marseille whispered in his ear, explaining what was happening. Her lilting accent both irritated him and pleased him. Drove him to distraction. He wanted her to stop but also wanted her to continue. He felt like Lysander who had inadvertently received Puck's spell to fall in love with Helena. Though not in love with Miss Marseille, he did feel charmed by the enchanting French lady. He was more like the Helena character, falling for someone who would never return his affections. The wrong person to have fallen in love with the lovely lady. Unlikely he would end up with the right beautiful maiden as Lysander and Demetrius would by the end.

Even he was smart enough to know this fair maiden could never be his. Her brother had told him as much. Even if he hadn't warned him, Montana knew.

The professor leaned toward Miss Marseille. "Stop hissing in the poor man's ear. How is he supposed to enjoy the show?"

"If he understands what is going on, he can enjoy it more."

The professor glanced at Montana. "I am sure he is doing fine without your help."

At the intermission, the foursome gathered in the hallway outside the theater with the other patrons. Professor Marseille paid little attention to Montana or Miss Marseille, his focus solely on Felicity. Though grateful to not be under the man's scrutiny, Montana was also uneasy about the professor's intentions toward his own sister. She seemed to enjoy the dandy's attention.

Miss Marseille touched Montana's arm to garner his attention. "Do not worry about them. I figured Felicity would enjoy herself more if she had a companion. They are getting along brilliantly."

A little too brilliantly for Montana's liking. But there really was no harm being done. Is this how the professor felt when he saw Montana with his sister?

What should he do? Focus on the lovely Frenchwoman? Or make a show of protecting his twin who didn't need protecting? First of all, Professor Marseille didn't seem threatening in the least and was behaving as a perfect gentleman. No ulterior motives with that man. Second, even if the professor was a cad, Felicity could take care of herself.

Which left Montana free to give Miss Marseille all of his attention. He smiled to himself.

Nine

In the cool evening air, Montana guided Cletus down the main street of Kamola with Felicity behind him. In spite of dressing up and trying to figure out what the play actors were saying, he'd enjoyed the day. Mostly because of being with Miss Marseille.

He had been pleased when his twin had come down, after having supper with the Marseilles, in her regular clothes rather than the fancy dress she'd borrowed. He had appreciated the professor not commenting on the buggy Montana had rented. "Do you wish I had a buggy for you to ride in?"

"What kind of question is that? I always ride on the back of your horse."

"I thought, being a woman, you might prefer it over a smelly horse."

"Like Miss Marseille? I'm not prissy like her. Riding here suits me well, and Cletus isn't smelly." She leaned around him and patted the horse's withers. "Are you, boy?"

"Don't call Miss Marseille prissy." His skin prickled.

Felicity resumed her position behind him. "I don't mean that in an unkind way, but she does want things just so and isn't used to getting her hands dirty. Though I liked the fancy dress, I wouldn't cotton to not being able to do much for fear of mussing it up."

"There's nothing wrong with having things a certain way." He had specific places in his small barn for his horse tack and other things. He knew where to find anything he was after and knew right off if anything was missing or out of place. He could even find whatever he needed in the dark.

It had been an adjustment when his twin had come to live with him for a while. She put his dishes in all the wrong places, so he struck a deal with her. If she did all the cooking and didn't move stuff around in the rest of his cabin—except her room corner—he wouldn't fuss about the kitchen area. So far, it had worked out fine.

Felicity rested her chin on his shoulder. "Miss Marseille is sweet on you."

The pretty lady was nice. But *sweet* on him? Not likely. "Why do you say that?"

"When Mr. Marseille climbed into the carriage at the hotel, he had tried to get me to move next to her. She pointed her finger and told him something in French. I think it was to sit down and not make a fuss. He replied in French but obeyed."

Montana liked the idea of her wanting him to sit next to her. All in all, it was a wonderful outing. He didn't even mind the play he could barely understand.

"Don't go getting any fancy ideas about the socialite. When all is said and done, their kind never end up with our kind. A family such as hers would never allow it."

Throw cold water on a fire. How could he forget with everyone reminding him all the time? He had also reminded himself.

After Deputy Montana and his sister had left, Geneviève's brother came to her room. "I have a favor to ask of you." When it was just the two of them, they both spoke French.

"If you are going to insist I no longer keep company with the deputy, I won't be able to capitulate." She enjoyed her new-found freedom, even if it couldn't last, and would take advantage of it as long as she could.

"It's not that, but do be careful." He crossed to the balcony doors, his hands clasped together at the small of his back. "Would you come to church with me in the morning?" He turned to face her.

She hadn't been to church in almost a month. She hesitated. Why had he asked her so hesitantly, and why did he call it a favor? *Ah.* "Will *that woman* be there?"

"*Oui.* I merely want you to see her. I want to know what you think of her."

"You don't expect me to speak to her, do you?"

"No. I have never spoken to her. She sits in the front. I usually enter at the rear after the service has started and depart a moment before it ends."

"Like some malefactor?" How unseemly.

He flashed his cocky grin. "A little."

The thought of secreting in and out of someplace without notice *was* intriguing. "Our grandparents would never approve."

His smile widened. "You'll do it?"

"I'll think about it." She wanted to, but she also didn't.

"Wear something less conspicuous. Nothing with big sleeves." He headed toward the door. "I'll come by your room first thing."

Geneviève liked her puffed sleeves. If she didn't feel inclined to go on the outing in the morning, she didn't have to go and probably wouldn't be up for it. She had never wanted anything to do with her brother's quest. Her blue checkered taffeta dress she'd gone fishing in could possibly be suitable.

However, by morning, curiosity had taken over. With Felicity having the day off, she wouldn't be pelted with questions about where she was off to.

Her choice for attire came down to her pink silk taffeta with gorgeous lace around the bottom of the slightly puffed sleeves, one of her walking suits, or the cotton calico dress, which was completely unsuitable for church. She settled on her burgundy walking suit as she could don that one without help which she had done on the train. The sleeves, though puffed, weren't as big as her other walking suit. She'd stepped off the train in it, and into Deputy Montana's arms. She smiled at the memory.

She slipped into the church behind her brother after everyone was already singing. Her emotions warred within, excitement as though she were a bandit and trepidation at what her brother asked of her.

Once in place with a hymnal open, Pierre inclined his head. "She's in the second row on the left, third one in."

Geneviève craned her neck to see. The woman had taken off her hat—if she even wore one. How unseemly.

Several other women also wore no hat. Was that the style out here?

As soon as the singing ceased, Geneviève sat quickly so as not to be noticed. Her hat brim—even though on the small side of her usual—scraped along Pierre's sleeve.

The vicar stood in the front. He wore no clergy frock, only regular attire as though he were taking a stroll down the street on a regular afternoon, doing nothing of significance. Not only did the vicar dress inappropriately, but many of the men were in dusty shirts and trousers with no tie or coat. Women wore simple dresses. Didn't these people out west know teaching about God was important? A function which required one to look their best? People attended church in a more casual manner on the frontier. It seemed disrespectful. But then wasn't God here too? Regardless of people's attire?

The vicar opened his Bible and preached on forgiveness.

Geneviève kept her focus on the back of the woman's head. That woman knew nothing. Pierre's quest was in vain. She would have nothing to tell him.

Midway through the sermon, something the vicar said arrested Geneviève's attention. "Matthew 18:21 and 22, 'Then came Peter to him, and said, Lord, how oft shall my brother sin against me, and I forgive him? Till seven times? Jesus saith unto him, I say not unto thee, Until seven times: but, Until seventy times seven.'"

The vicar chuckled. "Some of us can't count that high. But this verse isn't about keeping track of how many times you forgive another, it's about not keeping track at all. This is to show us to forgive without giving thought to it. Let God figure out the rest."

Didn't a person need to ask for forgiveness first? Some people didn't deserve to be forgiven.

"In case anyone is wondering how much seventy times seven is, it's four hundred and ninety. Do you want to try to keep track of so many transgressions?"

Only one.

"I'm sure you all have better things to do."

The vicar prayed and everyone stood for a final hymn.

Geneviève did have better things to do. She spirited out the back of the church before her brother could tell her it was time.

Outside, she waited for him. When he exited, she waved him over to her. "Let's hurry and go before the people leave."

Pierre took her by the arm. "Over here no one will notice us."

Soon the parishioners exited the building, flowing in a direction mostly away from where she and her brother waited.

The woman gathered with her family outside, her husband—presumably—her son or daughter with their spouse and their children. The woman had a nice tidy family.

Tears pricked her eyes. "I want to go."

Pierre didn't hesitate, guiding her away and toward their carriage.

As the conveyance rolled away, she kept her gaze fixed on the happy family.

"What did you think of her?"

"She was the same as every other woman there. No one noteworthy. I'll not discuss her any further." She needed to occupy her mind with something else to keep her tears at bay. The deputy was always a pleasant distraction. However, even thoughts of him couldn't lift her mood.

Ten

ON MONDAY, HENNY STOOD IN HER kitchen, preparing supper for her boarders. She'd spent half the day roaming around town again with Saul in search of the mystery man. She hadn't seen the stranger in nearly a week. Maybe he had left as he'd done before, if he had even been real at all.

Lord, I'm not ready to drop my search quite yet. If I don't find him this week, I'll quit.

If she went any longer than that, she would be bordering on obsessive. Perhaps she already was.

The front door opened then closed a moment later. That would be Professor Tunstall and Professor Lumbard home from another day of teaching at the normal school.

"Henny?" Mr. Lumbard called. "We have a new boarder for you."

It would be good to have the income from another resident. How long might this person stay? She set down the spoon she'd been using to stir the stew.

She strode out through the dining room and stopped short just before the parlor, her breath catching in her throat. What was *he* doing here?

Mr. Lumbard stepped forward. "Henny, this is Professor Pierre Marseille. He's a guest lecturer, a temporary replacement for Professor Inger." He appeared to be a similar age to Mr. Tunstall, in his late twenties.

This was the same man who had stood outside Henny's house and watched her in town. He had evidently *not* left Kamola after all. What was he doing *here*, in her home? At long last, she had found him. Or rather, he'd found her.

Mr. Tunstall jumped in. "He's been staying at the White Hotel, but we told him this is a much preferable place to lodge. Took quite some convincing."

Mr. Marseille gave a stiff bow, his fingers twitching as though he might be nervous. "*Mademoiselle* Henny. Pleased to make your acquaintance." Though his French accent wasn't strong, it was distinct. "I do not wish to impose. My fellow colleagues assured me it would be all right for me to come and see if you were amiable to another lodger." His gray-blue eyes seemed to hold some sort of pain. Grief, perhaps?

Since this was the man who had been watching her, Henny wanted to say she had all the boarders she could handle at the moment. Something about him reminded her of a lost child. Although he hid it well, she'd seen the look too many times not to recognize it.

Mr. Lumbard took her arm. "You look flushed. Are you all right, Henny?"

She straightened. "I'm fine. Overheated from working in the kitchen is all." She studied *Monsieur* Marseille. Certainly, the Washington State Normal School wouldn't have hired anyone who wasn't trustworthy.

She should say no to him moving in, but her curiosity wanted to find out who he was. She should simply tell Edric about him and send him away right now. Or perhaps, the times he'd been standing outside her house, he'd merely been contemplating renting a room with no ulterior motives. "I lock the front door by ten. If you aren't here by then, you'll need to find elsewhere to sleep. I don't tolerate any shenanigans. No ladies in your room. No foul language. No gambling or smoking."

"I would not do those things. If it will put your mind at ease, I am a God-fearing man."

That did help. A wounded look in this man's gray-blue eyes kicked in Henny's nurturing side. She never could turn away someone in need of a room. Wasn't that one of the reasons God had made it possible for her to purchase this large house, to help people? She sensed *Monsieur* Marseille's needs went beyond a place to sleep. "We can give it a try. See how you fit into the goings on around here."

With a gracious, yet disarming, smile, he dipped his head. "*Merci.* I will gather my belongings from the hotel tomorrow and come then. If that suits you."

Mr. Tunstall stepped closer to *Monsieur* Marseille. "Don't make the poor man spend another night at the hotel. It's nice and all, but it can't compare to your meals and your beds."

Henny forced an uneasy smile. "That will be fine. I'll make up a room after supper. The one across from you, Mr. Tunstall?"

"Perfect."

Monsieur Marseille held out a hand. "Tomorrow will be fine. I will not be able to gather my things so quickly. You have no idea how much I appreciate this."

Henny hoped she didn't regret her impulsive decision. She had tonight to further pray on this matter and decide if indeed she should allow this man to move in under her roof.

After supper, Henny approached the younger of her two boarders. "Mr. Tunstall, would you please hitch up my buggy."

He knit his eyebrows together. "You don't normally venture out after supper?"

She hadn't thought this through but appreciated her boarder looking out for her. "I'm going to visit a friend. It will still be light for another hour or so."

Soon enough the buggy was hitched and waiting for her. Mr. Tunstall held the horse's halter. "Shall I accompany you?"

"Thank you, but I'll be fine." Henny climbed in. "I shouldn't be too long." She put the rig into motion.

She had to tell Edric and Saul she'd found the mysterious stranger. The disappearing man. He *was* real. She hadn't imagined him after all. She wasn't sure if it made her feel better that she hadn't concocted him in her head, or nervous that the phantom was real.

This meant her ongoing search was over. How did she feel about that? Relieved she wasn't crazy. Glad to put a name to the stranger. But also, a little unnerved.

The Hammond men would be upset the man had so boldly come to her home. They would probably head over right now tonight to his hotel room to interrogate him. As they probably should, but that wouldn't be good. Professor Marseille might get scared off, then she would never know why he'd been lurking around corners and in front of her house.

But how could she not tell them? When they found out he'd been living under her roof, they would be cross with her.

She stopped the buggy in front of their house.

Monsieur Marseille didn't seem dangerous, and she would have the other two professors in the house. She wished she had someone unattached to this whole situation to consult. She couldn't think of a single person. Everyone she knew would insist upon telling the sheriff. Edric, as well as Saul, would forbid her from allowing him to move in. She did run a boarding house, after all. What else was the man supposed to do? The only way she was likely to get answers from him, was to have him close so he couldn't disappear around another corner.

She snapped the reins and sent the horse into motion. She would pray and sleep on her decision. If she had a different leading in the morning, she could talk to the Hammonds then.

Lord, please protect me and my boarders if this man isn't who he seems to be. Also, give me clear direction if I shouldn't allow this man to move in.

What was the saying? *Keep one eye on your friends and two on your enemies.* Problem was, she didn't know which category this stranger fell into.

Another thought assaulted her. What if he wasn't really the stranger she'd seen around town watching her? What if, as Saul said, she'd confused more than one person for a single man she'd imagined was watching her. She didn't want to cause him undue conflict because of her overactive imagination.

After driving a while longer so she didn't return home too quickly and cause anyone to have suspicions about where she had gone and why, she headed home. She would wait to see how the Lord directed her.

The following morning, Henny drove to Washington State Normal School. She stood before the desk outside the president's office. "Good morning, Melany. I would like to see President Black. Does he have a spare minute?"

"For you, I'm sure he'd make time." The lady behind the desk rose. "I'll only be a moment." She disappeared through the door behind her. Soon, she returned and waved Henny in.

The president sat behind his large cherry-wood desk but stood when she entered. "It's good to see you, Henny. Have a seat." He motioned toward the leather armchair.

She sat.

He retook his seat. "When are you ever going to tell me your family name?"

"When I'm confident people won't abuse the knowledge." She couldn't afford to have people start bandying about her family name. She'd been Henny or Aunt Henny this long, she would be for the rest of her time on this earth.

"Mysterious. You've always been an intriguing woman." He rested his forearms on his desk. "What can I do for you?"

"You have a new professor here, *Monsieur* Marseille. He's French."

"Yes, we do. We only have him for this spring quarter and a few classes this summer. Already as word has gotten out about him teaching this summer, our registrations are up. Mostly the ladies. Can't blame them with a handsome gentleman like him for a teacher. I'm hoping to talk him into signing on for a year starting this fall."

The president seemed to like him. "What kind of man is he?"

Mr. Black quirked an eyebrow. "What is your interest in my staff?"

More than she could admit right now. "He's requested to rent one of my rooms. Before I let him move in this evening, I would prefer to know a bit more about him."

"You're a smart woman. He's a good man. I'd trust him in my home."

That was reassuring. The president had children. "Anything else you can tell me about him?"

"Such as?"

"I don't know." But she did know. "Was he born in Europe? What brought him out west? Has he ever been to Kamola before?"

"I didn't ask, but I guess I assumed he was born in France. He said he'd heard stories of the Wild West and wanted to experience it for himself. He came to Kamola in the late summer and left sometime in November, I think."

So, it could have been him watching her last fall. "He hasn't been here this whole time?"

"No. He was in Virginia when I corresponded with him over the winter to talk him into coming to teach for us."

"Did you know him before? Is that why you asked him to teach?"

"I ran into him late last summer, heard his French accent, and knew it would be good for our students to learn a foreign language."

Late summer? Henny hadn't noticed him until mid-fall. Maybe he wasn't the same person. She would have to wait and see. "What is he teaching?"

"Obviously, a couple of units of French, one in geography, and one in mathematics."

Apparently, he was widely traveled in addition to well educated.

"Thank you, Mr. Black. You have eased my mind greatly." She still had questions for Professor Marseille. Those would have to wait until she got to know him a little and see if she could figure out why he had come. If anything. She still wasn't convinced one hundred percent he was the same gentleman she'd been seeing. However, if he started asking questions about Nicole and her cousins, Henny would go straight to the sheriff.

After dressing this morning, Geneviève dismissed Felicity for the day. She had chosen her garden party dress that she could put a jacket over for her outing during the day which would be adequate for supper tonight. People in the frontier didn't seem to care if one wore the same attire all day or dressed for supper. She relished the idea of not changing clothes many times a day. What a way to save time. Like walking, it freed something inside her.

She headed down to the front desk of the hotel. "Is my picnic lunch ready?"

The clerk greeted her. "It is, Miss Marseille. I'll go to the kitchen and get that for you. Also, the buggy and driver you ordered is waiting out front."

"*Merci.*" *Oui*, walking was freeing, but the basket would likely be heavy with food.

The clerk returned momentarily with a cloth covered basket and a blanket. "I'll take this out to the buggy for you."

"*Merci.*"

At the conveyance, the clerk set the basket on the floor with the blanket on top of it and assisted Geneviève aboard. She thanked him again, and the driver took her to the sheriff's office.

With the basket in hand—which would have been too heavy for her to carry all that way—she entered the building.

Two men were within, neither of them her deputy. One stood at a filing cabinet. The other sat in a chair with his boots on the black potbelly stove. He quickly dropped his feet to the floor with a double thud and stood. "Howdy, Miss Marseille."

She tilted her head toward him. "Good day, deputy."

The other man turned around. "Good morning, miss. I'm Sheriff Rix. What can I do for you?" He shot the deputy a look.

"I came to see Deputy Montana. Is he not here?"

"He's out at the moment. I can send for him." The sheriff turned to the deputy. "Sammy, Montana is at the bathhouse because of a disturbance. Go take his place and send him back."

The younger man heaved a sigh but did as asked.

"That was very kind of you. I fear I may be interrupting his work. Should I leave?"

The man shook his head and indicated a wooden chair. "Have a seat."

She did.

The sheriff sat behind his desk. "It looks as though you might have brought him food."

"If it is no bother." She didn't want to cause Deputy Montana any difficulties. She knew how upset her grandparents got when someone distracted the servants from their tasks.

"Not at all." He flashed a reassuring smile. "A man needs to eat. He'll be glad you came. By your accent, I presume you're from France."

"*Oui*—yes."

He settled in his chair. "What brings you all this way to our little town?"

"My brother. He is teaching at the normal school."

He bobbed his head. "Do you plan to stay long?"

"I have not decided. We were supposed to leave right away, but plans change." She had originally wanted to, but for the time being wasn't so against being here. For now. Her turn to inquire. "Has Deputy Montana always lived in Kamola?"

The sheriff shook his head. "He comes from Spokane."

"Is his sister the only family he has?"

"His folks and others of his kin are mostly on the east side of the state."

"What brought him here?"

"I was in Spokane, transporting a prisoner. There was some trouble. Montana helped out. I offered him a job. He accepted. That was four years ago."

"Was he a deputy there? Is that why he assisted you?"

"Naw. As I recall, he was working at a general store, unloading shipments."

The deputy had been very helpful to her as well, retrieving her luggage without being asked. A fine man.

Deputy Montana blocked Mimi Barker's path to the exit door, allowing Jeremiah Barker to escape the bathhouse. He didn't feel bad the man had nothing but a towel to cover himself. The spring day had warmed a little. Whatever had inflamed his wife was probably justified. "Now, Mimi, put the gun down."

As she swung the shotgun around, the three men still in bathing tubs ducked. "Out of my way, Montana. I have no ill feelings toward you."

"I can't have you going around town brandishing a gun." He hoped she would decide to be reasonable.

"I ain't giving up my gun."

She was rarely a threat to anyone but Jeremiah.

Even so, Montana couldn't have her wielding a weapon while she was so upset. "How about you sit in that chair and lay it across your lap?"

She glanced at the chair and gave a nod before sitting. "He spent my egg money on whiskey and a bath. We have a tub at home. I think he's getting scrubbed up for some floozy."

"Jeremiah wouldn't do that."

A voice from behind him spoke. "Hey, Montana."

He glanced over his shoulder at Sammy. "What are you doing here?"

"Sheriff sent me to take over. Figured you needed help."

That sounded a little fishy. Didn't sound like Sheriff Rix. "I'm doing fine."

Sammy shrugged. "All I know is he wants you at the office in an all-fired hurry."

It must be important if the sheriff was taking him off a task. However, Sammy made it sound as though Montana might have done something wrong, which he knew he hadn't. Fine, if Sammy wanted this one, he could have it.

Montana stepped aside. "Mrs. Barker has a gripe with her husband. Jeremiah skedaddled out the rear. You need to get the gun from her and take poor Jeremiah his clothes. If you can find him." He strode toward the door. "And make sure those other men don't get shot."

Sammy gave him an annoyed glare.

Montana left.

Sammy would be fine. Mimi just needed a bit for her ire to simmer down. Now to see what Sheriff Rix wanted, if anything at all. He swung up onto Cletus.

Once at the sheriff's office, he noticed one of the for-hire buggies out front. Who was here?

He dismounted and tethered Cletus to the hitching rail. He slowed as he approached the door. Should he interrupt the sheriff? Sammy could be playing a joke on him.

Did he hear a female French accent? He opened the door without delay. His heart galloped at the sight of Miss Marseille. She turned in the chair and gifted him with a smile.

What was she doing here? Each time he saw her, he figured it was his last. Yet here she was.

Sheriff Rix broke the silence. "Miss Marseille has brought a picnic lunch for the two of you."

"You have?"

"Mais oui."

"I don't..."

"Go. Enjoy. Be back in an hour or so." The sheriff stood, likely in anticipation of the lady standing.

She held out her hand to Montana.

He took it, helping her to her feet, then spoke to the sheriff. "Are you sure?"

Sheriff Rix nodded. "You need to eat. What was the trouble at the bathhouse?"

"Jeremiah and Mimi Barker."

"Say no more."

"I do appreciate getting to pawn them off on Sammy." Montana took the basket and escorted Miss Marseille outside.

"Where is a good place to picnic?"

"There's a pond at the edge of town that's nice."

"Very good. We go."

Montana told the driver their destination and helped Miss Marseille into the buggy.

At Ferguson Pond, the driver waited nearby with the buggy. Close enough to serve as chaperone, but far enough away as not to be a hinderance.

Montana wasn't used to having someone hanging about, waiting, but it was best for the young lady's reputation to have another person along. He spread out the blanket and assisted Miss Marseille to sit on it. She unpacked the tasty meal she had likely gotten from the hotel.

At first, spending time with Miss Marseille had been a lark. Almost like getting away with something when he was a boy. Now, he feared he might be developing true feelings for her. He couldn't afford to have those.

Miss Marseille's lilting French voice sent a ripple through his thoughts. "You seem all serious. What is the matter?"

"What are we doing here?"

"Having a picnic. Yes?"

"Not right now. All of this—fishing, the play, a picnic. We both know I'm not your social equal. We could never have a future, so why do you keep spending time with me?"

"Can we not merely be friends?"

He thought about that a moment. "I suppose we could." For now. As long as he knew that, and she wasn't trifling with him.

Now to wrangle his emotions into submission so they remembered where he stood with her. Friends.

Eleven

LATER THAT EVENING IN THE HOTEL dining room, Geneviève sat across the table from her brother. "Ask me what I did today."

"Besides wear the same dress all day?" He smiled.

"You noticed? It's very liberating. We waste so much time dressing and redressing for various portions of the day, and then every different event requires new attire as well."

"I suppose we do. Tell me, what did you do today?" He stabbed a piece of meat.

"I procured a basket lunch and had a picnic with Deputy Montana."

Her brother's smile faded. He didn't look pleased at all. "Vivi, what are you doing with this man?"

"Nothing to draw so much concern on your face. He was a perfect gentleman."

"That's not what I mean. Are you developing feelings for him? Real feelings?"

She might be. "What if I am?"

"You'll only get hurt. *Grand-père* and *Grand-mère* will never allow it."

She pushed the food around her plate with her fork. "What if I don't want to marry whomever they choose?"

"You won't have a choice."

"I could say no."

"They would disinherit you. Cut you off. You're accustomed to a certain lifestyle. Your deputy would never be able to provide that for you."

He was right, of course, but in the center of her chest, an ache longed to be with Deputy Montana. He freed something inside her. Made her believe life could hold more than lavish cotillions, fine dining, grand museums, and expensive clothes. Worrying about what one wore, where one went to be seen, and with whom one was seen. The deputy and his sister seemed happier and more content than she had ever felt, and they had little. They didn't have the constant pressure to always be perfect.

"You seem deep in thought."

His words pulled her attention back to him. "I suppose I was." She didn't want to discuss her future, one which would be foisted upon her. Her heart wanted to bathe in her freedom as long as she could. "Your turn. What did you do today, other than teach?"

"I'm glad you asked. I have something to tell you."

She leaned forward. "All right." This felt like a secret. She loved secrets.

He spoke hesitantly. "I'm checking out of the hotel."

Geneviève straightened. "We're going home?" Excitement and disappointment vied for control inside her. On one hand getting her brother to leave Kamola had been her goal in coming. On the other, she rather enjoyed spending time with Deputy Montana.

"No. I'm moving into the boarding house run by the woman whom I believe knew Anne Henderson."

Her blood ran cold. "What! You can't do that." This wasn't good. He was only supposed to teach and grow weary of his fallacious quest.

"I can, and I have made the arrangements." He took one of her hands in both of his. "You could come too. I'm sure she has room. From everything I've heard about her, she's a good and kind woman. I'm sure she will help us."

"Us?" Geneviève pulled her hand free. "I told you before, I don't want anything to do with that woman or anyone who knew *Madame* Henderson. You are the only one who wants to delve into the past. Let it stay buried. No good can come of this."

"You aren't even a little curious about what she might know?"

She would never admit that. "Not in the least." But she hated that she *was* intrigued.

The following afternoon, Henny knelt in her backyard flower garden weeding. Her favorite place in her whole yard. The budding daisies were coming up strong and healthy. They would start blooming in a week or two. All she had in memory of a once upon a time family from a lifetime ago. A place which brought her both joy and heartache. She blinked to clear her vision. She would not dwell on past mistakes today.

She wrapped her fingers around a pesky plant that didn't belong and tugged with all her might. When it wouldn't budge, she stood and gripped it with both hands. With a yank, she pulled it free and stumbled backward. Surprisingly, she didn't find herself on the ground. Instead, strong arms caught her.

Professor Marseille gazed down at her with his gray-blue eyes. "Are you all right?"

What was he doing here? She hadn't expected him until supper time. "Yes, thanks to you." Something about him, Henny couldn't quite grasp, created an ethereal feeling. Probably nothing more than the excitement of nearly tumbling to the ground. She righted herself and held up the tangle of green. "Troublesome weed. Trying to clear out the pests before they get too embedded. I'm obviously a little late if this one is any indication."

He nodded toward the flower bed. "These are daisies, no?"

"Yes, they are." He knew flowers. What did that tell her about him? She tossed the weed into her growing pile. "I wasn't expecting you until closer to supper."

"Pardon my forwardness. I had a break in my classes and wondered if I could drop off my luggage. If this is not a good time, I will hold off until later."

She wasn't prepared to be alone with this man until she knew him better. However, it wouldn't hurt for him to set his suitcases in the entry.

Saul strolled from around the side of the house. "Henny, you have a delivery wagon out front."

Professor Marseille faced Saul. "That is mine."

Henny stepped forward. "Saul, this is my new boarder, Professor Marseille. He's moving in today. This is my friend Saul Hammond."

The professor stretched out his arm. "Please call me Pierre, Mr. Hammond."

Saul shook the man's hand. "Pleased to meet you. And Saul will do." He pointed his thumb over his shoulder. "Is all that yours in the wagon?"

Pierre smiled, and Henny's mind scurried about, searching for answers to questions she didn't know. "It is a bit much, but I did not know what I might need from back East. I brought many books. Fortunately for the movers, several are at the normal school." He indicated Henny. "I was inquiring if I might leave my things now and then return after classes. If that will suit you."

"That will be fine." Henny rubbed her hands together to brush off the dirt and led the way around the house.

Two steamer trunks and two large carpetbags waited in the bed of the wagon.

Henny stepped inside her front door. "I'll meet you at the top of the stairs." She went to the second floor and opened the beige and blue room. Having each of her rooms decorated in different colors helped to distinguish them.

With Saul present, she didn't mind showing him to his room. It took both movers to haul one of the large steamer trunks up. Pierre and Saul each carried one of the oversized carpetbags. Pierre returned with the hired men to get the second trunk.

Henny stood in the front entry with Saul. "What do you think of him?"

"There's something about him."

"Good or bad?"

"Definitely good. He has an honest face."

Henny had felt the same thing, but there could be something deceptive under his friendly exterior. If so, she needed to learn what.

"I suspect a few of your younger quilting ladies will be swooning over that one."

No doubt. If Henny were twenty-five years younger, she might swoon. "I'm sure Professor Tunstall will give him pointers on how to avoid too much attention from the young ladies in town."

Pierre led the movers upstairs with the other trunk and they disappeared into his room.

Saul leaned in. "What do you suppose he has in those? Seems like an awful lot for a man."

It did seem like an abundance for a gentleman, and those trunks were expensive, the highest quality money could buy. "He said he had books. He might have brought other things he would need for teaching." His suit was expensive too. Even so, it was the kind one changed out of to dress for meals. Likely, he had many more in his luggage.

"Saul, would you come to supper tonight? I want to know what you think of my new boarder after spending some time with him."

"I would love to, but I don't think you have anything to worry about. Though, if you have suspicions, I can have Edric look into him."

"No. Your impression will do fine." She didn't want to taint his opinion of the man before he'd had a chance to form one.

Pierre tipped his hat to Henny as he left. "I will see you this evening."

She gave him a nod.

Who are you, Professor Pierre Marseille? Why have you returned to Kamola and chosen to stay at my boarding house?

Geneviève met her brother outside his final class for the day. This was her last chance to talk him out of his senseless quest. "I saw someone else go into your room at the hotel." Was she too late? Please let her be in time.

He headed down the hall. "I told you I was leaving the hotel. I took my belongings to the boarding house earlier today."

"Not so soon." She walked beside him. "What am I supposed to do?"

"You can come with me. It will be better that way."

She shook her head. "Never. We can get on the next train and return to Virginia. We can forget all about this town."

"What about the deputy?"

She doubted she would ever forget him. "You have been telling me not to keep company with him, which will resolve itself if you'll leave with me." Her heart constricted at the thought. She didn't want to part from Deputy Montana.

"I'm sorry," he said. "I have to do this."

She stopped short.

Pierre halted as well. "I have a carriage arranged to take me. I can give you a ride to the hotel."

She took a retreating step and then another.

He held his hands out from his sides. "Where are you going?"

Anywhere but here. She hurried away, out the door at the far end of the hall. She wanted to run and keep running. Oh, bother. Her rented vehicle waited on the other side of the building.

Pierre would likely go to his office before leaving.

She had time to get to her carriage. Once there, another conveyance pulled up behind hers. Likely Pierre's.

She climbed in without waiting for the driver to open the door or assist her.

He peered in through the window. "Where to, miss?"

"I do not know. Drive. Anywhere." She just needed him to hurry before Pierre came out. She needed to be away from her stubborn brother.

The driver shrugged and climbed into his seat. The carriage lurched into motion.

Tears rolled down her cheeks. How could her brother do this? It would do no good. He wouldn't learn anything.

After a few minutes, the carriage stopped.

She dabbed at her face with her handkerchief.

The driver appeared in the door's window again. "I didn't know where to take you, so I brought you to the hotel since this is where I picked you up."

She stared at the building. She didn't want to go in. "Please take me to the sheriff's office."

"All right." He disappeared, and the carriage moved again.

Shortly it stopped.

Geneviève didn't wait for the driver. She climbed out and handed him his fee. "Thank you. I will not be needing you again."

"You're welcome." He drove away, probably glad to be away from such an emotional woman.

She dabbed her eyes again and blinked several times. Then she put on a smile and entered the sheriff's office.

A deputy sat behind the desk with his boots up. She'd seen him before, eating at the hotel with her deputy. Widening his eyes as though afraid of her, he pointed toward the corner.

She turned.

Deputy Montana sat in a chair by the potbelly stove but shot to his feet. "Miss Marseille? What are you doing here?"

The desk deputy trailed a finger from the corner of his eye. "Looks as though she needs to talk to you. You go. I'll sit with the prisoner."

"Howdy, pretty lady." The man in the cell stood with his arms draped through the bars.

The desk deputy tossed an empty tin cup at the bars. "We'll have none of that." He tipped his head toward Deputy Montana. "Go."

Deputy Montana cupped his hand around her elbow and escorted her out. "Where's your carriage?"

"It is gone."

The deputy likely could tell she had been crying and didn't know quite what to do. "I can get another one."

She shook her head. "I want to walk." Not something she would have said before coming to Kamola.

"All right. I can escort you to the hotel."

"I do not want to go there." She sniffled.

He guided her around the building. "There's a meadow behind here." He showed her to a downed log a short distance from the building. "Have a seat."

She was too agitated to sit. She didn't want others telling her what to do. If her brother could do whatever he wanted, then so could she. She threw her arms around

Deputy Montana's neck and kissed him. Shocking, even to herself, but she didn't care.

He graciously returned her kiss but soon gripped her wrists behind his head and pulled himself free. "I may be the biggest fool in the world for stopping that, but I need to know. What's this about? Who upset you?" He gazed at her with great concern in his brown eyes.

That melted her resolve. She slumped down onto the log. Though she tried hard to prevent them, tears streamed from her eyes.

He sat next to her, offering his folded red bandana.

She took it and leaned into his side.

He wrapped an arm around her. "Did someone hurt you?"

Pierre, but not in the way he meant. She patted her face with his bandana. "My brother is making a fool of himself. He has left the hotel and moved into a boarding house."

"And left you there by yourself? Why would he do that?"

"He has misguided ideas about a woman."

Deputy Montana's mouth pulled up on the ends. "Ah. That makes sense. Men will do a lot of stupid things for a woman."

He thought it was some romantic affair. She must let him believe that because she couldn't tell him the truth. "You would not do that, would you?"

"I've been known to be stupid a time or two."

"I do not believe that." She gazed into his kind eyes. The reality of what she had done took her breath away. How could she have acted so rashly and kissed him? She'd behaved like a woman of ill repute. Ducking her head, she pressed the bandana to the corners of her eyes. "Please forgive me for my actions. I do not know what I was thinking."

"You were upset. It's best to pretend it didn't happen."

"You would do that? Forget about a lady's indiscretion?"

He widened his eyes like an innocent boy. "What indiscretion?"

"When I—"

"I don't know what you're talking about." He stood and offered her his hand. "How about I escort you to the hotel?"

She took it and rose to her feet. "You are as fine a gentleman as I have ever met." She was fortunate to have encountered him as soon as she stumbled off the train.

That evening after supper, Henny walked with Saul out to her front gate. The meal had been pleasant with good conversation. The men all got on well. "What do you think of my new boarder?"

"I like him. He seems to be a fine fellow."

"That's the impression I got as well. One can never be too careful. I wouldn't have taken a chance on him if not for Mr. Tunstall's and Mr. Lumbard's recommendations."

"You are a shrewd woman. He'll make a fine addition."

"I'm glad to hear you say so."

"Why do you say that?"

Should she tell him more? If she did, an inquisition would start. First with Saul and then Edric. Better to wait until Saul—and she—got to know this man better first. "I value your opinion." If Saul had sensed anything amiss with the man, she would have told him who he was. Or who she thought he was.

Twelve

THE NEXT MORNING, MONTANA RODE CLETUS through Kamola with Felicity behind him. He halted in front of the hotel, giving her a hand down. He wished *he* were the one going to see Miss Marseille. "Make sure she's all right."

His twin moved the fingers on her hand one after the other as though counting. "That's the fifth time you've asked."

"She was pretty upset yesterday."

"I know. I saw her after you did. She seemed all right. She had a light supper sent to her room."

He knew. He'd inquired at the front desk. Toast and jam. Hardly the makings of an adequate meal. "She didn't tell you any more about why she was upset about her brother and some woman?"

"I already told you she didn't."

"She gave no indication about who this woman is?"

"None. You're worrying too much about this and caring for her far more than you should. I'm sure her brother can take care of himself." She waved and entered the building.

Was he overly concerned? Miss Marseille had been distraught. That couldn't have been for nothing. Or else she never would have...

Pretend it didn't happen. That was what he'd told her. He didn't want to. He'd wanted to hold her in his arms and kiss her breathless. Yet, he'd been the one breathless.

It had been his duty to find out why she'd been so upset, not to take advantage of her distress.

He would have a talk with Mr. Marseille to find out what he had to say about the situation. Problem was, Montana didn't know which boarding house the man had moved to. Kamola had upwards of ten. He couldn't sit outside each one until Pierre Marseille appeared. Chances of missing him were great. He headed to the Washington State Normal School. The professor would come there eventually, and Montana couldn't miss him.

Once at the normal school, Montana debated whether it would be best to wait in the man's office or not. He opted for leaning against the railing of the outside steps to the main entrance.

After a while, teachers, staff, and students arrived in carriages, buggies, and on foot.

Mr. Marseille strolled up with three other professors. He stopped while the others continued inside. "Am I safe to assume you are here to see me?"

Montana nodded. "I saw your sister yesterday afternoon. I want to make sure she's all right."

"She is fine."

"She seemed to be upset over you moving to a boarding house and a woman you're seeing."

The man studied him a moment before replying. "She would prefer I remain at the hotel."

"How come you didn't?" Montana sensed this man was being evasive but couldn't put his finger on why.

"I had grown tired of the noise at inconvenient hours." He spoke through a veiled smile.

"But you left your sister at the hotel? With no chaperone?"

"I invited her to join me at the boarding house. She refused. Where my sister stays is between her and myself. I can assure you I will continue to look after her and be mindful of her activities." Even though Mr. Marseille said it with a cheerful French accent, that sounded like a warning.

"Which boarding house did you move to?"

"On Pine Street, run by a lady named Henny."

"Ah, Aunt Henny."

"I have heard people refer to her as such. What is her surname?"

"Don't know. Not sure if anyone knows. It's nothing to worry about. She's a wonderful person. I think you'll be happier there."

"That is good to know. Is that all? I have classes to prepare for."

"Thank you." Montana strolled away.

Mr. Marseille was a confusing man at best. Montana couldn't get a read on him. He appeared amiable yet there seemed to be a secretiveness with no evidence to back it up. Just a feeling. The man *was* watching out for his sister but not overbearing. He warned Montana about Miss Marseille, yet didn't forbid him from keeping company with her.

On Thursday, Henny drove her buggy with Saul at her side. She could no longer put off telling the Hammond men about the identity of the stranger who'd been watching her—her new boarder. With the quilting circle ladies coming over tomorrow, she wouldn't be able to keep the secret from them. Then Lily would be obliged to tell her husband—the sheriff. Which, in turn, would mean Saul would find out, and both men would be in more of a lather for sure if they didn't hear the news from her own lips.

Saul had understandably assumed he was going to help her search again today for the mystery stranger who had been watching her for several months. To avoid having to repeat herself and to get the grilling over with in one shot, she would tell father and son at the same time.

Stopping in front of the sheriff's office, Henny set the brake and looped the reins around the lever. She placed a hand on her midsection to calm her nerves.

After Saul climbed down and helped her out, he opened the door for her.

With a deep breath, she walked inside, wondering if she'd made the right decision.

Edric sat behind his desk but now stood and motioned toward a chair. "Good afternoon, Aunt Henny. Have a seat."

He was alone in the room. No deputies. No Prisoners. Good. The fewer people here the better.

"Good afternoon, Edric." Henny moved to the wooden chair and sat. "Thank you."

"Pa, would you like mine?"

"I'm fine." Saul stood at her side like a protective mother hen.

Best to begin with some pleasantries. "How is Lily adjusting?" She knew the young woman was doing well but needed a way to start the conversation.

Edric smiled. "Great. We're all figuring out how to work as a family. It's not perfect, but I'm enjoying the challenge of it."

"That's good. It's time she and her boy had a happy home."

"Indeed." The sheriff folded his arms. "I know you didn't come simply to ask after my burgeoning family, which I'm sure you already know about from at least two sources. So, what brings the pair of you to my office?"

Saul spoke before she could. "She wouldn't tell me."

Henny glanced from one man to the other. "Would you two sit?" Having them tower over her wasn't making this any easier.

Edric swung the chair out from behind the desk and indicated his father take it, while he sat on the edge of his desk. "What can I do for you?"

She drew in a breath to bolster her courage. "My new boarder."

One of Edric's eyebrows quirked up, transforming him from friend to sheriff. "Something wrong with him? He seems like a nice fellow."

Saul nodded. "Real nice. Good addition."

She hoped as much. "He's a most polite gentleman. Very attentive. Always trying to do things for me. If he were thirty years older, I might suspect he had designs on me."

Edric narrowed his eyes. "But...?"

Extending her index finger, she spoke. "First, I want the two of you to remember I am a grown woman and can make my own decisions."

After a moment's hesitation, both nodded.

Henny shifted in the chair. "I believe—though I'm not completely sure—my new boarder is the stranger who has been watching me." She braced for the rebuke that would come.

Saul jumped to his feet. "What? How could you let him under your roof?"

Though expected, she disliked being scolded. "Easy. I opened my door. I'm sure he was merely trying to decide if he wanted to rent a room. I read far more into things than I should have." Would they believe that when she didn't?

Both men remained quiet for a moment until Edric broke the silence. "What did he say when you asked him about his previous actions?"

She straightened. "I didn't mention them. He doesn't know I was aware of him watching me." She wanted to keep it that way.

Edric shook his head. "You should have come to me when you first realized who he was. I could have spoken to him. Looked into his background and character."

"As I said, I'm a grown woman who can make her own decisions. I believe the Lord is leading me to help him." Not that she really felt he needed help, not in a traditional sense.

Saul grumbled beside her. "You should send him packing."

She narrowed her eyes at the elder Mr. Hammond. "I'm not going to do that. No matter what either of you say. At least not yet. You, yourself, said he was a 'nice man' and a 'good addition'. There is something about him. Something that makes me want to...I'm not sure what...help him? But I can't imagine what he might need."

Edric sighed. "You have a big heart, Aunt Henny. Sometimes too big for your own good." He pulled out a sheet of paper from the top desk drawer. "What's his full name?"

"Why?" She didn't want the sheriff to scare him off.

"I'm going to make a few inquiries."

"You don't have to do that."

Saul thinned his lips. "But he's going to."

She supposed that was prudent. "Pierre Marseille. He's from France and is a guest professor at Washington State Normal School for a few months. He came from Virginia most recently. I already spoke to the president of the normal school, and he assured me Professor Marseille has a good reputation."

Edric wrote the information down. "Anything else?"

"Maybe the hotel has some information—permanent address or something. He was there before my boarding house."

"I'll send a few telegrams and let you know what I find out."

"I would appreciate it if neither of you said anything to him. I don't want to scare him off."

"Scare him off is *exactly* what I'd like to do." Saul folded his arms.

"Pa, Aunt Henny has asked, and the man hasn't actually done anything wrong."

The elder Mr. Hammond looked at her sideways. "Are we supposed to wait until he does?"

Henny was losing control of this conversation. "If I get any indication from the Lord he is no good, I'll let you throw him out, but until such time, please do as I ask."

"Fine." Saul harrumphed. "But I'll be keeping a close eye on him."

"Thank you." Henny stood, addressing the sheriff. "I appreciate you looking into this."

"Anything for you, Aunt Henny."

She crossed to the door then turned to Saul. "Are you coming? Or have I ruffled your ire?"

"You've ruffled my ire all right, but I'm coming. Someone needs to look after you."

Henny had been looking after herself for over twenty years, but she appreciated the sentiment.

Outside, she climbed aboard with Saul right behind her, and she set the buggy into motion. Even though he didn't say a word, she could sense his displeasure. He would get used to the idea of Mr. Marseille in her home and be fine with it. She hoped.

Saul pointed. "There's the cad now."

The topic of her conversation with the Hammond men stood on the boardwalk of the White Hotel, talking to a striking young lady. A lady of refinement. A lady not from around here. They appeared to be in a serious discussion. Professor Marseille implored the woman with his hands out from his sides, and she declined his request.

"Shouldn't he be in a classroom teaching?"

"He has free time in the middle of the day." Henny liked the professor and thought of him as a Christian man, but she was troubled by what she saw. The woman was refusing him, but he didn't seem to be accepting her answer. Maybe she had been wrong about him after all.

"Still think he's decent?"

"There could be a perfectly reasonable explanation for what we see."

"I'll go find out." Saul made a move to leave the buggy.

Henny put a hand on his arm. "Please don't. Vinegar won't catch flies. You stay here. I'll speak to him."

Folding his arms, Saul grunted but settled back onto the seat.

She climbed down and hurried toward the couple. "Professor Marseille?"

The young woman startled and darted inside the hotel.

Henny would get to the bottom of this. "I didn't mean to scare off your lady friend."

His face shifted from irritation to a neutral expression. "She had someplace to be."

That didn't explain why he had been detaining her. "Is she your sweetheart?"

"No. She's..."

"A friend?"

"Of sorts."

"You're welcome to invite her to supper some time at the boarding house." Then Henny could find out who she was as well as more about the professor.

"I would like that, but I'm afraid she might not be up for it."

What was that supposed to mean?

"The two of you seemed to be in a bit of a disagreement when I approached."

"She has opinions of how I should conduct my life."

"I see."

He tipped his hat. "It was a pleasure running into you, but I must return to the normal school. Good day." He walked off.

This was not as simple as it appeared to be. She entered the hotel and marched to the front desk, addressing the stocky fellow there. "The woman who came in a few moments ago, where did she go?"

"To her room."

"You wouldn't be inclined to tell me her name, would you?"

"I'm sorry. I shouldn't."

She didn't want to get the man in trouble. Too bad Grant wasn't on duty. He would have told her. "Thank you anyway." She left the building.

Saul stood on the boardwalk with his arms folded.

She held up a hand. "Don't say it. I know it was a bad idea." But not completely. She was more convinced than ever the man was hiding something. If she let on to either Saul or his son, she would never get to the bottom of this mystery.

On Friday, Henny sat in the circle with her dear quilting friends. She pulled her thread through two fabrics for her scrappy mountain star quilt. This would be the last block before sewing them all together.

Franny bit her bottom lip. "I hear the new professor at the normal school is ever so handsome and that he's staying here. What is he like, Aunt Henny?"

Henny had delayed telling the ladies about her new boarder as long as she could. "I agree, he is striking. He's a very private man." Both she and Saul had tried to get information out of him at supper last night, but the man had been evasive.

"Does he have a sweetheart?"

She didn't know. He hadn't said the woman was, but he hadn't said she wasn't. "I saw him talking to a young lady outside the White Hotel. Whether she's his sweetheart or not, I couldn't say."

"Is it true he has a French accent?"

"Yes." Henny remembered when inconsequential things like that thrilled her.

Lily eyed Henny. Edric and Saul had obviously told her.

Time to dive in with the real bit of information. "I wanted to thank you all for keeping a look out for that stranger I told you about."

Several women around the circle said they hadn't seen anyone suspicious.

"That's because I found him. Or rather he found me."

"Oh, dear."

"Henny?"

"No need for anyone to worry. The man I had seen was Mr. Marseille, my new boarder. He was merely looking for a more permanent place to lodge than at the hotel."

Marguerite thinned her lips. "Henny, don't be gullible. If he was truly after nothing more than a room, he would have come straight to your door and not been lurking about like a miscreant."

Others nodded.

"Honestly, I made a mountain of bread dough out of a pinch of flour. I'm sorry to have worried you all."

Though the topic was dropped, the conversations for the rest of the time were stiffer and more stilted than usual. Some of the younger ladies even commented quietly to one another how exciting it would be to be courted by a handsome, slightly roguish gentleman.

Henny was a little relieved when the hour came for the ladies to leave. Quite unusual for her, but the tension had remained until the end.

Lily Hammond stayed behind after the others left, helping in the kitchen. "Edric and Saul are very concerned about your new boarder."

Henny hadn't meant to make people worry so much. True, she had been concerned when she didn't know who he was—and she still didn't, not really. Now that she'd met him, those concerns were gone. "Please assure them all is well with Mr. Marseille. I feel perfectly safe with him." The longer he remained here, the less troubled she was over the whole thing. She still believed he harbored secrets, but she also didn't believe him to be dangerous.

The Lord would bring all things to light in His time.

Thirteen

After church, Henny sat in the White Hotel dining room, enjoying lunch with Saul Hammond. She had been pleased to have her new boarder eagerly attend services this morning.

Saul took a drink of his coffee. "Thank you for coming to lunch with me."

"Thank you for inviting me." She'd never eaten so many meals with him, but she knew this couldn't go on. "I always enjoy time with you."

"As I do with you."

"Lily says married life is going well for her and Edric." Generally, a safe topic.

He nodded as he set down his coffee cup. "Things are settling down at the house. I'm more in the way than not. Lily has taken over the cooking and cleaning and mending—well, most everything I did—and does them better. My son doesn't need me."

"Of course, he does. No matter how old, children always need their parents in one respect or another."

"He doesn't need me underfoot." Saul captured Henny with an intense, longing gaze. "And I'm not getting any younger. I've been thinking about what I want to do." He took her hand. "And who I want to do it with."

Henny's insides tightened at the direction Saul was heading. A direction she couldn't allow. Pulling her hand free, she settled it nervously in her lap. "Please don't say something you can never take back."

A crease pulled between his eyebrows. "Why would I want to renounce my feelings?"

Mercy. "It's best if you don't voice them at all."

"Keeping silent won't make them any less true. You must know how much you've come to mean to me."

This had been what she had been sensing from him while attempting to deny her own feelings. As long he didn't speak them aloud, she could ignore her own.

"What's this about, Henny?"

She'd tried not to dwell on this part of her past, it hurt too much, but she had little choice now. Time to dig up history. "I'm...not a free woman."

Saul stared at her as though trying to comprehend her meaning.

"That's to say—"

"I know what 'not free' means. If you've had a husband all this time, where is he?"

Good question. "Europe." At least last she'd heard. "He left over twenty years ago." Taken from her was more like it. She wouldn't—couldn't think about the rest, the pain too much to bear. "I arrived in Kamola a couple years afterwards."

"Why didn't you go with him?"

That was a complicated story. "I didn't have the means and didn't know where in Europe. I assumed Great Britain, but he could have gone to Italy, France, Belgium, Spain. Anywhere."

"If he could leave like that, he didn't deserve you. Seven years abandoned is all it takes to declare a marriage over." He reached across the table as though to take her hand again.

She held them safely in her lap. "Maybe in men's eyes, but I don't think God views it the same way."

He withdrew his arm. "You think God wants you living unprotected with a questionable man with unclear motives under your roof?"

She couldn't argue with the *questionable man* issue. "Is your declaration of ardor because of Mr. Marseille?"

"I haven't exactly declared it yet because you stopped me, but yes, this is partly about that man. You may be independent, but you are also vulnerable."

"I appreciate your concern. I don't believe I'm in any danger from him. You are worrying over nothing." At least she hoped that was the case.

"It's not nothing. The man has been evasive. Edric or I could get him to confess."

Oh dear, was he thinking of confronting Mr. Marseille? "Saul, don't say a word to him. I honestly believe the truth will be revealed in time. If you scare him off, I'll never find out why he's here. Perhaps, I imagined him watching me—as you and others believed."

"I always believed you thought he was watching you."

"That I *thought* he was, not that he *actually* was."

Saul shook his head. "How did this conversation get so off course?"

He'd insisted on being her protector. "You were trying to be gallant."

"That man will never sit well with me until he's gone."

"What happened to him being 'nice' and a 'good addition'?"

"That was before I knew better."

Henny withdrew one hand from her lap and covered his. "Would you trust me on this? I'm trusting the Lord. If you really want to help, pray."

"I'll continue to. It's the only way I get any sleep since you told me about him."

Unfortunately, she had done too good of a job convincing Saul and others that someone had been watching. Now, he wouldn't let it be. Long ago, Henny had accepted she would spend the rest of her life alone, but her friend across the table was making it more difficult. If Winston didn't want her, why couldn't she be happy with someone else?

On Monday, Henny turned her horse out into her small pasture and took her shopping basket to the house.

Mr. Marseille had been in her home for a week now with nary a hint of the man who'd been watching her. Had her witnessing the professor all those months ago been a dream? Or had it been some other man? If so, then who? She hadn't noticed anyone since her new boarder moved in, and she'd looked in earnest while she was out today.

Something vaguely familiar about him niggled at her, but she couldn't figure out what. Something about his eyes? The way he carried himself? The tonal quality of his voice?

Hmm. She didn't know. Some unidentifiable quality.

Henny set her shopping basket on the kitchen worktable and froze. A soft noise came from the other room. What was that? A rustling sound from the direction of her bedroom on the first floor. No one should be in there. Henny grabbed the rolling pin. She crept down the hall, sidestepping the creaky boards. It was probably only Miss Tibbins.

She peered through the partially open door. Mr. Marseille? She straightened and swung the door open wide. "Can I help you find something?"

The Frenchman pivoted. Guilt etched across his features. "Pardon. I will go." He resembled a boy caught with his hand in the cookie jar.

Henny stood in the middle of the doorway with the rolling pin in front of her. "I never would have taken you for a common thief." His clothes were too fine for that. "You must be after something in particular."

Mr. Marseille stopped in his tracks and stared a moment. He must have realized Henny didn't plan to move until she received an answer. "I wished to look for a Scripture and thought you might have a Holy Bible."

Most people wouldn't argue with a person wanting to seek out God's Word. In this situation, she would forge a different path. "That gave you the right to invite yourself into my private room?"

He ducked his head. "I was wrong. Please forgive."

Though he appeared contrite, Henny sensed there was more. She should ask him to leave her home altogether, but something told her she needed to keep him close. "Don't let this happen again."

"I will not. I promise."

Lowering her weapon, Henny stepped aside.

The man scooted past her, down the hall, and out the front door.

She should tell Edric and Saul about this but wouldn't until she received guidance from the Lord. The Hammond men would scare him off for sure.

What was it about this young man which made her want to find out more about him? What drew her to him? Though he apparently had everything he needed, he still had an air of being lost somehow. It made no sense. First, he'd watched her, then asked her odd questions, and now this.

She crossed to her bed, slipped her hand under the mattress, and pulled out the Bible the young man had been searching for. Too much incriminating evidence in here to leave it lying about for prying eyes.

On Wednesday, Geneviève spent the day at the river with Deputy Montana and Felicity. This time they didn't fish but ate the tasty picnic lunch Felicity had made.

Geneviève sat on the bank in her blue and green calico dress. Hers had far more details than most of the ones she'd observed ladies in town wearing. It had pin tucks, box pleats, ruching, ruffles, and lace. She'd needed something more than the simple dress of others. If she was to wear frontier fashion, she would do so in style.

The May day had turned out warm, so she had allowed Felicity to talk her into removing her shoes and stockings to dip her feet in the cool water. She would not wade as her lady's maid and Deputy Montana did. He had his trousers rolled up to his knees. Felicity had pulled the hem at the back of her dress forward between her legs and tucked it in at her waist. How brazen. However, not as unacceptable as it would be for Geneviève to do the same. For her lady's maid, the company wasn't so scandalous. If it were only Felicity, Geneviève would be tempted to tuck in her skirt and wade as well. It seemed fun. She envied her lady's maid's ability to be so carefree.

Felicity swished a foot through the water. "Come on in. You'll like it."

Geneviève shook her head. "No, I cannot."

Deputy Montana held his hand out toward her. "I'll steady you."

"Come on," Felicity coaxed.

Geneviève bit her bottom lip. Should she? It did look enjoyable.

Her lady's maid cupped her hands together, dipped them beneath the surface, and flung a heaving bowlful of the river.

Geneviève ducked and lifted her arms in front of her face to ward off the oncoming onslaught, to no avail. The full amount splashed down on her, causing her to suck in a startled breath. She couldn't believe Felicity had done that. No servant in her grandparents' employ would have ever acted in so bold a manner.

Felicity giggled. "Now you have to come in. You're already wet."

Deputy Montana put his hands together and hurled water at his sister in retribution. She splashed in return. Each time, Geneviève tried to guard herself, in a vain attempt to stay semi-dry. Since she was saturated, she decided to join in, so she slid off the boulder she sat upon and into the six inches of river. The sandy bottom squished between her toes. Her dress's skirt soaked up as much liquid as possible. She bent and splattered Felicity then the deputy.

Her lady's maid returned a volley, but the deputy came to Geneviève's side and assisted her in her attack against his sister.

In the ensuing chaos, Geneviève tried to duck behind the deputy, lost her balance, and fell into the water. On her way down, Deputy Montana reached out to catch her, and she inadvertently pulled him down with her into the cold water. Her breath caught as she stared into his handsome face a few inches from hers.

After laughing, Felicity offered a helping hand, and her brother tugged her in as well. She sloshed him in the face.

This had been more fun than Geneviève could ever remember having. Her grandmother would be horrified at such deviant behavior.

By the time she'd arrived back at the hotel, her dress had ceased dripping but remained damp. Geneviève halted at the hotel door and waited while Deputy Montana opened it for her. She smiled and dipped her head. *"Merci."* She stepped inside but kept her gaze on him.

"*De rien.* Did I remember how to pronounce that right?"

"You did." She appreciated him trying so hard.

"Geneviève Angelique Marseille." The even toned, foreboding French voice came from the matronly figure standing in front of the window.

Geneviève froze at the all too familiar tone. Though the sun's glaring backdrop darkened her identity, Geneviève knew the woman, having heard that voice many times, most often lately in her head.

The deputy pointed. "That lady knows you?"

Geneviève nodded.

"Do not point, young man. It is rude and obnoxious."

Pasting on a rigid smile, Geneviève faced her grandmother. Her insides tightened. Was she standing correctly? Was she holding her hands in the right position? Was she doing everything as *Grand-mère* had taught her? At precisely the right speed, she crossed to her and made a slight curtsy, instinctively replying in French. "I wasn't expecting you."

Grand-mère narrowed her eyes and continued in French. "That is obvious. Who is this?"

Geneviève switched to English out of respect for her companions. "*Grand-mère*, this is one of Kamola's deputies, Deputy Montana and his sister Felicity. May I present *Madame* Angelique Marseille."

Deputy Montana dipped his head. "Pleased to meet you, ma'am."

Felicity echoed the greeting and curtsied in the manner of which Geneviève had, although more awkward as she apparently stepped on her petticoat.

Grand-mère gave them each a nod of acknowledgement.

Geneviève adjusted her posture to ensure she stood properly. "This is a pleasant surprise. What brings you to Kamola?"

Grand-mère resumed in French. "You know exactly what I'm doing here. I've come to rescue you from this dreadful place."

Kamola wasn't so dreadful. Though Geneviève had thought so at first, she knew differently now. She wanted to contradict *Grand-mère* but nothing good would come of it. It would only make matters worse.

The deputy stepped forward. "If there is anything you need, I'd be glad to help."

Grand-mère flicked her wrist and spoke in English this time. "Your services aren't required. Neither of you. You may go."

Geneviève glanced at the deputy and shook her head. She hoped he wouldn't make a fuss.

He stood mutely.

Felicity, on the other hand, looked in a temper, seething, so Geneviève mouthed, "Please don't." She wouldn't win a verbal battle with *Grand-mère*.

Grand-mère scrutinized Geneviève then switched to French again. "We will discuss your attire later." She inclined her head toward the door. "I've already had your belongings packed and loaded into a wagon. We are expected at a friend's residence."

Grand-mère would have plenty to say about Geneviève's calico dress once they were alone. Hopefully, she didn't realize it was damp.

As *Grand-mère* ushered her out the door, Geneviève glanced over her shoulder at the deputy. She wanted to run to him but knew it would do no good.

At the sight of a stately carriage waiting out front, Geneviève had the oddest thought.

Trapped.

Why would she think that? Hadn't leaving Kamola been her plan since the moment she arrived? When the door closed, the click rang in her ears, signaling the end of her freedom. A weight the size of her steamer trunk settled on her chest. Her lungs labored to draw in air.

She peered out the window at Deputy Montana standing on the boardwalk. Confusion marred his handsome face, and Geneviève's heart broke.

The carriage jostled into motion.

Grand-mère tapped Geneviève's arm. "Stop gawking. You were raised better."

She faced forward with the familiar knot in her stomach. *Grand-mère* would scold her soon enough.

The tension her body was so used to returned like an old friend. An unwanted companion. She hadn't realized that for these past nearly three weeks that agitation hadn't accompanied her everywhere. After her first day and meeting the deputy, she'd felt more at ease than she used to. How could she have not noticed how fretful she had been before? The feeling had been so normal for her she hadn't known living could be otherwise.

But it could.

She had a certain kindhearted deputy and his sister to thank for that.

Fourteen

MONTANA STARED AFTER THE KESNERS' CARRIAGE with a "K" crest on the side. He wasn't sure what to think of recent events.

Though Miss Marseille seemed to know the older woman and went willingly, she hadn't appeared to be happy about it.

He would have intervened if not for the shake of her head. He had bristled at how the older woman had instantly dismissed him. Montana knew vaguely who the older woman was because Miss Marseille had called her something resembling grandma, but he hadn't liked the way she treated her.

Felicity pressed her lips together then blew out a frustrated breath. "*'Your services aren't required? You may go?'* The nerve of her." She put her hands on her hips. "Why didn't you stop that overbearing woman?"

"For the same reason you didn't say anything. Miss Marseille didn't want us to intervene." He'd desperately wanted to.

"Then what's the plan?"

"Plan?"

"To rescue her?"

His twin couldn't be serious, but the idea intrigued Montana. "*We* do nothing. I'll speak with her brother and decide what actions to take from there. He came across as a decent fellow. Take the buckboard home. I'll let you know what I find out."

She huffed but left.

He crossed to Grant at the desk. "Who was that woman?"

"Scary. She said she was Miss Marseille's grandmother and came in with an entourage, packing Miss Marseille's things and giving orders to everyone as though she owned the hotel. She even gave orders to a couple of the guests who smartly scurried away." Grant leaned forward. "The strangest thing was she didn't bark her orders as one would think. Her voice was even and almost soft, yet commanding. Then she'd give you that look." He shuddered. "I thought Miss Marseille was demanding. Not compared to that woman."

Montana needed to learn more about the elder Mrs. Marseille. If Miss Geneviève Marseille was actually being held against her will, he would need to do something about it. He tapped the registry desk. "Let me know if Miss Marseille returns."

Grant nodded.

Because Cletus had been hitched to the buckboard he'd sent with his twin, Montana strode out and went to the livery where he rented a saddled horse. If this woman was Miss Marseille's family come to return her to her society world, he would need to leave her alone. Of course, this day would come. But why so soon? He could no more live in her fancy world than she could live in his simpler one permanently. He'd fooled himself into thinking they had something real between them, but it had been nothing more than a lark for her. A way to irritate her brother as the professor had warned him.

Montana swung onto the horse named Turk and rode to Washington State Normal School. Inside, he flashed his badge and inquired after Professor Marseille.

The young man behind the reception desk looked up then consulted a schedule sheet. "Professor Marseille is teaching a class at the moment. It ends in ten minutes, and he should return to his office shortly afterward."

"Should? Do you anticipate him going anywhere but his office?" Montana didn't want to miss him.

"Not unless he's waylaid by a student or two. And the young ladies do favor the handsome, single professors and take every opportunity they can to garner their attention. One would think they came to find a husband rather than a teaching certificate."

"I see. Perhaps I'll wait outside his classroom. Which way is it?"

The young man gave him directions.

Montana strolled off. It helped to have a badge in a situation such as this. Though mostly a personal matter, he did have some concerns about the woman who briskly whisked Miss Marseille away, so he wouldn't feel guilty over his actions.

He peered through the window in the classroom door. Pierre Marseille leaned against the wall to the side of the room while a female student stood in front, giving some sort of speech or presentation.

Soon after the student finished, the professor dismissed the class. Both young men and young women filed out. A couple of the ladies gave Montana approving glances and smiled at him. He gave them each a quick nod but refused to encourage them. When the flow ceased, he stepped inside the classroom. Three female students clustered around the professor.

Did the man wish to be extricated? Or did he enjoy their attention?

Whether he did or not, Montana was anxious to speak to him on his sister's behalf, so he cleared his throat.

Four pairs of eyes turned to him. Pierre Marseille's face brightened. "That's all, ladies. You may ask your questions at the next class period."

As the students sulked out, one had pouty lips and another smiled at Montana. He ignored them and turned his attention on Mr. Marseille.

Once they had gone, the professor said, "I appreciate the interruption. As I do not have a class next hour, they have been known to linger far longer than they should."

Montana was glad to know Pierre Marseille didn't appear to be encouraging ladies so much younger than himself and to whom he was in a position of authority. One could easily abuse such power.

"What can I do for you, deputy?" The professor straightened a stack of papers and tucked them into his satchel. "I assume this concerns my sister."

"It does. An older woman claiming to be her grandmother had her things at the hotel packed up and whisked Miss Marseille away."

Pierre heaved a sigh. "I was afraid of this. I warned Geneviève *Grand-mère* would come."

"I didn't like the way she ordered your sister about and gave her no say in the matter. Miss Marseille didn't seem happy and gave the impression she wanted to stay at the hotel."

"I assure you my sister is perfectly safe. Happy? I am sure she is not. Do you know where our grandmother took her? Were they taking the next train out of town?"

"They rode off in one of the Kesner carriages. She's a prominent woman in town."

"No doubt, if *Grand-mère* was headed there."

Though grateful Miss Marseille wasn't in any danger, Montana was a bit disappointed he didn't have a reason to head over to see her. "I would like to go with you to the Kesners'."

"That is not a wise idea. As I told you, our grandparents would not approve of you." Professor Marseille hung his satchel over his shoulder. "You did not believe there could be anything more between you and my sister than this little dalliance, did you? I warned you."

That he had, and Montana had known, but still hope had grown. He'd felt something more and had thought Miss Marseille had as well. He'd been nothing but a fool and a distraction for her, and she'd been trifling with his affections. "Will you tell her I was asking about her?"

The professor nodded.

Geneviève and *Grand-mère* had ridden in scolding silence and disapproving shakes of *Grand-mère's* head. Geneviève dared not speak lest *Grand-mère* start reprimanding aloud. She would hear all about her scandalous behavior soon enough. Would she bother to inquire as to how Geneviève's clothes got drenched? Maybe they were dry enough for her to not have noticed.

Two footmen and a maid met the carriage outside of the Kesners' home. *Grand-mère* exited first. Geneviève took the servant's hand and stepped out of the carriage.

The other man addressed *Grand-mère*. "The trunk and luggage have been taken upstairs. Your granddaughter is in the room connected to yours."

That would ensure Geneviève didn't step one foot out of her room without her grandmother's notice. Back to life as it had been before. How had she born such a stifling existence? She dutifully followed her grandmother inside.

Grand-mère ascended the steps where a middle-aged woman opened the front door. "Tell Mrs. Kesner my granddaughter needs to tidy herself before introductions." She headed straight to the staircase and glided up.

Geneviève didn't want to follow but knew she must.

A maid opened a bedroom door.

Geneviève entered the opulent bedchamber behind her grandmother. Blue and gold fabrics. Wide open spaces between the massive pieces of furniture. Nothing like her little hotel room had been, though nice. But those accommodations had been pleasant and her own. This— like her various living quarters at her grandparents' homes—belonged to someone else. Someone else telling her what to do. Someone else making all the decisions.

Silvie stood at an open steamer trunk, removing clothes.

Grand-mère waved her hand at the lady's maid. "You may go for now. Return in ten minutes."

The maid curtsied and left, closing the door on her way out.

Grand-mère narrowed her eyes. "What do you have to say for yourself and your disgraceful behavior?"

Geneviève knew her grandmother required a contrite apology, but Geneviève wasn't in the mood nor one bit sorry. She'd enjoyed herself these past three weeks. Now the familiar ache in her mid-section had returned, a tautness which constricted more than any tightly laced corset. An ache she'd thought was normal. But was it? She hadn't experienced it with Deputy Montana or Felicity. She'd been at ease. Perhaps she shouldn't have been. In truth, she'd allowed herself to become a person she was not. "What do you wish me to say?"

"You have no explanation for your actions? I was worried about you. How do you think I felt, returning to the Virginia house to find you gone? I feared you had been kidnapped."

"No, *Grand-mère*. I merely came to visit with my *frère*."

"Is that all? It's apparent there is more to your little trip than missing your *frère*. What about that...that frock you're wearing? You look like a commoner."

Her grandmother had intended her remark as an insult and had no idea Geneviève received it as a compliment. "It's a calico dress and very functional. I'm not afraid to sit down when I'm wearing it."

"Sit down? Why on earth would you need to do that? Ladies must bear much discomfort to present themselves acceptable."

Geneviève had learned as much growing up, never questioning it, but now it struck her as a little silly. "Clothes make one acceptable or not?"

"Don't get impertinent with me. You know very well the outward appearance is the first thing people see on which to make a judgment. If they are revolted by the outside, they can never get to know the real you inside."

Who was the real Geneviève? She'd thought she knew, but now she wasn't sure.

"We must get that soggy mess off you."

So *Grand-mère* had noticed.

Though Geneviève had planned to get out of the dress before, now she wished to keep it on. She wanted to hold onto the girl who had spent time with the deputy. The girl whose insides weren't tangled in knots. She could never be that carefree girl again.

Grand-mère opened the door and nodded to someone in the hallway, no doubt a servant at the ready.

Silvie strolled in.

Grand-mère waved a hand toward Geneviève. "See that she's presentable and do it quickly. We don't want to keep our hostess waiting."

Silvie bobbed a curtsy. *"Oui, madame."*

Grand-mère left Geneviève in Silvie's capable hands, closing the door behind her.

Geneviève best change lest she get scolded even more, so she fussed with the top button. The damp fabric made the fastenings stiff.

"Mademoiselle, let me do that." Her lady's maid skillfully unfastened one button at a time down the front of the dress.

Out of habit, Geneviève allowed her arms to drop to her sides. Why was it that wealthy people couldn't dress and undress themselves? Other than the fact their clothing was designed to need someone else to help them. There had been something refreshing in the simpler clothes. Though she would never forgo all of her high fashion wardrobe, the occasional calico would be nice.

Silvie worked deftly with haste and soon had Geneviève out of her wet attire and into fresh, silk under garments. "Sit at the vanity, and I will repair your coiffure."

Geneviève did as commanded. "I'm sure you'll need to start from scratch."

Felicity had done a serviceable enough job, but she wasn't familiar with the Paris styles, and Geneviève had never paid close enough attention to what Silvie did with her hair.

Geneviève studied her reflection as Silvie unwound her damp blond locks and pulled a brush through them. Amazingly, *Grand-mère* hadn't feigned fainting at Geneviève's disheveled appearance.

Her lady's maid spoke with admiration. "I can't believe you traveled all the way across the country by yourself."

Exactly how Geneviève had felt as she had planned her escape and then traveled west. "It wasn't so much." She had continued to feel amazed at her actions after her arrival, but at some point, she had stopped seeing it as some great accomplishment. When had that happened? In retrospect, the incredibleness of her journey had begun to wear off when she'd met Deputy Montana on the train platform. From there, the wonderment of what she'd done had faded little by little. Now her lady's maid was in awe of her. "Silvie, if I had asked you, would you have come along with me without telling anyone or trying to stop me?"

"I am sorry, no, *mademoiselle*. I could not go against *Madame* Marseille. She would cast me out and ensure I never worked as a lady's maid again."

As Geneviève had suspected. The servants had all been loyal to her grandparents who paid their wages. They couldn't risk their livelihood for the whims of a débutante. All but the one stable hand she'd been able to bribe.

Silvie went on. "I do commend you for your bravery."

Was it bravery? Or desperation? If not for her brother's quest for answers about a dead woman—a malefactor— Geneviève never would have ventured out on her own.

Never would have known life could be different.

Perfectly dressed and coiffed, Geneviève strolled in the Kesners' garden with her brother. A welcome respite from the rest of the household. "I didn't get a chance to pay Felicity her wages for today. Would you see to that?"

"Of course." Pierre patted her hand resting on his arm. "You're different."

"What do you mean?"

"You are once again the withdrawn little girl you used to be. I think the deputy might have been good for you. Though you didn't hold yourself as stiff, you stood with more confidence."

"I did?" She never felt confident.

"*Oui.* How do you feel about the deputy?"

The corners of her mouth curved into a smile of their own volition. "He is very nice. I am quite fond of him."

"He came to see me at the school. He was worried *Grand-mère* had kidnapped you."

"In a way, she did. She left no room for arguments per her normal approach."

He motioned for her to sit on a bench under a blossoming apple tree.

She shook her head. "*Grand-mère* would disapprove of my sitting in this dress." With Deputy Montana, she wouldn't have hesitated to rest her feet.

Pierre guided her toward a pond on the property. "Were you trifling with the deputy, or have you developed true feelings for him?"

Her heart ached to acknowledge her affection for the deputy. "I suppose it doesn't matter. Our grandparents will decide the course for my life, including my husband, and that will be that. My life will be chosen for me."

"It does matter. *Père* married for love. He would want you to have love too. Is that what you want?"

She had hoped for love, but *Grand-mère* always told her to get such foolish notions out of her head. Love was for fools and the poor. And it kept them both as such. "If you see Deputy Montana, would you tell him I'm sorry for the abrupt end to our outing?"

"I'll be sure to tell him."

"*Merci.*" Her enthusiasm of the past few weeks drained from her. Her energy sapped. "Please don't let *Grand-mère* take me away." Something she never would have imagined saying a month ago before she'd ventured out on her own, heading west.

"I'll do what I can, but you should know, she has designs on the young Mr. Kesner as her future grandson-in-law. I'm sure *Grand-père* would approve of him."

Geneviève had feared as much. She was grateful business kept *Grand-père* from coming as well. "I pray she changes her mind."

"Would it be so terrible? He seems like a fine fellow."

She didn't even know him, so it would be terrible. "Will you allow our grandparents to dictate whom you will take for your wife?" She knew he wouldn't. He didn't have to because he was a man.

He thought a moment. "You really are trapped. I never thought about it much before. You could come to Henny's boarding house. She has room. She's invited you to supper."

That would be worse. "I can't. I wish you would leave her establishment."

He shook his head. "I'm close, Vivi. I can feel it."

She sensed it as well, but it didn't bring her the comfort it did her brother. It made her blood run cold.

Fifteen

AFTER TWO DAYS IN RESIDENCE AT the Kesner estate, Geneviève couldn't avoid an outing with the Kesner heir any longer. She sat in the high-end carriage with Lamar Kesner at the reins. Why had *he* chosen to drive and not have one of the footmen do it?

He guided the horse onto the thoroughfare. "Finally, alone." He seemed pleased with this arrangement of their grandmothers pushing them together. Hopefully, he wouldn't insist upon a long excursion.

She could always feign a headache, which would likely manifest itself in due time.

When the horse slowed, Mr. Kesner flicked the reins to keep the animal from deciding to stop altogether. "I think you know, as well as I do, our grandmothers would like to see us together."

Mr. Kesner probably fancied the idea too. Now that Geneviève had asserted herself by traipsing across the country on an unapproved trip, *Grand-mère* would increase her efforts to find her a suitable husband. Preferably one her grandparents could control. "I suppose they do."

"Are you fine with that?"

"I hardly know you, so how can I say?"

He looked at her out of the corner of his eye. "That doesn't answer my question."

No, it hadn't. Most men wouldn't pursue the matter, allowing a lady a small air of mystery. Apparently, he wasn't like the others. "I doubt I will have much say in the matter."

"You will marry anyone she tells you to?"

She took a deep breath. Men didn't always understand how the world worked for women. "I do not have the same privileges and freedoms as a man. I cannot simply marry anyone I choose."

He switched to French. "How many appropriate gentlemen from approved families with the right lineage have your grandparents paired you with?"

Geneviève tilted her head and spoke in English. "You speak French?"

"*Oui*. I thought you would be more comfortable conversing in your native language."

Geneviève transitioned to French. "You have very little accent."

"I had a tutor since age six and studied abroad for four years. Paris was one of my favorite cities."

She loved Paris. Though she'd missed hearing her beloved French, she also enjoyed listening to and speaking English. "You had very good instruction."

"*Merci*. But you never answered my question."

That was right. He had asked her something. "What was your question?"

"How many approved suitors has your family tried to foist upon you?"

She gave him a sidelong glance. "You sound as though you've had experience in this area." She mentally schooled herself. She never would have been so bold as to make such a forward comment to a gentleman before traveling west by herself, but she wouldn't withdraw it.

"I have. My grandmama has *encouraged* me toward no less than twenty-seven suitable young ladies."

He had obviously kept count.

Geneviève considered herself fortunate at fewer than ten. "You didn't find any of them to your liking?"

"Most were insipidly boring with no original thought. A few were intriguing, but those seemed to be the ones whose heart yearned for another."

"Does that mean you wish to marry soon?"

"I surprise myself to say I do." He turned down a residential street. "I look forward to having a wife and children, but she must be the right wife. I don't think I would marry simply for the sake of marrying. Although Grandmama thinks heirs are an acceptable reason. Do you wish to marry?"

"*Monsieur* Kesner, that is a highly personal question."

"But it was all right for you to ask me? I think you are an adventurous sort who will answer it. Or are you, *Mademoiselle* Marseille, going to artfully dodge this one as you did my other question?"

Ah, he had noticed.

"Like you, I wish to marry for love." She tilted her head. "Nine, to answer your earlier question. My *grand-mère* is afraid I will be an old maid."

"You have years before anyone would think that of you."

Not as many as he might expect. She was often mistaken for younger than her twenty-three years.

He flicked the reins again. "Which are you? Insipidly boring? Or has your heart been captured by another?"

Bold of him to ask such a direct question. A question she didn't know how to answer. She dreaded thinking of herself as insipidly boring—how grievous—but she didn't know where her heart stood. "Is there a third choice?"

He lifted one eyebrow in an intriguing way. "That you would venture to ask, suggests you aren't boring. Option three is you would welcome romantic overtures from me to see if we would suit."

She didn't care for that alternative either. "Do you fancy me enough to care if I were eager for your attention or not?"

"Just wondering if I should bother to put forth any effort or merely devise a believable front for the sake of others." He understood the pressure of family on one to marry and marry well—*and* to the right kind of person.

She knew how *Grand-mère* would want her to answer, but she couldn't bring herself to say it. "It couldn't hurt to put on a front to see if anything develops." Which she knew wouldn't.

He gave her another sideways glance. "That tells me all I need to know."

She supposed her veiled dismissal would.

As Mr. Kesner meandered around town, they ended up on the main street. Ahead, Deputy Montana headed toward the sheriff's office. She must speak to him. "I only now remembered I have a fitting at the dressmaker's.

Would you mind dropping me off and returning in two hours?" That should give her sufficient time.

"Of course not." Mr. Kesner pulled the carriage over in front of the French lady's dressmaker shop and helped Geneviève out. "Will two hours be enough?"

Men were usually eager to avoid activities concerning fashion. "I'm sure it will. *Merci.*" She made the pretense of entering the establishment until he pulled away.

Once he was safely down the road, she hurried across the street. Then she feigned interest in her reticule as she listened to the deputy's boot steps advancing from behind her.

They stopped.

She brushed her hands over the front of her skirt while waiting for him to address her. But he didn't. What was he doing? She couldn't fake interest in nothing much longer.

"How long are you going to pretend to be brushing invisible dirt from your dress while waiting for me?"

Caught. He'd seen through her ruse. She formed her mouth into an oh. "Deputy Montana. I did not see you approaching."

He folded his arms. "I'm sure you did."

"Very well. I did see and was hoping to speak with you."

"Then why didn't you say so? Why put on a false front?"

After the way her grandmother had treated him and Geneviève's sharp departure, she wasn't sure he would want to see her again. "It is not ladylike to appear so forward."

"Another one of your fancy rules?"

"They are not mine, per se, but yes."

He hitched his hip against a support post. "What can I do for you, Miss Marseille?"

His cool attitude hurt but was to be expected. "I must apologize for my hasty exit the other day at the hotel."

"I understand. You didn't want your grandmother to know we were acquaintances. I've always been aware I could never measure up. It's all right."

"No. That is not it at all." She rested her hand on his arm still folded across his chest. Very much against those fancy rules she followed, but she didn't regret it. She wanted a connection to him "I feared my *grand-mère* would say something disparaging to you. I did not want that to happen."

He stared at her hand on his arm. "I'm a big boy and don't get hurt so easily."

"It still would not have been right, and it would have hurt me."

His eyebrows pulled together. "You seem as though you might actually care."

"I do. Why would you think otherwise?"

"Do you truly not know? I'm so far beneath your station, I'm surprised you ever allowed me to escort you to the hotel and even more surprised you agreed to my company again. I always knew I wasn't good enough, and your brother warned me this day would come. None of this is unexpected."

Her vision blurred. "Not good enough? What makes one good? Money? Or character?"

"There are good people with money. I'm sure your grandmother would prefer you spend time with one of them. We both know she would never approve of me."

Grand-mère had indeed found a suitable gentleman of means, and so far, Mr. Kesner exhibited no unfavorable behavior. She didn't care for him in that way. Or was it simply because *Grand-mère* approved, so Geneviève didn't? "Maybe we could take a walk."

Montana eyed the pretty French lady. Did he want to go walking with her?

Definitely.

Should he?

Definitely not. "A walk would be nice." He pushed away from the post.

"Geneviève?" Felicity headed across the street, dodging a wagon and a pile of droppings. "It's so good to see you. We were afraid your grandma was going to take you away from Kamola."

"I am still here."

So much for taking a walk. Probably best.

Felicity stepped onto the boardwalk. "Did they tell you I stopped by to see you at the Kesner house?"

Miss Marseille's eyes widened. "No, they did not."

"I was afraid of that. Montana stopped by as well."

Geneviève turned her attention on him. "They did not tell me."

He figured as much. Why should they? Like Lysander in that Shakespeare play, he would never win the approval of the fair maiden's guardians. He didn't matter to society folks, but Miss Marseille did seem concerned. "Just doing my job." He tapped his deputy star, but it had been more than duty. A lot more.

No future with this one, Montana. No future at all.

Even knowing that, he couldn't convince his heart to let her go.

Sixteen

After church, Henny marched along the road toward home. She had sent her two boarders, the two younger professors, off with her buggy. Saul had offered to take her, but after she had argued with him over her new boarder, she'd decided to walk. He had no right to tell her what to do. Practically an order.

A buggy approached from behind her and slowed. "I'm sorry, Henny. I spoke out of turn. Let me give you a ride."

She turned to face Saul, a kind man and dear friend. He'd only acted due to his feelings for her. Perhaps his affection was the reason she'd snapped back. "Apology accepted, but I prefer to walk. You gave me a few things to contemplate, so the stroll and solitude will give me a chance to do that."

"Can't you think at home?"

"One would assume so, but all the things that need doing whisper to me, beckoning me to pay attention to them. I'm less distracted this way. Nothing to do but reflect and ponder while I walk."

"I didn't mean to upset you so."

"I know. You're concerned for me. I've been on my own with no one to worry themselves over my welfare for a very long time. I'm not used to it." She enjoyed having the freedom to make her own decisions without being questioned. However, it was nice to have someone care.

"I wish you'd let me drive you home."

"I appreciate your offer, but I'm still spry enough to make the trek."

"You're a stubborn one."

"Thank you."

He drove off.

If not for her stubborn streak, she doubted she would have survived so well on her own for all these years.

On the other hand, there was wisdom in the midst of counsel.

Lord, give me clear direction on Professor Marseille. Is it safe for him to remain under my roof? Or should I ask him to leave?

At the crossroads that led in the direction of the Hammonds' place, Saul waited in his buggy. How sweet of him. Henny's house was in sight. She waved to him, and he returned the gesture before continuing on his way.

She was glad to be home. Though she could walk the distance, she wasn't used to it and was tuckered out as well as hungry. Entering through the kitchen door, she set her reticule on the worktable and poured herself a glass of water.

A noise from her room stopped her. Like a drawer being opened. Was someone in there again? This time, she snatched the shotgun from her pantry and inched toward her room. Though the weapon wasn't loaded, it gave her a sense of security.

Please don't let it be Professor Marseille again. Would she prefer a stranger? No. *Let it be my cat, Miss Tibbins, after a mouse.* Maybe the sound hadn't been a drawer.

She knocked the door open with the barrel of the gun.

Professor Marseille crouched in front of her open bottom bureau drawer. He startled and straightened, knowing he was caught. For a second time.

Maybe Saul was right about sending this man away. "Snooping again?"

Though he appeared contrite, he remained silent.

How many times had he rifled through her things without her knowledge? "Exactly what are you after?"

He put his hands out in front of himself. "I mean not to hurt you in any way. You can put that down."

She lowered the shotgun but kept it at the ready. "It was you last fall watching me, wasn't it?"

He hesitated then nodded.

Good to know she wasn't touched in the head. "Tell me why you are going through my belongings, or I'll have no choice but to send you away and inform the sheriff." She would still do both. She couldn't tolerate someone invading her privacy.

He opened his mouth, and his lips moved, but no words came out. He seemed to want to explain. So why didn't he?

"You need to move out of my house immediately."

He took a long, slow breath. "I have reason to believe you might have information about an Anne Seymour or Anne Henderson."

Henny's insides twisted into a tight knot. Names she hadn't heard in over two decades. She'd thought she'd been careful. How had she been found? The room seemed to close in on her. The shotgun slipped from her grasp and clattered to the floor.

Mr. Marseille's eyes widened, and he rushed to her side, taking her arm. "Are you all right? Let me get you to the settee." He helped her to the other room to sit. "I will get you water." He returned momentarily with a glass.

She took a drink, finding it hard to swallow. "Who are you? A Pinkerton or some other detective?"

"No. My interest is purely personal."

What should Henny do? Throw him out? Get the sheriff? She would need to explain to Edric her sordid past if she did. Or talk to this nice, young man? "Who is this Anne woman to you?"

"I am not sure, but I think she might have information about my *mère*—my mother."

It couldn't be. "Your...mother?"

"*Oui.* My *mère* passed away when I was very young. Are you Anne Henderson? Or know of her?"

Her hand shook as she set the glass on the side table. "What if I do?"

"I want to find out about my *mère*. My *père* gave me this and told me to find Anne Henderson Seymour." He pulled a card from his pocket. The same one Henny had seen him with before. "This is her. Her name is on the reverse side."

Henny gazed at the photograph of herself from twenty-five years ago. The past rushed in and took the air from her lungs. She studied the young man's face. His eyes were the same color as Winston's, and the same wave to his hair. And the Seymour jawline. But the shape of his eyes and his eyebrows came from his Henderson forefathers. Henny's voice came out barely audible. "Winston?"

"Excuse me?"

Why did he have a different name? Was he merely a look-alike? "What is your father's name?"

"Jacque Marseille."

Her voice quivered. "Not Winston? Winston Seymour?"

"When I was young, he once called me Winston. *Grand-mère* got very upset and told me to forget I ever heard that name."

This was indeed her son. Her vision blurred. No wonder she'd been drawn to him. Henny lifted her hand to his cheek. "My baby. I thought I'd never see you again."

"I do not understand. You think you are my *mère*? You cannot be. She is dead."

"That's merely what they told you." Henny wasn't surprised. As she stood, a tear slipped down her face, and she swiped it away. "I'll be right back."

Pierre rose as well and reached out to her. "Are you all right to walk? You nearly fell over a few moments ago."

"I'm fine." Very fine if this was indeed her son. She hurried to her room, retrieved her Bible stuffed with papers and photographs, and returned to the parlor. Drawing in a calming breath, she retook her place on the settee and thumbed through the mess until she found the photograph. "This is Winston Seymour the second...my husband."

"*Père*? That is my father." He lifted his gaze to Henny's face and squinted as though trying to pull her from long-lost memories. "You are my *mère*?"

Henny nodded, aching to take him into her arms—arms that had missed so much—to hold him, and never let him go again. She realized he probably wouldn't appreciate such affection from a relative stranger. He'd only just learned his mother was alive. Eventually, she hoped she could hug him, but for now, she would refrain.

She shuffled through her Bible's pages, along with the papers and photographs it contained. Finding the family tree page, she laid it open and pointed to his name with his birth date next to it. *Winston John Seymour* III. "This is you." She hadn't been given a choice when naming her son.

"I was named after my *père*?"

"And his father."

"I never knew." He touched the name and date below his. "Who is this?"

"Your sister."

He looked from her to the Bible. "Geneviève's name was *Daisy*?" He chuckled.

"Yes." She had fought to be able to choose at least one of her children's name. The name held a special meaning for her as it was her mother's name. "Is she the young lady staying at the hotel?" Henny's heart stilled with hope.

"*Oui.*"

Unbelievable, her children had found her. All the years in between started to fall away.

She had lost hope and thought God had forgotten her heartache. Her prayers hadn't been futile all these years, after all. *Thank You, Lord.*

He was silent for a moment. "I understand now. *Père* planted every kind of daisy he could find in our garden. *Grand-mère* was not happy. They often fought over it."

Henny's eyes watered. "He did?"

"Once, when I was nine or ten, I overheard *Père* arguing with *Grand-mère*. She told him he needed to marry again, said Geneviève and I needed a *mère*. He said he already had a wife. *Grand-mère* said he did not. He said if she did not stop, he would take me and Geneviève away and she would never see us again."

Winston had wanted Henny. Leaving hadn't been his idea. Henny had always hoped.

She stood. "Come with me." She headed to her back door and out onto the porch.

Mr. Marseille—Winston—her son—held out his elbow to her.

She steadied herself on his arm, not because she needed to, but because she wanted to. "Thank you." A thoughtful gentleman, like his father. She led him to her prized patch. "In this flowerbed, as you know, are daisies. I've planted every variety I could find as well." The first bloom had opened with a few more on the way. "I know they don't look like much, but they'll be bright and lovely soon."

"*Père* planted Queen Anne's lace in his patch. Now I understand why he tended it so carefully. *Grand-mère* hated it. Why?"

"Your grandmother didn't approve of your father marrying me. She wanted him to marry someone better than me." Cora had apparently continued to despise Henny even after she and her husband had stolen everything from Henny. "She and your grandfather had plans for him which didn't include me." They had been furious when they discovered their son and Henny—Anne—had married secretly, but softened a little when they learned they were going to be grandparents. Henny's son didn't need to know all the ugly details of his grandparents' venom. Let him keep whatever happy memories he had.

Henny pointed to two boulders, one a good height for sitting on, the other bigger. "Winston means joyful rock. The daisies for your sister and the rocks for you and your father. Pierre is Peter which means rock."

"I remember a kind woman tucking me into bed, singing me a lullaby, and kissing me on the forehead." He paused and whispered, "'*Good-night, my sweet.*' I thought it was a nanny. Was that you?"

Her son remembered her even though he'd been so young. Henny's eyes blurred, and her throat constricted her words. All she could do was nod.

He shook his head. "I am confused. When I thought you were dead, I understood why you were not with us. But if you have been alive all this time, why did you leave us?"

Henny blinked away her tears and cleared her throat to talk. "I didn't leave you or your sister and your father. I would never have left any of you. Your grandparents took you away from me, all the way to Europe."

"Was I born in America?"

Henny nodded. "Daisy too."

"I dreamed so many times of you coming for us. Why did you not?"

She didn't like to speak ill of people. "Your grandparents made it impossible for me." They had fabricated charges to have her thrown into jail if she followed them or ever tried to find her children.

"What about *Père*?"

"It's very hard for a son to go against his parents. That's why we married in secret. We figured there was nothing they could do about it once we were expecting you. We underestimated them, and they found a way."

"I am sorry they treated you in such a way."

"Is your father in Kamola as well?" She hadn't recalled seeing any other new people in town from when she'd started noticing her son. Her son. If she had known from the start, she would have run to him.

"He died on our country estate near Cologne ten months ago. That is when he gave me the picture and letter and told me to find you."

"Letter?"

"To you, but I want to know what he says in it."

"I understand."

"It is in my room."

Henny was torn. Although curious as to the contents of the letter, she longed to go to her daughter. "I want to see Daisy."

"That will not be so easy."

"But she's in town?"

"She does not want to see you. She never wanted to come. She tried to talk me out of this and get me to leave."

"Why? Never mind. Your grandmother." The woman's hatred for Henny held no bounds.

"She believes you abandoned us. *Grand-mère* told us over and over you had, before she told us you died."

"So why are you willing to speak with me?"

"I guess because I remember you. I want to know the truth."

Bless her little boy's heart. Though he wasn't so little anymore. "I still want to see her. Now that you know the truth, maybe she'll be willing." The last time Henny held Daisy, her baby girl was ten months old. Henny's heart ached for her daughter. Her sweet little girl.

He covered her hand with his. "I should speak to her first."

Henny ached to run to the hotel and wrap her arms around her daughter. A daughter who had grown up without her. A daughter who didn't know her. A daughter who despised her. "I'll pray she's receptive." She tried to conjure the face of the young woman she'd seen outside the hotel with Winston. All she could remember was the poised woman had scowled and hurried away.

Her daughter would need patience and time. Henny didn't know if she had enough. She'd already missed so much. She would try for Daisy's sake.

Seventeen

HENNY LEFT IN HER BUGGY ON Monday right after her boarders had departed for work at Washington State Normal School, including her son. She had to tell Saul about Winston right away. First, to ease his mind about her safety where the professor was concerned. Winston was no threat. But mostly, Saul was the one person, above all others, she wanted to share her good news with—to share in her joy.

Hopefully, he would receive what she had to tell him well. He hadn't come to supper last night as expected. Was he still upset with her over their spat earlier in the day? Or was he punishing her, leaving her to her fate with the stranger in her home? Or was he simply being considerate to give her some space? She would find out soon enough.

She parked the buggy outside the Hammond residence and set the brake.

Lord, please open Saul's heart to be receptive to what I have to say.

Unlike before when she had information about the stranger being her new boarder and told both Hammond men at once, she would tell them separately this time. Saul deserved the privacy to react to the information without his son as witness.

She climbed down and trekked to the front door.

Lily answered her knock. "Aunt Henny. What a surprise. Come in."

Henny entered. It was good to see this young mother so happy after the trials she'd been through. "When is the baby due again?" She already knew, but it was a good conversation starter and distraction from her mission.

Lily caressed her protruding belly. "Early August."

"Are you and Edric hoping for a boy or a girl?"

"We already have both, so we don't care. I'm hoping for a boy for Edric's sake. A man longs to have a son of his own blood."

"We both know he treats your son as his own, as you do with his girls."

"I know. Toby and I are blessed to have him." Lily motioned toward the kitchen. "Would you like a cup of coffee and a cookie?"

"That sounds wonderful, but I'll have to pass. I came to speak to Saul. Is he here?" Her stomach soured.

"He's out in the garden, fussing." The young mother crossed to the kitchen door.

Henny followed in her wake. "Don't call him in. I'll go out to him." It would be best that way so she could speak to him in private. "Before I go, would you be able to come to my house tomorrow morning? I'm inviting all the quilting ladies. I have something to share with everyone and don't want to wait until Friday when the word might have already traveled around town."

"I would love to. I can't wait to hear your news."

"I'll see you tomorrow then." Henny exited to the backyard, hoping this wasn't a mistake.

Saul stood hunched over fledgling plants. He glanced up at the tap of the screen door closing and smiled.

That boded well. Henny crossed to the edge of the garden.

He met her there, brushing dirt from his hands. "I wasn't expecting to see you. I figured you'd be vexed with me for a good long while."

A part of her was, for him trying to dictate what she could and couldn't do, but her wonderful news overrode that. "I've been independent for most of my life. I'm not used to others poking their opinions into my business."

"For that, I'm sorry." He guided her to a bench nestled under a tree. "I don't want to see you get hurt."

She sat. "I appreciate your concern. That's why I came to tell you about my new boarder in question." Her insides tightened even more. How would her friend receive the news?

Saul's expression turned hard. "What has he done? He didn't harm you, did he?"

Henny shook her head. Far from it. Rather than blurting out that the young man was her long-lost son, she'd decided to start at the beginning. "Remember when I told you I wasn't free?"

He nodded. "What does one have to do with the other?"

"I'll get to that." This was going to be harder than she thought. She hadn't spoken of these things in over two decades. "As many young people are, I could be a reckless fool in my formative years. Unruly, you might say."

"You, Henny?"

She nodded and continued. "Even though I had all the right clothes and attended all the débutante events, some people in polite society wouldn't accept me or my parents."

"Society?" Saul knitted his eyebrows together. "You come from money? I can't picture it."

"That was a long time ago."

"What happened?"

So many things, but it was best if she kept this as straightforward as possible. "I fell in love with a man my parents warned me against. Not because he was bad or anything like that, but because of his family. I didn't listen to them and saw him anyway. Later that same year, my father died. His heart just quit. My mother became ill and passed away in a matter of weeks. I was devastated and suddenly a wealthy young débutante. My beau and I continued to see each other even though his parents forbid him. We married in secret so they couldn't stop us. I was so happy to become Mrs. Winston Seymour."

"Ah, so your last name is Seymour. The secret is out now."

"Yes and no. I'll explain that in a minute. We kept our union concealed for several months. I was naïve in thinking nothing could come between us or stop us. As soon as his parents discovered our deception, they tried to have the marriage terminated. By then, I was with child. The idea of a grandchild softened them. Or so I had thought."

Saul remained blessedly silent, either out of shock or consideration, she didn't know.

"We named our boy after his father, Winston John Seymour III. Three years later, we had a little girl. Life was seemingly perfect. I didn't know my in-laws were scheming while I was carrying my daughter. When Daisy was ten months old, they presented me documentation of charges which would have sent me to prison for the rest of my life. Things they invented. Affidavits from witnesses. They convinced my husband I wasn't a suitable mother, and to protect our children, they should take them away."

"That's terrible." Saul shook his head. "I can't imagine anyone believing you to be an unfit mother."

"It was complex." She'd tried to simplify it as much as she could and still make it understandable. "I was a bit unorthodox. My in-laws called me wild, but I never did anything which would put my children in danger. They were my heart and soul."

"I don't know what I would have done if someone took Edric from me. It was horrible when my first daughter-in-law kept our granddaughters from us."

She could identify with him. The ache of losing her children had been unbearable at times. "I was young and afraid. I didn't know what to do. I had no one to turn to. When I married, all my assets became my husband's. I had nothing. A man came with a small velvet bag containing some money and a few of my family's jewels. He told me to take it and run before I was arrested. I did. I had hoped Winston would come for me, and I planned to go back for my children. Before I could return, they were whisked off to Europe with the threat of putting me in an asylum if I ever tried to look for them. I made a few discreet inquiries but found no trace of them. I now know their names were changed."

"Oh, Henny. Why would they go to such lengths to keep you away from your own children?"

"My in-laws were people who needed to control everything and everyone around them. I traveled west and ended up in Denver. A pair of widowed sisters helped me. They led me to the Lord. They taught me to cook and keep house so I could get employment as a maid or cook's assistant. They advised me to keep moving and never let my guard down and to go by my maiden name. After a couple of years, I grew weary of never staying in one place very long. When I arrived here, I decided to make Kamola my home. I figured I was far from my in-laws' reach. When I first introduced myself, I got as far as Anne Hen—before I faltered. My maiden name was Henderson. The person thought I said Aunt Henny. And so, I was reborn."

"That is some story. Anne Henderson. I like it. It suits you. I don't understand what any of this has to do with our disagreement yesterday?"

"Mr. Marseille…" A lump formed in Henny's throat. "…is my son. My son found me."

Saul's eyes widened. "Are you sure? He could tell you anything in hopes you would believe it."

No doubt in her mind. "It's him. He has my husband's small portrait cabinet card of me when I was a young woman. He has my husband's eyes and smile. My daughter is in town as well."

"Is that the woman you saw him with in front of the hotel?"

She nodded then shook her head. "She doesn't want to see me yet, but I hope, in time, she will." A tear slipped down her cheek.

Saul caressed it away with his thumb, sending a shiver through her. "And your husband? Is he here also?"

She shook her head. "Before Winston passed away, he told our son to find me."

"I'm happy for you, but I'm still suspicious of this man."

In time, Saul would see he had nothing to fear from her son. "Thank you."

Saul was silent.

All she had told him was a lot to take in.

He cleared his throat. "You know what this means? You are a free woman. Free to marry."

She was indeed but didn't feel that way. "Saul, I've only just found out my husband passed away. I know our marriage died over twenty years ago, but I feel newly widowed. Then there is getting to know my children. They need to come first."

Saul clutched her hand in both of his. "I understand. I'll wait for you as long as it takes." He cupped her cheek and placed a tender kiss on her lips.

Her roiling emotions paused as she savored his touch. It had been ages since she felt cherished by a man in such a way. When she opened her eyes, reality gripped her once again. "Please don't tell anyone about my children. I don't want to be the topic of town gossip." It was inevitable, but she would prefer to hold it off as long as possible.

"What about Edric? He should know."

"I'm headed to his office next, so he can stop worrying as well."

"I'll go with you."

At the sheriff's office, after filling Edric in about Mr. Marseille's identity, her children, and her past, Henny headed to the mercantile. She bought sugar and powdered chocolate for the cake she planned to make and serve tomorrow as well as a few other items.

Franny totaled her order. "Are you making something delectable for circle on Friday?"

"I'm baking a cake for tomorrow. I'm inviting all the quilting ladies over in the morning. I have something I wish to share. Can you come?" Her friends deserved to hear the soon-to-be-gossip straight from her.

"I'm sure I can. What is this about?"

"I'll tell the whole group all about it tomorrow."

"How intriguing. I can let Trudy and Dorthea know. Guy Jones was just in here. I think he was heading over to the livery before going home. If you catch him before he leaves town, he can tell Betsy and Neva. He could also probably swing by the Keegan Ranch to let Nicole know."

"Thank you. I would appreciate it." That only left Agnes Martin and the three Atwood ladies.

Saul escorted Henny out to her buggy and helped her in. "I'll see if I can catch Guy. You go ahead and see to the others." He covered her hand with his. "This is going to be all right. Your friends will stick with you."

She hoped so.

Geneviève bid Lamar Kesner good day outside the normal school. He had been kind enough to provide her a means of escape again. He was the only excuse *Grand-mère* would accept which allowed Geneviève off the Kesner grounds. Not even to see her brother. If not for the possibility of a match between her and the Kesner heir, *Grand-mère* would have whisked Geneviève back East the moment she'd dragged her out of the White Hotel. If Geneviève wished to remain in Kamola, she needed to play the game.

Though she planned to see her brother, she also hoped to spend a little time with Deputy Montana.

As she strolled along the walk to the school, a woman called her name.

Felicity approached from the other direction on the street, waving to her.

Geneviève stopped. Her temporary lady's maid could give her news about the deputy.

Felicity wore the yellow calico dress Geneviève had bought her at the mercantile. It suited the girl. Where this young woman could dress for the entire day at one time, Geneviève didn't have that luxury. She'd already changed twice today, and it wasn't even noon. Once into a morning gown appropriate for mingling over breakfast with the rest of the household. Then again into an outfit suited for an expedition into town. When she had suggested remaining in the same dress to go out, *Grand-mère* had given her a scalding look.

Felicity likely thought Geneviève extravagant. A part of her said it didn't matter, but another part wished for the girl to not view her poorly.

"I'm so glad to have run into you. It's like they are keeping you prisoner in there."

Indeed. "It is not so bad as that."

"Well, I would hate to be so restricted."

Geneviève didn't care for it either, even though it had been her life before. She hadn't known any different. Time to change the subject. "Is your brother at the sheriff's office?" She hoped to make her way over there in one of the waiting buggies.

"He's generally in and out of the office all day. We could walk there now and find out."

"I must see my brother first." That way if Lamar asked, she could tell him Pierre was well. "I will see you later." She hoped.

Felicity touched Geneviève's arm. "Before I let you go, I just heard the news. I think it's wonderful about Aunt Henny."

Geneviève bristled at the woman's nickname. What kind of person allowed those who weren't related to her to call her by such an endearment? "What about her?"

"She's a wonderful woman."

If these frontier people only knew. "Everyone is entitled to their own opinion."

Felicity scrunched her eyebrows. "She's your mother."

What a terrible thing to say? "Where did you hear that?"

"Sheriff Rix got it straight from Aunt Henny herself. He informed my brother on the case of the man who had been following her. My brother told me. He wasn't supposed to, but he was acting squirrelly, so I wormed it out of him."

"You are mistaken. My *mère* passed away years ago, when I was quite young." She'd cried many times over not having a *mère* to tuck her in at night.

"But—"

"I must go." Geneviève hurried away before Felicity could say anymore, hoping not to be followed.

Did the whole town believe this falseness? This lie? Why would people spread such inventions?

Geneviève entered the building and soon stood in her brother's office at the normal school. Gazing out the window, her knotted stomach tightened. Her middle threatened to cave in on itself. This sensation reminded her of the time *Grand-mère* had caught her without her stockings and shoes on their lawn at home in Paris. She had loved the feel of the dew-kissed grass on the souls of her feet and tickling between her toes.

Footsteps approached the door, and then it opened. Pierre smiled wide. "Vivi. I'm so glad you are here." He greeted her with a kiss to each cheek. "I have some news to tell you."

She doubted she would like what he had to say. With a shuddering breath, she spoke. "I have heard some terrible gossip. Felicity said people are spreading a malicious rumor that the Henny woman is our *mère*. You need to put a stop to this."

He took her trembling hands in his. "She *is* our *mère*."

"No, she cannot be. I will not believe this." Her *mère* had abandoned her and then died. Or rather their *grand-mère* had told them she'd died. Then when they had found out she hadn't died at first but died later, she told them their *mère* had abandoned them. What *mère* could do that to her own children? "How can you believe these things?"

"Because it's true. She has a photograph of her and *Père* on their wedding day."

She pulled her hands from his grasp.

"She wants to meet you."

"No." She faced the window again.

"Please, Vivi. For me."

Geneviève would not meet this deceiver who had drawn her brother into her web.

"She has a daisy garden the same as *Père's*. Do you want to know why?"

Even though Geneviève shook her head, she did want to know.

"It's for you. Your name before we were taken away was Daisy."

How pedestrian. She swung back around to face her brother. "No. I am Geneviève. As I have always been."

"Daisy's the name you were given at birth. I saw it along with mine in her Bible. I'm Winston after *Père* and *Grand-père*."

"Those aren't our names." Her heart wrenched in her chest. "Merely telling you they are to make you believe."

"Our birthdates were written beside each of our names."

"She could have written those in at any time."

He shook his head. "There's no way she could know both of ours."

A small voice within whispered it was true. No, no, no. She would not believe.

"Please come to her house and meet her." His eyes pleaded. "Please."

Oui. If she met this woman, she could disprove her lies. "Not at her house. I don't want to go there." She put a hand on her tormented middle. Her stomach threatened to expel her breakfast.

Pierre took her hands again. "Thank you. I'll arrange everything. You won't regret this."

No, she wouldn't.

She would put an end to this woman's lies.

Eighteen

On Tuesday, Henny made sure everything was perfect. She cut into the chocolate cake she'd made.

Her son hadn't been home for supper last night. He'd eaten with his sister at the Kesners', having told her about the existence of her mother earlier in the day. Though Daisy was reluctant, he'd convinced her to meet Henny on Wednesday. However, he cautioned Henny to keep her hope in check. Would her daughter indeed show up? She would be praying extra hard that Daisy would sit down with her.

Fortunately, her quilting friends had all been able to join her today, so no one would be left out.

After serving them each a slice of cake and something to drink, she sat in her usual spot on the settee.

Agnes Martin started off. "Henny, you are obviously out of sorts. We are here for you no matter what."

No matter what. Henny hoped so. She hadn't realized her distress had been so evident on her face. "I have some news and wanted you to hear it from me and not someone else. I owe all of you that." She set about explaining her past, her children, and Mr. Marseille's identity. Then she held her breath.

After a lingering silence, comments ensued.

"He's your son?"

"I thought he looked familiar."

"Why didn't he say so instead of skulking about?"

"Is he unattached?"

"Franny!"

"What? He's handsome and related to Henny. What could be better?"

Henny hadn't thought to ask him if either he or Daisy were married. She could have grandchildren. *Mercy.* Certainly, her son would have told her if she had any. She couldn't think about that right now. "I will understand if some of you don't wish to associate with me any longer."

Agnes stood. "There is not one woman in this room who would turn her back on you."

Henny appreciated Agnes's tenacity. "Each lady needs to decide for herself and not be treated harshly in any way if she chooses to excuse herself. I will understand. I'm not who I presented myself to be."

Dorthea stood. "You presented yourself as a good woman, and you are."

Isabelle stood. "And unselfish."

"And helpful."

"Kind."

One by one each of her friends stood calling out a word. Henny appreciated everyone's generosity and loyalty.

Only Marguerite Atwood remained seated. The room stilled as all eyes rested on her. They all held a collective breath until, she slowly rose. "A dear friend."

Now Henny stood. "You all are dear friends to me. I can't begin to thank you." She had been right to call Kamola her home.

If her daughter would show even the tiniest bit of the compassion these women had lavished on Henny, all *would* be well as Saul had said.

On Wednesday, Geneviève's stomach contorted as she entered the White Hotel on Pierre's arm. Though she had changed her mind about coming, she also didn't want to disappoint her brother. With *Père* gone, her brother was the one person she could confide in. She halted outside the dining room barely able to draw a breath, which had nothing to do with her corset. "I need a moment. You go on ahead inside."

He squeezed her hand on his arm. "You'll be fine. I'm right here with you. I won't leave your side."

Smart of him. If he left her alone, she might flee. Her whole body felt like a tightly twisted cord ready to snap from the tension. Every nerve frayed.

"Take a deep breath."

Though not deep, she took as much of a breath as her agitated lungs would allow.

"Ready?"

No. She would never be ready but nodded anyway. Stepping through the doorway, she saw the woman immediately. Geneviève could still leave, but her feet carried her across the room.

The woman stood as Geneviève and Pierre reached the table. "Hello, Daisy. I'm so happy you came." Her eyes filled with tears.

Geneviève would not be moved by this woman. She held on to her anger to keep her own emotions from overwhelming her and narrowed her eyes. "Hello, *Madame* Henderson. Or is it *Madame* Seymour? My name is *Geneviève Marseille*." She felt rather than saw Pierre's disapproval of the emphasis of her name as he sharply pulled the chair from the table and held it for her. She lowered herself into the seat, dismissing her big brother's discipline.

"I'll remember to call you Geneviève. Please call me Aunt Henny or Henny." The woman reseated herself and then Pierre sat.

"I do not make it a practice to refer to people by anything other than their actual name."

Madame Henderson's bright expression dampened. "I've had coffee served for each of us."

Geneviève gave a nod in recognition of her thoughtfulness, but she wouldn't be drinking the bitter beverage. For if she did, her stomach would revolt for sure. Best to keep the status quo.

Pierre picked up his cup and took a sip. *"Merci."*

"My pleasure." *Madame* Henderson returned her focus to Geneviève. "You've grown into a lovely young lady. You have your father's eyes."

Geneviève had always been told that, but they had failed to mention she had this woman's face shape and cheek bones. Did this woman believe flattery would soften her?

Madame Henderson had Pierre's eyes, brow, and mouth. "I'm sure you don't remember me, but I remember you."

"I am sure you are correct. I have no memory of you whatsoever." Even so, her heart leapt at something familiar, like a whisper in the dark.

Geneviève switched to French so the simple frontier woman couldn't understand her. "*Frère*, you can't possibly believe this woman's claims. She is *not* our *mère*." No matter how much she resembled Pierre.

"Don't be rude," Pierre admonished in French then switched to English with a smile. "Remember your manners and speak in English."

Geneviève forced a smile. "Pardon."

Madame Henderson hesitated before continuing. "I remember the day you were born. You came a month early. You were so tiny but perfect. I held you in my arms and knew my life was about as wonderful as one could get."

"I do not know who you held, but it was not me." Geneviève felt nothing but contempt for the woman.

At least that was what she told herself.

Madame Henderson implored, "I know you were told otherwise, but I never abandoned you. Neither of you. I would never do that."

Geneviève had had enough of this woman's lies and wanted this to end. "I *do* believe you on that issue. Since I do not believe you to be my *mère*, then you could not have possibly abandoned me." She stood, which forced Pierre to get to his feet. "Good day."

Madame Henderson remained seated. "I hope we can become friends."

This woman couldn't be serious. "I do not believe that will be possible."

"I'm still going to pray for it."

Hope in the woman's eyes tugged on Geneviève's emotions. She headed toward the exit as quickly as etiquette would respectably allow.

"Vivi!"

"Let her go." The compassion in *Madame* Henderson's simple statement pulled at Geneviève's heart, but she didn't stop.

She didn't want this woman to be her *mère*. Her life had been less complicated with her *mère* deceased. She wanted that simpler life again.

Then Pierre wouldn't have come to Kamola. She wouldn't have either and never would have met the deputy. She hurried to the sheriff's office to see Deputy Montana.

The man behind the desk stood. "He's not here. He doesn't work today."

What should she do now? "Do you think you could find me a carriage to take me...someplace?" She didn't know where to go.

"Will do." He pressed on his hat and scurried out.

Montana swung his ax down on the flat end of a log, lifted it with the hunk of wood holding on, and brought it down again, causing the piece to split in half. If he cut a little wood every day, through the summer, he should have plenty come winter. If he chopped twice or three times as much on his day off, he wouldn't think so much about Miss Marseille. He shifted his gaze to his growing pile, five times what he cut any other day.

As he set one of the halves on the chopping block, hoofbeats approached, fast. He rested the ax head on the top of his boot.

Deputy Sammy brought his horse to a stop in front of him but didn't dismount. "You're needed at the sheriff's office."

What was Sammy up to? "It's my day off."

"Your French lady came in."

His heart leapt at the mention of her. *Best to cut all ties where she was concerned.*

"She was looking for you and seemed upset."

Did it have something to do with Aunt Henny being her mother? Felicity said Miss Marseille had been distressed when she had mentioned it to her.

Don't take the bait, Montana.

"She asked me to fetch a carriage for her, but I came here instead."

The worst thing Montana could do was go to her. There could be nothing between them. All that nonsense was in the past. "I'm not presentable to be in the company of a lady." *Don't do it.* "I'll wash up and saddle my horse." Miss Marseille was upset—Sammy said so—Montana *had* to go.

By the time he reached the office, she was gone.

He was such a halfwit. Once again, he acted as the Helena fool from the play, chasing after the wrong person.

Sammy came in behind him. "I swear she was here."

Under different circumstances, he would assume Sammy was playing a joke on him. Not today. He liked the idea of Miss Marseille coming to him seeking comfort. More dreams and delusions. Perhaps he was more the Lysander ninny thinking he could ever have a chance with someone like Miss Marseille. He shook his head. When had he begun thinking of himself in terms of Shakespeare characters? He must be losing his mind. What a dolt. "Thanks for trying. She must have gone to the Kesners'."

He headed out the rear of the building to the place he'd taken Miss Marseille when she'd been distressed before.

His breath caught, and he halted.

Like an apparition he'd conjured from his longings, Miss Marseille sat on the very log they had before...after she had kissed him.

And he'd kissed her in return.

Dare he approach? If she was nothing more than a figment, he didn't want her to disappear. If she was real, he didn't want to disturb her. Except, she had been the one who sought him out.

His feet took him to her. "Miss Marseille?"

Startling, she gazed up with red, tear-filled eyes. "You are here?"

"Sammy got me." He sat next to her and handed her his blue bandana. "What's wrong?"

"*Merci.*" She dabbed the cloth at her eyes. "Pierre has been completely taken in by *Madame* Henderson. I cannot talk reason to him."

"By who?"

"That Henny woman."

"I don't understand. I thought Aunt Henny was your mother."

She turned a withering glare on him. "My *mère* died years ago. Now that woman has deceived my poor *frère.*"

He suspected she wished him to drop the matter, but Aunt Henny deserved a little defense. She wouldn't say something which wasn't true. "I thought she had proof."

"Are you going to side with her as well?"

"I'm not siding with anyone, merely trying to understand." He might as well stick his foot clear in it. "Why wouldn't you want her for your mother? She's a wonderful person."

"If she is, as you say, my *mother*, then she abandoned me, Pierre, and *Père*. If she is not, then she is a liar and a cheat. Either way she is not a *wonderful* person and does not deserve the endearment of *mère.*"

Put that way, he could kind of see her point. "So, you don't believe she's your mother?"

"It is best that way. I already got over the heartache of her betrayal once before. I do not want to do it again."

He couldn't imagine Aunt Henny abandoning anyone, let alone her children. How could he help both Miss Marseille *and* Aunt Henny?

Miss Marseille held out his bandana to him. "I am sorry about your kerchief."

He waved it off. "Keep it." He liked the idea of her having something of his. It kept them connected, even if only tenuously.

Later that afternoon, Henny sat at her kitchen table with Saul, each with a cup of coffee. Her stomach shifted and contorted into a tight ball within her as it had at the hotel when meeting her daughter.

Saul covered her hand with his. "What's wrong?"

She tried to block her emotions but couldn't. She replayed her encounter with Daisy, and her vision blurred. "She doesn't want anything to do with me."

He squeezed her hand. "I'm sure that's not true."

The young woman who strolled into the dining room on Winston's arm had stood poised and full of grace. She carried herself the same as Henny's mother-in-law had, with a touch of distain in her gaze. "She thought I had abandoned her and was dead."

"Then this has all been a big shock to her."

"She doesn't even believe I'm her mother."

"She merely needs time." He patted Henny's hand.

Strangely the small action comforted her. "You didn't see the expression on her face. It was the same one my mother-in-law would give me. She never approved of me either. And since she raised my daughter, Daisy—or rather Geneviève—has her predilections."

Saul shook his head. "What could your mother-in-law have possibly found in you to disapprove of?"

There were always so many things, but they all stemmed from her main bone of contention. "I didn't come from old money as they did. Both her family and my father-in-law's. Very old money. Old money should only marry old money. My father earned his, so we were the dreaded new money lot."

"Oh, fiddlesticks. That's stupid. No amount of money, new or old, can compare to good character, of which you have a whole meadow full."

She put her free hand atop Saul's. "Thank you. I don't know what I would do without your friendship."

He stacked his other hand on top of hers. "I'm always here for you."

The comfort in those simple words ministered to her heart. "Knowing my daughter wasn't ready for an endearment such as *mother*, I asked her to call me Henny. To which, she informed me she didn't refer to people except by their actual name. I was so tempted to remind her Geneviève Marseille wasn't *her* actual name. Nor her brother's or grandparents."

"But you didn't."

"Was I wrong in not calling their bluff and let them put me in jail? Or worse, an asylum?" Death would be more humane.

Saul gave a dramatic shiver. "It sounds as though your in-laws had a bit of power or knew powerful people, so they would have had you locked up one way or another. Retreat isn't a bad option. You stand to fight another day. Leaving all those years ago has made it possible for you to see your children now. If not, you probably would have never seen them again."

"I thought I *would* never see them again. If not for my husband telling our son to find me, I wouldn't have this chance. They would still think I abandoned them and was dead."

"They know the truth now. Your son believes you, and your daughter will too in time."

Henny hoped so.

"So, what shall I call you? Henny? Or Anne?"

She'd been Henny more than half of her life. The name had grown on her. "Henny. Anne was a different person." Henny was a nickname, much like the deputy going by Montana. Henny suited her. Henny was stronger than Anne had ever been. Anne depended on others, first her parents then her husband. Henny had only ever had herself to rely on. Anne wouldn't be able to weather Daisy's rejection. Henny would fight for her daughter this time. Fight for the woman—Geneviève—her daughter had become.

Nineteen

THE NEXT DAY, HENNY STOOD IN line at Waldon's Mercantile, holding three spools of thread. She had planned to get these on Monday when she'd purchased cake ingredients, but the excitement of learning about her children had pushed that item off her list. She could have bought the thread on Wednesday after meeting Daisy, but she'd been too upset after the encounter to think of much of anything. Was she turning into a forgetful old lady? Fifty-one was much too young for that.

She made her way to the front and set the thread on the counter. "Hello, Franny. I hope you're having a good day."

"Hello, Aunt Henny. Good enough. I have a crick in my neck. I must have slept catawampus on it." She tallied the thread and gave the total.

"Put some dried beans in a flour sack and set it on the stove until the beans warm clear through." Henny handed over some coins. "Place it on the sore part of your neck. Make sure it's not too hot. You don't want to burn your skin." That method had worked for Henny on more than one occasion.

"Thanks." Franny put the money in the till. "I'll see you tomorrow and let you know how the beans worked."

Henny stepped outside and prepared to climb into her buggy.

"Anne."

Henny's blood ran cold, and she turned slowly. Her nemesis stood before her. "Cora." She should have guessed she would be in town if Henny's children were. "I'm surprised to see you here."

Her mother-in-law's eyes narrowed. "I'm sure you are. Thought you could get away?"

She had hoped so, but evidently not. "Not the sort of town I'd expect you to step foot in." The reason Kamola had been a good choice for Henny to make it her home.

Cora sneered. "Exactly the sort of place I'd expect to find you. I see you've returned to your squalid roots."

Cora and the eldest Winston had never viewed Henny—or rather Anne—as good enough for their son. Old money looked down their nose at new. Her parents with or without money had always been better and kinder people than the Seymours.

The old feelings of needing to cower before this woman reared up. Henny's insides bunched, and she had an overwhelming desire to flee.

Upon marrying, she had foolishly assumed she could look to this woman as a mother, having lost her own.

"So, you are the reason my grandson came here. I should have known his desire to be a teacher was a ruse. He's sneaky and deceptive, exactly like you."

Henny took the jab as a compliment. Even half a world away, her son retained something of her. Did Cora's surprise at Henny's presence mean this was the first knowledge her in-laws had of Henny's whereabouts? "Actually, Winston—my Winston—sent him to me. Daisy too."

"Her name is Geneviève. You know she's here?"

This wasn't the time or place to quibble about Daisy's name. "I've spoken to her." Henny wouldn't divulge that her daughter didn't want anything to do with her.

"I don't believe you. She would have told me. Both of my grandchildren have thrived splendidly without you. I'll take her away from this little town."

How had Daisy made it all the way to Kamola without her grandparents' permission? *Good girl, Daisy.* There was hope in her daughter's rebellion against her grandparents. "Are you sure? I don't think *my* daughter will go with you."

"You stay away from Geneviève, or Mr. Marseille will take our evidence to the authorities."

So not only Henny's children's names were changed, but the whole family.

Her insides recoiled at the threat, even though Henny knew the evidence was fabricated. "Be careful, Cora, or you will push her away as you did your son. Remember where he ended up? Right in my arms." She couldn't believe her boldness. She had never before countered Cora or the senior Winston. It felt good. Maybe if she had done so before, she wouldn't have lost her family.

"She doesn't even know you."

True, but Henny had seen the struggle in her daughter's eyes. She would continue to pray for Daisy's heart to be softened—or rather Geneviève's. It would take some doing to think of her as such. "Good day, Cora." Henny climbed into her buggy, released the brake with a shaking hand, and encouraged the horse forward.

Though her insides were all a jumble and concern niggled at the edge of her thoughts, it had felt good to speak her mind to her mother-in-law.

After supper when her other two boarders had retired to their rooms for the evening, Winston—or rather Pierre— handed her an envelope. "This is the letter *Père* left for you." He sat in the chair opposite her on the settee.

Henny had forgotten all about the letter her son said he had from his father. She had been too excited learning about her son and meeting her daughter. She glanced up from the envelope. "The seal is broken."

"*Oui.* I read it. I could not turn over information which could be potentially hurtful without knowing what it contained."

"Then, this contains nothing of importance?"

"They are my *père's* words, so yes, they are important. But his words are to you. I will not deny you, or him, this opportunity."

Henny appreciated that. Apparently, he was going to sit and watch her read it. She wanted to pour over it in private, but since her son already knew what it contained, his presence was of little consequence. Then there was the matter of the brown-paper wrapped parcel on his lap. Was that for her as well? She would find out soon enough and took a deep breath before beginning.

My Dearest Annie,

Her breath caught. She could hear his voice in her head even after all these years.

I am not worthy nor deserving to use such familiarity or endearment. I am weak. I have always been weak. You made me a better man, but sadly, I wasn't strong enough to keep you. If you can ever find it in your heart to forgive me, I would be forever grateful and in your debt.

Of course she forgave him. She had never held it against him but laid the blame with his parents.

I imagined myself as your knight in shining armor. But alas, it was you who rescued me.
If I could fold back the years to our wedding day, I would do things very different. After the ceremony, I would whisk you away to where no one could find us.

He had wanted her. Henny didn't know if that made the situation better or worse. Bittersweet at the very least.

Instead, I allowed my parents to convince me you were unfit and our children would be better off without you. I knew they were wrong, but I didn't know how to fight them. I take the full blame. I should have been stronger. I should have returned for you. I should have been a better husband, a better person. My whole life they told me what to do. You were my one defiance. I didn't know how to deal with their disappointment and buckled to their wishes. I am so ashamed of myself.
I ruined my life.
I ruined your life.
I ruined our children's lives.

Henny's life hadn't been ruined. In spite of everything, she had a good life.

I hope fate has been kind to you. I hope happiness has shone down upon you. I hope our children have inherited your good sense and will get to know you. They will be better for it.

Our son has grown into a man you would be proud of. He takes after you. Not letting things or people stand in the way of what he wants.

Our daughter is a beauty like you, but unfortunately, I fear she might have more of my propensity to please my parents.

My mother is a hard woman to oppose, my father impossible. They will not bend or waiver.

Henny knew that all too well. If she had defied the Seymours all those years ago, would she have been able to keep her children? Or would she have still lost them *and* been locked away forever? She would never know, because she, too, had been weak.

I have given our son all of the incriminating evidence my parents counterfeited against you, to give to you. Do what you wish with it. Keep it or burn it.

"He says he gave you something else for me." She pointed to the bundle on her son's lap, loosely wrapped in brown paper with twine to tie it closed. "Is that it?"

"*Oui.* Are you finished?"

"Not quite." She read to the end of the letter and refocused on her son. "I assume you read what was in there as well."

"I did. Is the evidence in here against you true?"

From what Henny could remember from over twenty-two years ago, it wasn't. "No. But I had no way to prove my innocence."

"There is more than information on you. *Père* has some which could be very harmful to my grandparents. Is it false as well?"

"I have no idea." It was the first she'd heard of it. Her son wouldn't likely turn over the package now, but as long as he held the incriminating evidence rather than her in-laws, Henny could breathe easier.

Surprisingly, he handed the parcel across the tea table to her. "*Père* wanted you to have this. Please don't use it against my family."

Henny *was* his family, but she knew he wasn't counting her—at least not yet. She had no intention of doing harm to others. "So why are you giving it to me?"

"For two reasons. First, these were *Père's* wishes. Second, I have gotten to know you and do not believe you would intentionally hurt someone."

A part of Henny did want to hurt the people who had stolen her children and the life she should have had, but she knew she wouldn't. It would do no good and cause more harm. "Thank you for all this, and for your trust in me."

He stood. "You are welcome. I will retire now." He headed upstairs.

A part of Henny wanted to call him back and soak in his presence, but another part wanted to dive into the package of malice on her lap.

She untied the string, refusing to cower to her in-laws anymore.

Twenty

On Sunday afternoon, Geneviève eagerly agreed to a carriage ride with Lamar. She'd had enough of *Grand-mère's* constant picking at everything she did—how she stood, the angle of her hand, breathing too loudly.

How could Geneviève not have noticed before how nitpicky it all was? If a potential suitor found her undesirable because the ruffle on her blouse cuff was a quarter of an inch longer than the latest fashion... The thought seemed ridiculous now. How could she have believed all that? It had been the only way she had known. Her grandparents meant well. *Grand-mère* fussed to ensure Geneviève would catch the best husband possible. But was a man who cared more about what she wore better than one who cared about her heart and character? Deputy Montana seemed to accept her as she was regardless of whether or not her dress and manners were perfect.

Lamar would be a good person from whom to seek advice because he had no vested interest in the outcome. "Do you mind if I ask you for your opinion?"

He glanced sideways at her. "Don't mind at all."

"Everyone thinks they know what is best for me. I do not know what to do. My grandparents want me to do one thing, my brother and Henny another. If I choose my grandparents' way, I will lose Deputy Montana. If I choose that Henny woman, I lose my grandparents."

He reined in at a street intersection to allow a wagon to pass. "How do you normally make decisions?" He put the carriage into motion again.

How indeed? The root of her dilemma. "Until now, my grandparents made them all. Except when I decided to defy them and came west on my own. I am a grown woman and should be able to make a decision on my own. So why can I not?"

"It sounds as though you've never had the opportunity to develop that skill."

"Decision-making is a skill?"

"In a way. You learn how to make decisions by making them and learning from the outcome." He guided the horse around a corner. "Consider your choice to come west. Given your experiences here, would you judge this a success or failure?"

She thought a moment. "I do not know. I am very confused."

"List the good things about coming to Kamola and the bad things, then decide if you would do it again based on the knowledge you have now."

"I merely want things to return to the way they were before."

"Before what?"

"Before *Père* died...and I found out my *mère* is alive." She didn't know which pained her most.

"Answer me honestly. Would you rather be ignorant of the truth?"

Though she wished things to be as they were before, a part of her was glad to know the truth. Did she honestly wish not to know?

Lamar reined the carriage to a halt on a street lined with houses.

"Why did you stop?"

"We've arrived." He climbed out and assisted her down.

She straightened her dress front. "I do not understand."

His expression turned apologetic. "Please don't be angry with me. Your brother asked me to bring you."

Geneviève glanced around, taking in the modest mint-green exterior of the house, white picket fence, and the chaos of wild flowers starting to bloom. She noted the sign out front, *Aunt Henny's Boarding House, Home to the Weary Traveler.* She didn't have to wonder why she was brought here. "I want to leave."

"Are you sure? You wanted to know if you had made the right decision in coming all the way from back East."

She settled her gaze on the older man and three small children on the porch with that Anne Henderson woman who was supposedly her mother. One part of her loathed for the familial tie to be true. But her heart...*ached* for it to be so.

Madame Henderson wrapped her arms around the littlest girl. That should have been Geneviève she was hugging at a young age. Why hadn't this woman wanted to be *her mère*? What had Geneviève done to turn this woman away from her? Why couldn't she love Geneviève?

The woman lifted her gaze and looked directly at her. "Daisy." She came down the steps to the other side of the gate.

Geneviève bristled. "My name is Geneviève Angelique Marseille."

The woman smiled gingerly at Geneviève. "My apologies, Geneviève. I'm trying to make the change in my head, but I have only ever thought of you as Daisy until now. I will endeavor to do better. I can't tell you how much it means to me to have you at my home."

Geneviève couldn't believe she was here. "I see you replaced your real family with a new one."

"Of course I haven't."

But she had. Geneviève could see with her own eyes.

Pierre sauntered along the walk and out through the gate. "Vivi, you're here." He turned to Lamar. "*Merci* for bringing her. You may go."

Geneviève's voice caught. "Please do not."

Lamar nodded. "I would be glad to stay."

"As you wish." Pierre motioned toward the yard. "Come and join us."

She shook her head. "I cannot believe you did this."

"I have done more." Pierre looked resolute. "I gave her the bundle of papers *Père* wanted her to have. In there is not only evidence of false wrong doings of our *mère*, but some real ones of our grandparents. She can use it to keep our grandparents from sending her to jail for things she did not do."

"How could you do that to them?"

Her brother leveled his gaze at her. "No one deserves to go to jail for crimes they did not commit."

"She could use the information to send our grandparents to jail!"

"I do not think she will, but she has it as a security to protect herself." He turned to *Madame* Henderson. "Is that not right?"

"I promise you I will never use it to hurt anyone."

A false promise. "You could say anything to protect yourself."

Pierre took Geneviève's hand. "She did nothing wrong. Our grandparents committed many illegal acts. Like framing her and kidnapping us."

"They did not kidnap us, we had *Père*."

Pierre countered. "They basically kidnapped him as well."

Geneviève turned from her brother to *Madame* Henderson and glared. "You have papers which could condemn my grandparents."

The woman hesitated. "I do. Your father wanted me to have them. To protect myself."

"He should not have done that. What will you do with them? I am sure you would like nothing better than to pay back my grandparents for the pain and suffering you believe they caused you."

"I'm not after retribution. That won't erase all those years. It won't make anything better. More than likely, it would make matters worse. I plan to hold on to the information as a precaution in case your grandparents have other fabricated evidence and try to send me to jail."

"What would stop you from doing likewise to them?"

"I suppose nothing, but I won't. I promise you."

Something inside Geneviève longed to believe this woman—did believe her—but she couldn't risk her grandparents' future. "Am I supposed to blindly take you at your word?"

"I have nothing but my word to give you." *Madame* Henderson held out her hands.

Geneviève wanted to trust her, but that would mean her grandparents had done terrible things. "I do not know you, so I cannot trust you."

The woman was silent for a moment. "You're right. Wait here." She headed up the walk and inside the house.

Geneviève put her hand on her midsection. "I have bees in my stomach."

Lamar had remained silently at her side. "Don't you mean butterflies?"

"No. These are stinging me." An all too familiar feeling.

Pierre took her hand. "If you are not ready to trust her, then trust me."

She did trust her brother, but he couldn't control another person's actions.

Madame Henderson returned with a brown-paper wrapped package. "These are all the documents which incriminate your grandparents." She held them out. "As well as the false ones against me."

Geneviève took them. "What do you expect me to do with these?"

"Whatever you choose. My life is in your hands."

"But...you said you were keeping them." What was this woman up to?

"I've changed my mind. I want you to have them."

"It makes no sense for you to give these to me."

"I've waited a long time for the day I would hopefully see my children again." The woman's eyes teared.

Geneviève found hers tearing as well.

"I hope this measure of trust will start repairing the distrust between us. I never wanted to lose you. I didn't know how to find you."

Geneviève was at a loss. She couldn't believe this woman had given her something so valuable. She could get rid of her for good. She hugged the papers to her chest. *"Merci beaucoup."*

"You're welcome."

"I must go now." Geneviève turned and hurried into the carriage without waiting to be assisted.

Pierre called after her. "Do not go, Vivi."

Then the woman said, "Let her. She needs to do this." She called out to Geneviève. "I love you. I always have and always will."

Tears pricked Geneviève's eyes. How could that woman claim to love her when she didn't even know her?

Lamar climbed aboard and put the horse into motion. "I was surprised you didn't stay after her gesture of trust."

"This is all too much. I must see what is in here." She tightened her fingers around the brown paper, causing it to crinkle. "Maybe it is nothing and the woman has fooled me."

"That's not the kind of person Miss Henny is. Do you believe her that she loves you?"

Honestly, she didn't know what kind of woman *Madame* Henderson was. "It does not matter. I will not see her again." That thought both pleased her and bothered her.

"Why not?"

"I do not wish to get to know her." But maybe a part of her did.

"What is the worst that can happen? You realize you don't like her as you'd always thought?"

No, a small niggling inside had already warmed to this woman a little. "What if she does not like me?"

He lifted his head in a half nod. "Ah. That's the real trouble. We all want to be liked, and being accepted by our parents is paramount. We want them to be proud of us. Miss Henny is a good person. I think she will surprise you. In a good way."

She had already been rejected by her *mère* once all those years ago. She couldn't bear to be rejected again.

Twenty-One

GENEVIÈVE HAD HIDDEN THE PAPERS IN her room at the Kesners'. Hesitant to learn what the documents revealed, she put the task off until there was no risk of *Grand-mère* catching her.

The next morning between breakfast and dinner proved to be such an opportunity. *Grand-mère* had an outing with *Madame* Kesner. Geneviève could put it off no longer. She retrieved the package from under her mattress and sat on the bed, not caring if her dress got wrinkles. She read every word on every page. Evidence mounted against *Madame* Henderson as well as her grandparents. Was it *all* true? Was *any* of it true?

She never imagined her grandparents to be mean spirited. They had always been so loving to her and Pierre. Doted on them. They had high expectations, for certain, but that was because they wanted the best for them.

When her door opened, she startled.

Grand-mère loomed in the doorway. "You best have a good excuse for not being in the dining room for dinner. You should have come down fifteen minutes ago, and you haven't even changed. You're making people wait."

A maid had come a half an hour earlier to let her know it was nearly noon. But Geneviève had had more important matters on her mind. She studied her grandmother for a moment. Were she and *Grand-père* truly capable of what these documents suggested? "*Père* gave Pierre a bundle of documents which gives evidence against my *mère*."

Grand-mère blanched. "I'll take those. You needn't concern yourself with them."

Rising to her feet, Geneviève shook a fist full of papers. "*Grand-mère*, tell me you and *Grand-père* didn't do these things. Tell me you didn't fabricate evidence against an innocent woman."

"She was hardly innocent." *Grand-mère* narrowed her eyes at the documents. "It was for your own good. We were protecting you and your brother from her. And your father as well. She beguiled him."

Geneviève couldn't believe this. Everything she had known in her formative years might be a lie. "How could you do those things?"

"We did what had to be done."

Geneviève couldn't believe her grandparents had committed such deeds. She bundled all the documents in the brown paper and hurried from the room. She didn't want to be around her grandmother at the moment. Too many conflicting emotions and thoughts jumbled together inside her. She needed to sort it all out in her mind.

At the bottom of the stairs, she stopped. Where to go?

A maid approached. "They are waiting in the dining room."

"Geneviève," came from above her, and *Grand-mère* descended the stairs at an unhurried pace fit for a lady.

Geneviève felt trapped, so she spun toward the front door, yanked it open, and escaped, without bothering to close it behind her.

At the base of the veranda steps, a footman dipped his head to her. "How may I assist you?"

"I want to leave."

"I will have a carriage and driver readied for you."

From behind her came, "Geneviève, what are you doing? Return inside at once."

Geneviève couldn't face *Grand-mère* at the moment and took off at a brisk, unladylike pace.

"Where do you think you're going?"

Geneviève hiked her skirt with her free hand and bolted.

"Geneviève Angelique!"

She wouldn't stop. She wouldn't go back. Even before she reached the end of the long drive between the house and the road, she ran out of breath. She paused and put her hand on her midsection. Corsets were not designed for running. She wished she had on her less restrictive calico dress. She would get caught for sure, but she wouldn't stop. Heaving in a breath, she hurried to the road and turned out of sight from the house behind the wrought iron fence and bushes which protected the estate from the outside world. A world Geneviève had experienced and liked. She leaned against a tree to catch her breath. But only for a moment. She couldn't risk it any longer than that.

She pushed away from the tree before she was ready but knew she should. She headed along the road, skirting around the heart of town. When someone came after her, they would likely take the most direct route.

After a few minutes, a carriage approached from in front of her. She must appear foolish, walking along the road in a fancy organza dress, hugging a parcel. She kept her head ducked to keep from being noticed. Though doubtful she'd go unseen, the person would probably drive on by.

"Geneviève?"

She glanced up to see Isabelle Dawson driving a small carriage. Felicity had introduced her to the young woman at the viewing of *A Midsummer Night's Dream*. "Good afternoon, *Madame* Dawson."

The woman reined in and glanced around. "Where is your carriage?"

No sense fibbing about it. "I do not have one. I would appreciate it if you would not tell anyone you saw me." Felicity had told her this woman was of a similar station as the Kesners and Geneviève's own grandparents. Chances were, she would go out of her way to inform on Geneviève.

She smiled. "So you're running away. I did my fair share of escaping. I can take you into town if you like."

This woman wasn't going to turn her in? "Why would you do that?"

"I understand the need to get away from all the fuss. Climb aboard, and I'll take you where you want to go."

Geneviève weighed her options. Continue on foot where more people could spot her or trust this woman whose kind eyes invited her in. *Merci.* She gripped the side of the buggy and stepped inside. Fortunately, it was a low step and then another to get aboard.

Once Geneviève was seated with her package on her lap, Isabelle snapped the reins. "Where to?"

Where? The hotel? No, that would be the first place *Grand-mère* would look. She had no place else to go. "I do not know. I only knew where I did not want to be."

"Well, that's the first step. You can think about it while we drive. When you figure it out, you can tell me."

"You are not going to ask me why I ran out?"

"It's probably none of my business." *Madame* Dawson glanced at her. "If you want someone to listen to your woes, I can do that."

Too many muddled thoughts to sort out on one buggy ride. "I would rather not." She needed to untangle her woes before speaking them to another person.

"Then it's settled. We are two young ladies out for a nice drive on this overcast, gray day."

"*Merci.*" Geneviève wouldn't mind getting to know this lady better. She seemed like a person who could be a friend. "I appreciate you helping me."

"Not a problem. But do let me know where you would like me to take you, or else you'll wind up at my house."

"I will." Geneviève didn't know this woman well enough to go to her home nor did she want to. She wanted to disappear and be alone. Since the hotel wasn't an option, she would like to see her *frère*. But no. He would either be teaching or with that woman—their *mère*—at her boarding house he lived in. That would never do.

If she couldn't see Pierre, then she wanted to see Deputy Montana. She could go to the sheriff's office, but if he wasn't there, the other deputy or sheriff might ask too many questions. "Do you know where Deputy Montana and his sister Felicity live?"

"Hmm. I think so. Is that where you'd like to go?"

"Yes, please." Felicity would help her.

Madame Dawson hesitated. "It might not be appropriate to be going to the deputy's cabin without an escort."

"His sister will be there. She has been an adequate chaperone for many weeks."

"All right." Isabelle drove along until she stopped in front of a moderate cabin. "Hulloo! Anybody home?"

No one responded and no one appeared.

"There doesn't appear to be anyone home."

Geneviève climbed down. "That is all right."

"Are you sure?"

"I am. I promise you, I will be perfectly safe." She did feel safe with the deputy. The only person she felt more so was with her brother. "I will sit on this nice porch until they return." Her grandmother would never find her here. She would be safe.

"All right. If you're sure, I'll be on my way."

"*Merci beaucoup.*" She sat in a rocking chair on the small covered porch.

"It appears as though it might rain. If it does come down, go on inside. I'm sure they wouldn't mind."

Geneviève could never do that, but if she told *Madame* Dawson, the woman might not leave. "I will."

Isabelle drove away.

Geneviève heaved a sigh of relief as she sank deeper into the comfortable chair. She had made it. She had escaped. Though the cabin wasn't isolated in the woods, the street it was on seemed to have little or no traffic.

Now what? What would she tell the deputy and his sister when they arrived? She couldn't stay here for the long term.

How could her grandparents have done such things? How could her own *mère* not come for her? Anne Henderson was in no way innocent in all this. She had to have done something for *Grand-mère* and *Grand-père* to think her unfit.

Tears welled in her eyes. Her life was a mess. Was everything she knew of her life a lie? What was the truth? Could she trust anyone?

She heard horse hoofbeats coming up the street. She glanced in the direction of the sound and could tell it wasn't Deputy Montana. What if it was someone sent from the Kesners' to search for her? She had to hide. Should she go around behind the cabin? *Oui*, that would be good. She scurried around the building and waited for the hoofbeats to draw near.

She held her breath.

Then they faded away.

A crack of thunder rumbled overhead. Within a minute, huge drops splatted on the ground and dotted her dress. Holding the incriminating documents close, she darted to the threshold of the rear door and scrunched under the slight overhang.

She couldn't risk the papers getting wet and smearing the ink. The rain increased. It wouldn't be long before she and the package were drenched. Staying out in this weather was ridiculous. Deputy Montana wouldn't mind, and neither would Felicity. *Madame* Dawson had said so. She tried the handle and stepped inside.

She shivered from being wet and rubbed her arms while waiting for her eyes to adjust to the dim interior. Slowly, the room came into focus. A rough-hewn table with a candle in a pewter holder with ring-shaped handle. A fireplace at one end of the room and a potbelly stove at the other. A counter and shelves were nestled into one corner with canisters and jars as she'd seen in the kitchens of the various homes she'd lived in. Only the necessities here. Though very rustic, it was clean. Something inviting about the place seemed to welcome her.

Her teeth chattered. She wished there were a fire in the hearth. She didn't know the first thing about building one. Left to her own devices, she wouldn't survive. Something which never used to bother her. In fact, she prided herself on not having to do much of anything because it meant she had enough money to have others do everything for her. Now she realized how useless she was. She still liked her finery, but it would be good to be able to survive if no one else was around. A shiver coursed through her. Without a fire, she needed to find something else to keep her warm. She didn't like the cold.

A curtain half drawn in one corner revealed a narrow bed. Dropping her package on the bed, she snatched the quilt folded on the foot of it and wrapped it around herself.

How resourceful. Pitiful was more accurate. How could finding a blanket make her feel somehow useful and capable?

Life had been so much simpler back East and in Europe, before she'd had the stupid idea to follow Pierre out here. She wished she could return to that. Why did life have to change? But it had. She would never be that naïve, protected girl again. Now a woman of the world, she sighed. Not really. As Lamar had pointed out, she didn't want to revert to not knowing the truth.

Sinking down on the bed, she curled her legs and drew the blanket tight.

Part of her still longed to have *Grand-mère* telling her what to do. Life had been easier and less stressful in some ways. She didn't have to worry about making poor choices. If a wrong decision was made, it wouldn't be her fault. She could never be blamed.

The other part of her thrived on making her own decisions. Granted she hadn't made any truly bad ones yet. Unless one were to ask *Grand-mère*, then all the decisions she had made of late were bad.

Choosing what she would do and what she would wear had been invigorating if not a little scary. But she had gotten used to it and came to resent all her decisions being made for her. When she'd insisted on wearing a dress Silvie hadn't suggested, *Grand-mère* had picked at it all through supper. Geneviève found out later *Grand-mère* had always been choosing Geneviève's clothes by way of Silvie. Like Geneviève, Silvie took her orders from others.

Grand-mère had indeed controlled every aspect of Geneviève's life. Before this trip, had she made any decisions? Ever? She couldn't think of one.

Because of what she'd learned about her past, she wished she had never ventured to Kamola. Although, coming and asserting her independence had been the best thing for her. She was a different person than she was two months ago.

If she had learned the information about her mother and her grandparents while back East or in France, she would have believed her grandparents rather than the truth. But she did know the truth.

She snuggled deeper into the quilt to contemplate what her future might look like. She hoped the deputy might be in it, but she didn't see how. *Grand-mère* and *Grand-père* would never approve of him. They would choose someone more fitting. Someone who suited her station. She paused.

Maybe she didn't care if they approved of Deputy Montana or not.

Twenty-Two

Montana had waited until the rain died off before heading home with his twin behind him on Cletus. No sense getting soaked for no reason.

He couldn't help feeling sorry for himself. He'd foolishly fallen for a gal he had no business even considering having an interest in. Miss Marseille was out of reach for a fellow like him. He never should have deluded himself into thinking there could be anything between them, any future for them. Regardless, he had allowed the thoughts and feelings to take root and grow. And grow they had, until he fancied himself being accepted by her wealthy family.

They would see what a fine gentleman he was and overlook his lack of assets. And of course, they would insist he keep his job as deputy because it was such a worthy occupation. In truth, he hoped they would insist upon him quitting because it was far too dangerous, then he could enjoy a life of leisure. He didn't think he would be content with a life of leisure, though. Nothing more than fanciful dreams he had no business letting take root. He'd set himself up for a fall. A very bad, long fall. One he didn't know if he could recover from.

Montana reined in Cletus in front of his cabin and reached his hand around behind him where his sister gripped his forearm and swung down. The ground splatted beneath her feet.

"I'll start supper." Felicity headed toward the door. "Don't track in mud or you'll be the one on your hands and knees scrubbing the floor."

A little dirt never hurt anything, but he'd be considerate of her hard work. Besides, he preferred a tidy place. He swung off as well with a small splash. "I'll take care of Cletus and check on the chickens and be in shortly."

Felicity stepped inside then reversed direction. "Montana, we got company."

He tossed his horse's reins over the hitching rail. "Is that raccoon inside again? I thought I patched the hole." He leapt onto the porch, wiped his boots as best he could, and strode inside.

He stopped short.

Curled on his bed he was letting Felicity use, bundled in a quilt and apparently fast asleep, lay Miss Marseille.

He must not be seeing things right. He'd been thinking about her and pining for her so much he was now imagining things. He shook his head to clear his vision.

She didn't disappear.

He turned to his sister. "Do you see what I see?"

She nodded. "That ain't no coon. Never saw one wear a fancy dress before."

He rolled his eyes at her wisecrack. "Why is she here?"

Felicity shrugged. "How should I know?"

"What should we do? Wake her?"

"Probably."

He nudged Felicity's shoulder with his own. "You do it."

His twin put her hand on his spine and shoved him forward. "Your place, your gal, your responsibility."

He stumbled toward the bed. After hesitating, he stretched out his arm and touched her shoulder through the quilt with one finger, and whispered, "Miss Marseille?"

She made a soft sound like a kitten.

He turned to his sister and shrugged.

"You're going to have to do more than that and speak louder." She made a shooing motion with her hands.

He jostled Miss Marseille a little harder and spoke at about the same volume. "Miss Marseille?"

She shifted this time.

He stepped back.

Her eyelids fluttered open. She jumped to her feet, and a brown parcel tumbled off the bed, causing the papers within to slide onto the floor. With them lay the bandana he'd given her the other day. Shedding the quilt to the end of the bed, she scooped the papers along with the blue cloth into her arms and hugged them to her chest. She spoke rapidly in French then switched to English. "Oh, my. I did not mean to fall asleep. Please forgive." The big sleeves she was partial to had mostly mashed flat along with the ruffles and fluff of her pale purple dress. "It started to rain, and I got cold. It was rude of me to enter your home without being invited."

"That's all right. We wouldn't want you to stay out in the rain. You were right to come inside." Montana wasn't sure how to ask her why she was in his cabin.

Felicity did it for him. "If you don't mind, what are you doing here? We thought we would never see you again."

Miss Marseille rubbed her arms. "I learned some dreadful things, and I did not want to be at the Kesners' any longer. I would have gone to my brother, but he is staying at the boarding house, so I could not go there."

"Of course you could go to Aunt Henny's. She would welcome you. She has rooms you could rent." Though Aunt Henny wouldn't charge her own daughter.

"No. I cannot go to that woman."

That woman? There was something more here she wasn't saying. "What's wrong with going to Aunt Henny's? She is your mother. Don't you like her?"

"I do not. Or at least I thought I did not, but now I do not know. I am very confused."

Montana was as well. "I don't understand."

"It is a long story. When I was very young, my *père*, my *frère*, my grandparents, and I moved to Europe after my *mère* passed away. When I was ten, I learned my *mère* had not passed away, but that she had abandoned us all those years ago, but she was now dead. My *père* became ill a year ago. Before he died, he told my brother our *mère* did not abandon us and she might not be dead. He told him to find a woman named Anne Henderson."

She took a shaky breath. "I did not want to find her. I did not want to learn about the woman who abandoned us. Pierre wanted to know about her. He wanted to find Anne Henderson so she could tell him about our *mère*. I begged him not to. He came last fall and found a woman he thought might know *Madame* Henderson. She is the woman you call Aunt Henny. But that is another lie. *She is Anne Henderson—my mère.* She is not dead at all. Why did she not ever come to find us?"

Being told someone was dead who wasn't *was* dreadful news. "I'm sure she would tell you what kept her away if you asked her."

"I spoke with her briefly yesterday. I do not want to talk to her anymore. Am I a terrible person for that?"

"No. It's still hard to believe you are Aunt Henny's daughter. As far as I know, no one even knew her real name. Although, I suspected Sheriff Rix did."

"See. How can I want to know someone who deceived a whole town for years? She cannot be an upstanding person."

"I can assure you Aunt Henny is of high moral character. She must have had a legitimate reason to not reveal her true name." Montana could tell by the taut expression on Miss Marseille's face she wasn't open to talking to Aunt—her mother. He glanced around his cabin. "If you don't want to go to Aunt Henny's and don't want to be at the Kesners', what do you want to do?"

"I do not know. I have nowhere to go. I have no money for a hotel."

Felicity stepped forward. "You can stay with us. Montana will sleep in the barn."

The deputy shook his head. "She can't stay here. That would sully her reputation regardless of where I slept. I'll pay for a room at the hotel for tonight. You'll be far more comfortable there and can figure out what you want to do tomorrow."

"*Merci beaucoup.* But I do not have anything else to wear." Miss Marseille waved her hand in front of her dress. "This is not suited for anything anymore. It is ruined."

"I'll lend you a night dress, and we'll figure out what to do about clothes in the morning." Felicity gathered the nicest skirt and blouse Miss Marseille had purchased for her. "These should fit you all right for tomorrow. I'll have Montana drop me off first thing to help you dress."

"*Merci.* But I have no money to pay your wages."

"You don't have to pay me anything. Friends help out friends."

"You consider me a friend?"

The expectancy in her eyes stabbed Montana's heart. Did she ever have true friends?

Felicity nodded. "Of course."

"Your kindness makes me want to cry."

Please, no. He didn't want to deal with tears. "I'll hitch the wagon. Be back in a jiffy." Montana left and led Cletus to the barn. "I'm sorry, boy, but I need you to do a little more work." He unsaddled the horse and hitched him to the buckboard. Then he walked it to the front of the cabin.

The ladies stood on the porch. Felicity had her arms full of quilts. His whole winter stash.

"What are all those for? It's not that cold." In fact, it wasn't cold at all. The rain had taken the heat from earlier out of the air.

"True, but the wagon seat is *that* hard." She heaved them toward him, and he caught them. "Would you spread them on the seat for us?"

He did and then helped Miss Marseille aboard first. She no longer had her brown-paper package but did have his bandana. He liked that. Had she given the bundle to Felicity? It had seemed important to her by the way she clutched it so tightly.

Miss Marseille turned. "Where should I sit?"

"In the middle. You aren't used to sitting on a wagon seat with the short sides. We wouldn't want you to lose your balance and fall off." The middle was exactly where Montana wanted her so she would be next to him.

"*Merci.* You two are always so thoughtful." She sat.

Maybe not as thoughtful as she might think. Now he felt guilty for being selfish.

Felicity eyed him. "I know the real reason, and I don't fault you for it." She climbed aboard.

He got in from the other side and took the reins. Yeah, the guilt wasn't going to bother him with the pretty French lady beside him.

At the hotel, Montana paid for the room as well as supper to be sent up to her. He didn't want her to have to come down and risk her grandmother seeing her. Certainly, the woman would have people out searching for Miss Marseille.

The clerk held a pen poised over the registry. "Would you like the same room as before?"

Miss Marseille's eyes widened. No doubt she feared her grandmother would find her too easily.

Montana didn't want the woman whisking Miss Marseille away again either. "Do you have a different one? Perhaps in another hallway?"

"Of course. How about the third floor?"

"*Oui*—I mean yes, I would prefer that."

The clerk filled in the room number on the registry and handed the key to Montana.

He immediately relinquished it to Miss Marseille. He didn't want anyone to think there was anything illicit about this arrangement. "Felicity, go on with her to get her settled in and whatever else she needs."

"Thanks. I was going to suggest that." His sister and Miss Marseille trekked up the stairs.

Montana turned to the desk clerk. "If anyone comes asking for her, don't let them know she's here. The only person you can inform is her brother. Understand?"

"Yes, sir. I'll make a note of it for others."

"If she wants breakfast in the morning before I get here or if she needs anything else, see she gets it. I'll settle any further charges tomorrow."

"Yes, sir."

Satisfied Miss Marseille was safe, Montana drove to Aunt Henny's instead of loitering in the lobby until his sister came down. He knocked on the boarding house door.

Aunt Henny opened it with an expectant expression that faltered. "Deputy Montana, what brings you here?" No doubt she'd hoped it to be her daughter.

"I need to speak with Mr. Marseille."

"I am right here." The professor stepped out from the interior doorway.

Aunt Henny waved Montana in. "Join us in the parlor."

Montana entered and faced Mr. Marseille. "It's about your sister."

Sucking in a small gasp, Aunt Henny's hand flew to her stomach.

"Is she all right?" Mr. Marseille asked.

"She's fine. I just thought someone should know her whereabouts." Someone other than himself and his sister. "I left her at the hotel. She didn't have any money, so I rented her a room."

After hesitating, Mr. Marseille sighed as he retrieved his wallet. "How much do I owe you?"

Though paying for a hotel room was no trifling matter on a deputy's pay, he waved the offer away. "That isn't why I've come. She seems to have run away from the Kesners'. I would go there and let your grandmother know she's safe, but I don't think I would be well received. I thought you might inform her of Miss Marseille's well-being. She doesn't want her grandmother to know where she is."

"I do not doubt that. *Grand-mère* would retrieve her again."

"But I didn't want your grandmother to worry."

"I appreciate your consideration. It was good of you to let me know."

Montana would have liked nothing better than to keep Miss Marseille hidden away at his place, but that would have been wrong in so many ways. He needed to be satisfied her brother would take care of her. Sort of satisfied. He would find out from Felicity what had happened.

Geneviève's stomach bunched at the knock on her hotel door. Had *Grand-mère* found her? Or worse...her so-called-*mère*? She didn't want to deal with either one right now. Felicity had left, so there wasn't anyone but herself to answer the door.

The knock came again. "Vivi, it's Pierre."

She breathed a sigh of relief and rushed to greet her *frère*. "You are alone?" She glanced along the corridor.

"*Oui.*" He came in with a large suitcase. "I brought some of your things. Silvie packed them. *Grand-mère* wasn't happy she helped me."

"Does *Grand-mère* know where I am?"

"No. She demanded to know, but I wouldn't tell her. I think she believes you are at the boarding house. You could come. Our *mère* would welcome you."

"I cannot. I don't know her."

"You can get to know her."

"What if I don't want to?"

His expression softened. "You will. When you're ready."

Geneviève wasn't so sure. The woman hadn't ever been part of her life. Why should she be now?

Pierre cleared his throat. "Since you seem to be avoiding *Grand-mère*, can I assume you haven't given her nor told her about the information our *mère* gave you, incriminating our grandparents?"

She bristled. "I wish you wouldn't call that woman our *mère*."

"What would you prefer I call her?"

"I don't know. Anne? *Madame* Henderson?"

"She goes by Aunt Henny here."

Geneviève scrunched her nose. "Whose aunt is she?"

"No one's and everyone's."

"That's ridiculous. How about Henny?" That way there was less of a reminder of her true identity.

"So, what do you plan to do with the information she gave you?"

"I don't know."

"You didn't give any of it to *Grand-mère*, did you?"

"Not yet. I told her about the papers before I left." Though reluctant to give the documents to her, she also felt comfort in having them so *that Henny woman* couldn't use them to harm her grandparents.

He glanced around the room. "Where is the bundle? You didn't leave it at the Kesners', did you?"

"No, Deputy Montana's sister is safeguarding the parcel for me."

"Those documents are our mother's only real assurance our grandparents won't send her to jail."

As well as the only assurance Henny wouldn't send her grandparents to jail. "They wouldn't do such a thing."

"They proved they are prone to drastic measures by spiriting us away to Europe and changing our names. I'm not sure what they are capable of anymore."

"They love us. They raised us." She didn't want to believe anything else, but she'd had grave doubts when she'd left the Kesners'.

"Their love was distorted by their belief Henny wasn't good enough. *Père* mostly raised us."

"All three did." A distorted love was still love, wasn't it? "You can't simply discount everything they did for us."

"If they hadn't taken us, we would have had a different life. *Père* would have had a different life. I think he would have been happier."

Père had always been melancholy.

What would her life have been like if they all hadn't moved to Europe? "I'm sure their threat of jail was all bluster and smoke."

"What if it wasn't?"

Geneviève didn't want to think about any of this right now. She wanted everything to return to the way it was before *Père* had passed away.

"Our *mère*—Henny has taken a great risk in giving you that information. She's trusting you not to betray her. Was she right to trust you?"

"I don't know. It's a huge responsibility." She needed someone she could trust to tell her what to do. She couldn't trust Henny nor her grandparents as they would each be looking out for their own interests. Her brother had sided with Henny.

"I want to get to know her. I can't do that if she's locked away. Come to the boarding house with me and talk to her."

Geneviève's insides twisted. "I'm not ready to do that."

"Deputy Montana told me he found you at his cabin. He's worried about you."

Kind of the deputy to say *that* rather than inside sleeping. She'd run away from *Grand-mère's* betrayal. *To stoop to such a level.* "I'll have to go back. *Grand-mère* confiscated the money I had brought. The deputy paid for my room here tonight, but I can't stay. I can't afford to."

"What would you do if you could stay?"

The thought pleased her.

"*Père* left you money."

"He did? I could stay? Or do whatever else I pleased?" She thought of the deputy.

"Anything. Anywhere. Within reason. I have control of your money until you turn twenty-five."

Less than two years.

"He bequeathed all three of us money."

"All three? Don't you mean both?" Certainly, *Père* wouldn't have left money to their grandparents. They had plenty of their own.

"He left money to Henny as well."

"What? Why would he do that?"

"Apparently, it was her money to begin with. Her parents were of moderate means, neither wealthy nor poor. Her father made some wise investments and became wealthy. Her parents died and left everything to her at age twenty. Being a woman, when she married *Père*, everything she owned became his—property, business, money. When we all went to Europe, our grandparents arranged things so Henny had nothing, presumably so she couldn't follow and try to retrieve us. They held the threat of sending her to jail to keep her at bay. *Père* didn't spend any of her money and safeguarded it for her and us."

This was all too much for Geneviève to bear.

"Henny didn't mourn the loss of her wealth, but she did grieve losing us and *Père*."

Geneviève felt sorry for the woman but wasn't ready to embrace her. She needed time to sort through all the recent events and decide what she wanted to do about it all and not what everyone else said she should do.

Twenty-Three

THE NEXT DAY, MONTANA SAT IN the sheriff's office. Though yesterday had cleared up to a blue sky, clouds had rolled in over the mountains again today. Miss Marseille's brother had brought her clothes, paid for additional nights at the hotel, and given her money. Montana wasn't needed. He was envious of his twin getting to spend time with her first thing this morning to get ready for the day. Miss Marseille had everything she required...which didn't include him.

At the sound of a cantering horse, Montana rushed out of the building. A two-wheeled trap raced down the street. Why did some people refuse to travel at a safe pace? That person could hit or injure someone, not to mention risking their own life.

He leapt onto Cletus and gave chase. At the edge of town, he caught up to the racing beast, grabbed the horse's halter, and brought the vehicle to a stop.

A terrified Miss Marseille sat upon the seat, no reins in her hands.

He leapt to the ground and went to her. "Are you all right?"

"*Merci, merci, merci.*" She leaned over and threw her arms around his neck, speaking softly in French against him. "I am unharmed."

Thank goodness. He pulled her from the seat and lifted her down. "What happened?"

"I do not know. The horse reared and bolted. The reins were yanked from my grasp." She held out her hands. Red leather-burn marks marred her palms.

Those looked a bit painful but not too bad. Good to know she hadn't been driving recklessly on purpose. "Where did you get the buggy?"

"I rented it."

"Where's the driver?"

"I did not want one. I paid him to let me take the carriage by myself with the money Pierre gave me."

The sum she said she'd paid the man was outrageous. Providing there wasn't damage to the vehicle or horse, Montana would see to it the man refunded some of the money. "Let me drive you to the hotel."

She shook her head. "*Grand-mère* came there. I did not want her to see me. I am tired of people telling me what to do and ordering me about. I wanted to drive in the country, to be away from people."

Out west, anything not in town would be the country. "I can drive you someplace quiet if you like." Which might not be a good idea without a chaperone. Despite that, she didn't sound as though she would be amenable to any of the places he could think of with other people around. Neither of them would allow anything inappropriate to happen.

"Yes, please."

He tethered Cletus to the rear of the trap and ushered Miss Marseille to the buggy.

She hesitated. "Will it be safe? The horse will not run again?"

"I promise to keep control of him." Whatever had startled the horse was back in town, and this time he would be holding the reins, so there shouldn't be a problem. He helped her in, then climbed aboard and set the horse into motion.

He drove out of town, contemplating stopping no farther than Ferguson Pond where they had picnicked before, in the shade under the old elm. The older school children referred to it as the "kissing" tree. There would be none of that today. Best to remove himself from temptation, so he drove on by.

A roar echoed from someplace in the distance. The horse nickered and flicked its ears. He'd heard it too.

"What was that?"

"Only a cougar. There are a few of them which roam around on the mountain. Don't fret, it wasn't nearly close enough to concern ourselves with." It sounded as though it could be as far away as Coulter's Gap.

He continued to a wooded area near some craggy rock cliffs. After reining in, he set the brake.

Miss Marseille looked around. "Why have we stopped?"

"To go much farther, we would start heading up the mountain. I thought this would be a good place to stretch our legs, unless you'd rather return to town."

She shook her head. "This is a nice place. It is so quiet."

He jumped down and lifted the pretty French lady to the ground, allowing his hands to linger on her waist a little longer than necessary. He walked with her to where some wildflowers bloomed and picked an orange flower with speckles on the petals. "It's a tiger lily."

She took it with a smile. *"Merci."*

It would be lovely in her hair, but he dared not.

A twig snapped and a pebble rolled down the embankment. Montana searched for the cause and pointed above them on the hill. "See that stag?"

Miss Marseille turned in the direction he indicated and sucked in a breath. "He is beautiful. Is he dangerous?"

"Not unless he feels trapped. He would run off long before we could get close enough to trap him." Too bad Montana wasn't in a position to be hunting. It would make some fine eating.

The animal swung his massive head of antlers toward them.

Miss Marseille squeaked. "He is staring at us. Are you sure he will not attack us?"

"I'm sure."

"I visited Spain where bulls with horns would charge matadors."

He hadn't meant to frighten her. "We can go."

As they took the first few steps in retreat, a clap of thunder rattled the air, startling the buck into bounding away. He kicked loose several large stones that tumbled down the hill, picking up momentum as well as company.

This wasn't good. Montana might be able to get out of the way in time but not Miss Marseille. He wrapped his arms around her and pushed her near the ground behind an outcropping.

Rocks crashed into the boulder they hid behind, some smashing to pieces. Bits pelted Montana, causing him to flinch. Miss Marseille jerked, likely having gotten hit by a shard. A bigger one didn't break apart and bounced off his back. That was going to leave a nasty bruise.

The horse hitched to the rented buggy reared and neighed loudly.

Ugh. He didn't need the horses getting frightened.

If not for protecting Miss Marseille, Montana would risk dashing to the horses and buggy, but he couldn't leave her alone.

After a second rearing protest, the horse bolted, dragging the buggy and Cletus along with him. Hopefully, they wouldn't go far.

When the rock onslaught slowed, Montana peered over the barrier to see if it was safe. A few smaller stones rolled slowly, but one raced and bounced along the ground, heading straight for them. He ducked as the tumbling rock ricocheted off a corner and sliced across the side of his head. That smarted. He slapped a hand on the injured spot. It hurt like the dickens. Tiny twinkling lights danced in the air around him, like sparks from a campfire.

"Deputy Montana? Are you all right?"

"I...I think so. I have a pretty hard head." He did feel lightheaded but would be fine. He had to be.

"Let me see." Miss Marseille pulled his hand away and gasped. "You are bleeding."

"It's probably nothing. Head wounds bleed more than other ones." This could be serious, but he didn't want to scare her any more than she already was.

"This is not nothing. You need help. I do not know what to do, but I do know we need to stop you from bleeding." She pressed his hand back onto his wound.

Montana winced. It did seem bloodier than before. He reached around behind his neck and pulled at the knot in his bandana but couldn't manage to get it loosened. It was as though he couldn't get his hand to work properly.

Miss Marseille pushed his effort aside. "I see what you are trying to accomplish. I will do it." She untied it quickly. "What should I do with this?"

"Tie it around my head to staunch the bleeding."

She chuffed out a breath. "Even I know this will not be enough."

"It's all I have. If I had another piece of cloth, that could go on first to press into the wound, but I don't, so this will have to do."

"I have an idea. Turn away. Do not look."

He wasn't sure why she said that, but it wouldn't matter if he turned away or not. His vision had blurred, and nausea roiled inside his gut. He would die before he allowed himself to throw up in front of Miss Marseille. He pinched his eyes shut to stop the dancing lights and quell the sickness in his stomach. He heard something tearing. He wanted to ask what she was doing but didn't have the strength.

Geneviève folded the torn piece of her silk petticoat and gently pulled the deputy's hand away from his injury. A dreadful wound. She hoped he was right about head injuries merely bleeding more than other ones. She pressed the cloth to his head.

He winced.

"I am sorry."

His words slurred. "Didn't hurt. I've a hard head."

It had hurt. That was obvious enough. His head wasn't as hard as he claimed.

Lord, please let him be all right.

With her other hand, she wrapped the neckerchief over the wad of silk petticoat and around his head then tied it in place.

He winced again.

She hated to hurt him, but she didn't know what else to do.

Blood still dribbled out. This was not sufficient, so she tore two more strips from her petticoat. She folded one to put over the first bandage. The second strip she wrapped three times around his head then tied it as tightly as she could. The bleeding seemed to cease.

A large raindrop slapped her on the cheek. No, she didn't need rain. Then one hit her arm. Then her shoulder and each hand.

Deputy Montana must have felt them too. He pointed. "Go to that overhang. It will protect you."

"What about you?"

"I'll be right behind you."

She stood and prepared to run for the protection of the protruding rockface.

The deputy staggered to his feet. Though a short distance, he wouldn't likely make it. At least not before getting drenched.

She draped his arm over her shoulders.

Montana shook his head and stopped the motion. "Go without me."

"I am not leaving you."

The rain turned to little white hail balls.

"We must hurry." She tried to speed him along.

Though he seemed to be trying to go faster, he was actually slogging slower. She tried to take more of his weight. The hail grew in size and stung. With all her might, she hauled him as quickly as she could to the overhang. The hail smarted as it pelted her, stinging her skin.

She sat the deputy in the protected area of the cleft and lowered herself next to him. The temperature had dropped, and she rubbed her arms. She had no idea what to do now.

Deputy Montana opened the front of his vest. "Come here, and I'll keep you warm."

How could he think of her comfort when he was injured? "You need to rest. I am supposed to be taking care of you. Not the other way around."

"Don't argue with me. It makes my head hurt more than it already does."

She moved against his side, and he wrapped his arm and a little bit of his vest around her. The heat from his body immediately warmed her. *"Merci."*

"Sure." He was silent for a few moments. "When the hail and rain lessen, we'll need to walk back to town. I don't see the horses."

"You are in no shape to do that." Her insides curled into a tight ball. She doubted he could make it so far. Would Deputy Montana die here because she was too inept to help him? Then she would die as well for lack of knowledge.

He squeezed her shoulder. "Stop fretting. We'll be fine."

She faced him, but his eyes were closed. "How can you say that?" She blinked tears away, threatening to overwhelm her. "I do not know what to do or how to help you. I am useless."

"You've already done a lot. You bandaged my head and got me out of the rain and hail." He squeezed her shoulder again. "You are stronger and more capable than you believe you are, more than people have made you believe."

He was wrong. She had no skills to survive out in the wilderness. She had no skills to survive anywhere. Without the comforts of fancy clothes, a big house, servants to wait on her, and people telling her what to do, she wouldn't survive. But no more. If she lived through this, that would change. No more being told what to do. No more not being able to take care of herself.

He put his finger under her chin and tilted her head to face him. "You're still fretting."

How could he tell? "I cannot help it. You are going to die out here, and it will be all my fault."

He brushed his knuckles across her cheek. "None of this is your fault."

"It is my fault, and you know it. I was trying to escape, and you came to my aid."

He put his fingers on her lips. "Stop talking."

She needed to confess her poor choices. She took his hand away and held it in hers. "If not for my stubbornness, we would not be in this fix. You are injured, and we do not have a horse."

"Please stop." He closed his eyes and seemed to be in pain.

Pain she had caused. *Oh, dear.* "I cannot. I feel so badly about—"

In an instant, he covered her mouth with his and kissed her, interrupting her words and vanquishing her thoughts and worries.

She had hoped he would kiss her again for ever so long and leaned into him, wanting him to never let her go. If she died here in his arms, that wouldn't be so bad.

The deputy pulled away and rested his forehead on hers. "The hail stopped." He leaned back into the rock face behind them with his eyes closed.

She missed his lips on hers. Sunbeams streaked through the gently falling rain. She glanced at Deputy Montana. His eyes remained shut. "How could you tell?"

"I could hear it."

"Should I try to find my way to town and return with help?" She doubted her ability to not get lost and wander in the wilderness forever. Or until the cougar found her.

"That's not necessary. When the rain slows a little more, we'll walk together."

He didn't think she could make it on her own either. "You also believe I would get lost."

"You wouldn't get lost. It's not hard to find Kamola from here."

"Then why should I not go for help? You are injured."

"If we run into that cougar, I have a gun to scare him off."

"Oh." Knowing about the wild animal made her not want to leave his side and made her want to return to town as quickly as possible. "We should go."

"Agreed."

She stood and assisted him to his feet.

"I'm supposed to be the gentleman and help you." He wavered.

She nestled next to him, hooking her arm around him and draping his over her shoulders. "Let me aid you."

"I don't like this one bit. I feel as weak as a newborn calf, wobbly legs and all." Though he protested in words, he didn't in actions.

They staggered along the path they had come on.

Geneviève had not worn the appropriate shoes for a long walk in the wilderness. "Do you think the cougar got the horses?"

"I doubt it. There's far easier prey for a big cat."

She hoped he didn't mean them.

Twenty-Four

AFTER A WHILE, GENEVIÈVE GLANCED ABOUT the countryside. Everything looked the same to her. Shouldn't they be to the town by now? Had she been taking them in circles? Her shoulders and back ached from supporting Deputy Montana. Her feet hurt from inappropriate footwear, so she wiggled her toes inside her satin shoes. New points of pain flared, but she wouldn't complain. The deputy was far worse off.

Her clenched stomach growled. So embarrassing. How could she possibly be hungry with her insides knotted with worry?

Deputy Montana spoke in a raspy voice. "I'm hungry too. Town's not too far off."

"How can you tell? I don't see any signs of civilization."

"I know the terrain. Less than a mile to the first houses."

Less than a mile. That didn't tell her much. How much time would that take on foot? At least they weren't lost—according to the deputy—but he did have quite a blow to his head.

Soon the rooflines of a few buildings came into view. She had never been so glad to see this little frontier town as now. She would survive after all.

The deputy swayed more and more with each step. But would *he*?

He stopped outside the gate of a mint-green house. "I'll be fine from here. Thank you." He removed his arm from over her shoulders. "Continue on this street until you get to the White Hotel."

He expected her to walk farther? Her feet had ceased hurting and gone partially numb. Or perhaps, she had merely blocked out the pain. "I do not know if you can make it."

"I'll manage. I know you don't want to go in there."

Glancing again at the modest building, her breathing halted. This was *her* house. He was right. She didn't want to go inside, no matter how badly her feet and body hurt, but Deputy Montana was in no condition to walk even the short distance on his own. She could at least get him to the door. She wouldn't leave him—didn't want to leave him. Gripping his wrist, she draped his arm back over her shoulders. It had been kind of him to think of her feelings even in his injured state. "I can get you to the porch."

"I'd appreciate that." Leaning on her, he shuffled through the open gate and along the walk. At the steps, he gripped the railing but still leaned on her for support.

No matter how tired she was and how much pain she experienced, she wouldn't leave him until he could stand at the door on his own.

He reached out a hand to brace himself on the front of the house. He removed his arm from around her again. "I'm all right now."

He swayed. He wasn't all right.

She kept her arm around him and knocked.

That Henny woman opened the door and immediately smiled at Geneviève.

Geneviève's heart leapt out toward this woman with the accepting gaze, but she reeled it back in. She could have none of that. She shifted under Deputy Montana's weight. "He is hurt."

The older woman's gaze turned to him. "Oh, dear." She pushed the screen open. "Bring him inside." She ducked under the deputy's other arm, and the pair aided the injured man into the parlor.

Pierre and two other men rose and took the weight of the deputy. They deposited him on the settee.

Though Geneviève was free to leave, she didn't want to. She stood rooted in place as the other four fussed over the deputy. With the others preoccupied, Geneviève could easily slip out unnoticed. No one here would miss her. All the same, she wanted to be with Deputy Montana and to see what kind of person this Henny woman really was.

Henny said something to Pierre who then separated from the group and came to her. "Here is a chair. Sit."

She didn't want to. She wasn't staying. Her exhausted body sat anyway. She must look like a drowned garden dormouse, having been caught in the rain and walking across half the countryside.

He studied her in earnest and spoke mostly in English. "*Merci* for coming inside."

She hadn't realized how much her being in Henny's house would mean to him. She spoke in French, not wanting *others* to know her words. "He needed help."

Pierre gave her his knowing slight smile and switched to French as well. "The young lady who stepped off the train nearly two months ago wouldn't have come in. She would have left him on the porch and hurried away."

She pictured her first horrified glimpses of Kamola and how desolate it had seemed. She'd been so naïve then and full of pride, incapable of taking care of herself or making simple decisions. Deputy Montana had swept her off her feet. Literally. Since leaving Virginia, she had traveled across the country, lived on her own in the hotel, gone fishing, made friends with common people—who she found extraordinary—walked across the countryside, and kissed a deputy. All things she had never dreamed of doing before.

She *had* changed.

Geneviève shook her head. "You are wrong. That young lady would have left him on the street outside the gate. That is if she aided him at all." How cold and callous of her. She couldn't imagine not helping him now.

"See, everyone can change. Our *mère* regrets not trying harder to find us early on. She was young and scared."

Geneviève understood how that felt. She studied the woman tending to the deputy's wounded head, unwinding the makeshift bandages.

When Henny spoke, her voice held both authority and compassion. "Professor Tunstall, would you get the medicine tin from the pantry shelf?"

The younger of the two men hurried off for what appeared to be the kitchen.

Geneviève gripped her brother's arm. "Is he going to be all right?" She didn't want to imagine anything worse happening to Deputy Montana.

Pierre patted her hand. "I think he will be fine. Once his wound is cleaned, he'll need to rest." He glanced over his shoulder. "I'm going to see what I can do for your sweetheart."

She relished the sound of that—sweetheart.

"Stay here and don't go anywhere. *S'il vous plaît.*"

Now that she was seated, she couldn't go anywhere even if she wanted to. She gave a limp nod.

Her brother returned to the activity at the settee.

The bloody strips of her petticoat and the deputy's bandana were pulled away, but she couldn't see his injury from her vantage point. He had people who knew how to help him. He would be safe.

Every muscle within her wilted. She shouldn't relax in the chair—not ladylike—but she couldn't keep her body poised properly. If not for her corset, she would have already folded into a heap. She allowed herself to rest against the soft, plush back. For just a minute or two. No one would notice.

Henny dabbed witch hazel on Deputy Montana's gash.

He winced but had ceased complaining or telling her not to fuss over him.

She'd made it clear she was tending to his wound whether he liked it or not. While working on Montana's head, half of Henny's attention remained on her daughter seated across the room. Though she hadn't looked in that direction, the young woman hadn't left, unless she had been quieter than a mouse.

Henny glanced over her shoulder. Nope, still there. She'd somehow managed to fall asleep sitting up, and Miss Tibbins had taken advantage of a free lap. It warmed Henny's heart to have her daughter close and not glaring.

Henny wound a strip of torn, clean-cloth bandage around the deputy's head and secured it in place. "Now that I'm sure you'll live, what happened?"

Deputy Montana shrugged. "My hard head got in the way of a rock careening down a hillside."

"Let me guess. It hit you because you were protecting my daughter. Thank you."

He shrugged again.

The deputy had no idea what it meant to Henny to have him protect her daughter. "You're fortunate it didn't do more damage."

"The Good Lord seems to want me here on earth a mite longer."

"I think a certain young lady will be glad for that." Henny adjusted the cloth to keep it in place better.

He gazed at Dais—Geneviève. "She didn't want to come inside."

"I know, but she did so for you. She cares a lot about you." Henny turned to her son. "Do you think she'll stay?"

Now Winston shrugged, in the same manner his father used to. "It is hard to say. I hope so."

Henny hoped so too. She'd longed for her children for over two decades. It felt like a dream to have them both here. She would do all she could to make her daughter feel welcome and to not push her.

Montana's stomach growled.

Henny looked at him wide-eyed. "You both must be famished after your ordeal. I have biscuits and apple butter. How does that sound?"

"Delicious. I'm so hungry, you could serve me dirt and I'd eat it."

She patted his arm as she stood. "Let's try the biscuits first."

Professors Lumbard and Tunstall excused themselves and went to their rooms.

Henny retrieved a tray with the biscuits and a cinnamon spread along with cups of tea. She served the poor starving deputy first, then her son, then took portions over to her sleeping daughter. She set the dishes on the side table but would let—Henny stopped herself from thinking Daisy—and let Geneviève rest. No, it didn't feel natural to think of her as Geneviève. She would call her daughter what Geneviève wished, but in Henny's thoughts and her heart, she would always be Daisy.

Poking from under the hem of the girl's fancy dress were muddy shoes. She had trudged through the rain and who knew what else to get her and the deputy to safety.

Henny knelt in front of her and wiggled one satin slipper off.

Her daughter shifted and woke. She stared at the cat on her lap and lifted her hands away from it. "What does it want?"

"That's Miss Tibbins. She only wants to sleep on your lap."

"Why?"

"She must like you. You can pet her." Henny ran her hand down the calico's spine.

Daisy repeated the action and set Miss Tibbins to purring. The girl smiled, warming Henny's heart.

Henny continued to remove her daughter's shoes.

Daisy frowned. "What are you doing?"

"Your shoes are muddy. I'm going to clean them. I hope they aren't ruined."

"You don't have to do that."

Henny doubted the girl had the energy to resist and removed the other. "I don't mind." She trained her gaze on the blood-stained, creamy-white hosiery. She set the footwear aside and untied the ribbon holding the first stocking around the girl's upper calf.

"Don't." Daisy moved her foot away, aiding Henny in pulling the stocking down.

Henny tugged it slowly the rest of the way off to not further injure the girl's foot. "We don't want the sores on your feet to get infected."

Her daughter sucked in a breath through her teeth as Henny freed the cloth from the half-dried blood. She removed the other stocking in the same manner. Henny stood. "I'll be right back with warm water. While I'm gone, you can start on your tea and biscuit."

In the kitchen, Henny filled a rectangular dish pan with warm water and dissolved Epsom salts in it.

Throwing a towel over her shoulder, she returned to her daughter who nibbled on a biscuit.

Henny knelt again and lowered Daisy's feet into the medicinal water.

The girl sucked in a breath as her feet adjusted to the Epsom infused bath.

"Let your feet soak in there for a few minutes."

She nodded and sipped her tea.

Henny stood and gave a nod to her son and Montana then took the girl's shoes to the back porch and wiped off as much of the dried mud from the satin as she could. Then she took a soft brush, dipped it in water, and removed the rest of the dirt. For a socialite like Daisy, these slippers were ruined. Many other girls would love to have ones such as these even with the wear and scuffs.

After about fifteen minutes, Henny knelt again in front of Daisy and gently dabbed at the injuries on her feet. She delighted in her daughter allowing her to minister to her in this way. Henny would take any interaction she could get with her daughter. She proceeded to dry her feet, applied ointment to the open blisters and raw spots, and wrapped them in bandages to keep the medicine in place. Daisy must have been in agony as she helped the deputy. That told Henny a lot. "You look exhausted. Would you like to lie down? I have a vacant room upstairs you can use."

"No. I am fine."

Henny expected as much. "Very well then. I'll be in the kitchen getting supper started if you need anything." She turned to the deputy still stretched out on the settee. "That goes for you as well. I'll have supper enough for both of you to join us."

Daisy ran her hands along her outer thighs as though not to disturb Miss Tibbins. "I do not have proper attire."

"We aren't formal here so we don't dress for meals. What you're wearing will be more than adequate."

Though her daughter didn't appear convinced, she didn't protest further.

"Aunt Henny?" Deputy Montana said. "My sister will be waiting at the hotel for Miss Marseille. Is there anyone who could get word to her that we are here?"

"I'm sure Professor Tunstall will be glad to go for you. I'll ask him." Henny was happy Daisy hadn't refused her help or rushed out as soon as she could. The poor girl looked bone tired. No wonder she didn't protest. "I'll have the professor invite her for supper as well."

Henny resisted the urge to skip as she headed toward the staircase. She would have both of her children at her supper table. Tears blurred her vision. *Thank You, Lord!*

Twenty-Five

Geneviève sat between her brother and Deputy Montana at Henny's table with an assortment of people. She was grateful Henny hadn't insisted she sit next to her. She had never eaten a meal in this manner. Rather than a servant offering the various foods to one person after the next, each person took a portion and then passed the dish to the next. *Grand-mère* would have a fit about this breach of etiquette. Even though Geneviève had eaten all of her biscuit, her stomach still growled at the unusual yet divine smelling food, fried chicken, fried potatoes, green beans, and more biscuits.

Everyone chattered amiably, but she didn't feel pressure to hold up a conversation with one person or another. She merely let the discussions wash over her.

Midway through the meal, the older professor directed a question to her. "Did you ever visit the Louvre Museum?"

"*Oui.* My *grand-mère* made sure I experienced all the cultural attractions possible."

"Then you saw *Winged Victory of Samothrace*?"

"*Oui.* She was very beautiful. She almost made me believe I could fly."

The other professor took a turn. "What was your favorite thing about living in Europe?"

"There are so many things. How is a person to choose only one? Let me think." France, Spain, Italy, England? That was it. "I fancied not having to travel far to be in a new country. Here, one travels and travels and remains in the same country."

Professor Tunstall gave a nod. "I suppose it is quite a jaunt to enter another one from here. Even so, the various parts are so different, it feels as though you are in a different country."

"This is true." Geneviève had seen it from the train window as she journeyed to Kamola.

Geneviève hadn't seen one servant the whole time she was in Henny's home. Did Henny do all the work? Cooking and cleaning? Geneviève didn't know the first thing about how to do any of that.

Though the food wasn't what Geneviève was used to, it was tasty, and she enjoyed it more than she would have imagined for the simple fare.

After supper, Montana adjusted his position on the too-short settee. He did have a herd of pillows behind him, but they could do only so much. His moving disturbed the cat on his lap, causing her to purr louder than before. He scratched the calico's head.

He knew he should go home but didn't want to part from Miss Marseille. Besides enjoying her company, if he left, she would leave as well. Aunt Henny seemed so happy to have her daughter here.

He gazed at Miss Marseille across the room, who gazed back at him. "How are your feet?"

"They are feeling much better."

He was glad. He'd known she was hurting pretty badly by the time they reached Aunt Henny's, but Montana had needed her help. The clonk to his head had made him too dizzy to stand straight. Without her to support him—and the need to see her safely back to town—he would have been slumped on the trail someplace. He did feel much fortified, having rested and eaten a good meal.

He thought about how worried she'd been for him, and rightly so, but he tried not to let on how troubled he had been as well. She had been unwavering in her desire to help him and adorable with her concern over his well-being. Then she had been snuggled next to him and smelled so sweet.

The lump on his noggin had knocked what little sense he had right out. Her prattling on and on had hurt his head. He hadn't been able to think clearly. He had needed her to stop talking. So, he'd done the only thing he could think to do in his weakened state. He'd kissed her.

He was done-for now. He'd avoided kissing her because he knew they had no future. He knew it. She knew it. Her brother had warned him. He could slough off his feelings for her as long as he kept a little distance, kept their relationship chaste. Kept their interactions to walks, suppers, and buggy rides. Kept his lips to himself. Then he could wrangle his emotions into submission.

Even with her feet bandaged, Miss Marseille looked as though she might bolt like a skittery horse. She hadn't wanted to come inside, but she had done so for him.

He stretched out his arm toward her. "Are your feet well enough to venture over here?"

She nodded.

Felicity sat in a dining room chair that had been moved to the parlor. "She is in no condition to be traipsing across the room."

Miss Marseille stood. "I am well enough." She limped her way over to him and scooped up his hand. "How are you feeling?"

Her touch sent a shiver along his arm. "Good." He scooted back as much as he could to make room for her and patted the settee.

She lowered herself to the cushion like a delicate flower. "You are not good. Your head is cut, and you left blood from here to the mountainside."

Felicity puffed out a breath. "He's been thrashed worse than this."

Montana gave his twin a withering look before answering Miss Marseille. "I'll survive." He rubbed his thumb across the back of her hand. "*Merci* for bringing *moi* here and staying. I know it's not easy for *vous* being here."

A small grin made a shy appearance on her face but was quickly shoved aside by a quivering lip.

He hoped she wouldn't cry. He couldn't take it if she cried.

"Your French is atrocious." Ah, the tiny smile overcame the cloud of emotion and broke through like a sunbeam.

He chuffed out a laugh and immediately regretted it. "Ow." His head pounded like a dozen sticks of dynamite had gone off in it.

"See, you are not good."

He closed his eyes against the pain. "I concede. You win."

"You scared me. I thought you might die out there."

"I wouldn't do that to you." He never wanted to do anything to put that fret on her face. He squeezed her hand. "I'm sorry you were so frightened. I'm fine. I'll heal as though nothing happened." He smiled to encourage another one from her.

It worked, and his heart thumped its pleasure, sending new pain to his head, but he didn't mind.

Geneviève reluctantly moved from the settee to the chair closest to Deputy Montana, while Henny served dessert in the parlor.

Henny handed Geneviève a china plate with a slice of spice cake with white frosting. Did the woman know Geneviève adored this?

Henny gave a slight smile. "This is one of my favorites. I hope you like it."

Something they had in common? "I am sure it will be fine." She wasn't ready to admit the connection.

The cake was both light and moist. The frosting, though different than what she was used to, was just as delicious as the ones her grandparents' expensive chefs had made.

How could this capable woman who made her own way in the world with no help from others be the same débutante her father had married? Geneviève knew no ladies of her social standing who could frost a cake let alone bake one. Geneviève might like to try, then she would bake sweets all the time.

A knock came on the door. Henny left the room, then her voice filtered in along with a male voice asking about Montana.

Henny re-entered the parlor trailed by another deputy.

The man shook his head. "Montana, what fool thing have you done?"

Montana cocked a smile. "Wrestled a grizzly."

"Wrong kind of wounds for that."

Geneviève enjoyed this playful banter between these two men.

Deputy Montana indicated Geneviève. "Cord, have you met Miss Marseille?"

"I haven't had the pleasure." Deputy Cord pressed his doffed hat to his chest. "Very pleased to meet you, miss."

"Enchanté."

"Oh, a fancy one. You might want to think twice about cavorting with this fella." He indicated his fellow deputy.

Deputy Montana cast him an annoyed look. "No one invited you."

Deputy Cord smiled. "I was over at the hotel, and Grant said you were here. Wanted to check on you and bring you your horse."

"Where did you find Cletus?" Deputy Montana asked.

Henny approached Deputy Cord. "Would you like a slice of cake?" She handed him a plate before he even answered.

The new deputy took a bite and swallowed. "He was standing outside the sheriff's office, like he was waiting for you to come out and take him home."

"He spooked and ran off."

"We thought the cougar might have gotten him." Geneviève wasn't sure why she'd jumped into a conversation which wasn't hers to intervene in. Maybe it was the relaxed atmosphere and easiness between these two men that made her feel it would be all right to do so.

Deputy Cord raised his eyebrows.

Montana spoke again. "Cougar was real. Heard her up the valley by Coulter's Gap."

"Was she headed for town?"

"Not likely if Cletus came this way. Was there a trap and a tawny colored horse with him?"

"No, but Billy said his rig returned without the lady who rented it. He assumed she didn't tether him tightly enough, and he wandered off."

"Cletus must have come loose from where I tied him to the back. Was the other horse unharmed and trap undamaged?"

"He didn't say anything was amiss, so I assume all was well."

"I am pleased the horse is all right." Geneviève's curiosity rose. "Why do you call the cougar she when we never saw it?"

"People saw a cougar with a couple of cubs earlier this spring and last fall. Probably the same cat."

They spoke of this as though having a wild animal so close to town was a normal event.

"Will you go shoot it?" Though the idea of a wild beast wandering into town was scary, she didn't wish it to be killed either.

Deputy Montana answered. "Not necessary. As long as there is plenty for her to hunt on the mountain, she has no need to come this far down. She no more wants to be around townsfolk than we want her around us."

These people seemed far too casual about wild animals in their proximity.

The other deputy took his empty plate to the kitchen then returned and spoke to Deputy Montana. "You need me to take care of Cletus? He's tied to the hitching rail out front."

"He'll be fine for a little while. Thanks for bringing him."

Everyone seemed to be welcome here, even those who stopped by unannounced. Invite them in and feed them then bid them good night. So many social faux pas committed this day, but it made for a more relaxed atmosphere. Nothing formal about this household. Rather refreshing.

With all of Henny's kindness, Geneviève's heart softened toward her.

Another knock on the door, this one gentler than the deputy's had been. Almost a whisper. Professor Tunstall answered the door this time and trailed *Grand-mère* into the parlor.

Geneviève impulsively sat straighter.

Grand-mère let her gaze scan the room, alighting momentarily on Pierre and settling on Geneviève. "Here you are. Let's go."

Geneviève instinctively stood, and pain shot through her feet. Though she hadn't wanted to come, she wasn't sure she wanted to leave either. She still couldn't believe what her grandparents had done. "I—I..."

"Don't stutter. Come along. You don't belong with these people."

This was how *Grand-mère* spoke to everyone. Giving orders and making decisions for them.

After having a taste of making her own decisions, Geneviève rather enjoyed the freedom. "No, *Grand-mère*." Her stomach clenched at her open defiance. "I am not leaving yet. I have been invited to stay."

Grand-mère narrowed her eyes at Henny. "This is your doing."

Henny shrugged. "I'm as surprised as you are. If my daughter wishes to stay, she may for as long as she likes." Henny faced Geneviève. "You *always* have a place here."

Geneviève did feel welcomed but also a little guilty because she didn't so much want to stay at Henny's as she didn't want to go wherever *Grand-mère* was at the moment, able to order her around.

"Geneviève, don't do something you'll regret."

She had already done things she would regret, but she suspected staying wasn't one of them.

Grand-mère switched to French. "I know what this is about. This man is not right for you. You deserve better. You have been bred for better. You come from a long line and heritage of Marseilles and Seymours."

Geneviève seethed at *Grand-mère* speaking derogatorily of Deputy Montana. She was glad he could not understand. She replied in French. "You don't know who is better for me. Who I should and should not care for."

"You can't possibly believe yourself to have true feelings for this man." *Grand-mère* cast a disparaging glance toward the deputy.

He spoke to Henny. "I think they're talking about me."

Henny nodded. "That they are."

Geneviève squinted at Henny. Had the older woman figured it out like Montana? It wouldn't be difficult to discern the general topic *Grand-mère* was going on about with her contumelious glares. But Henny spoke with more conviction than the deputy had. Geneviève couldn't worry about that now.

Grand-mère narrowed her eyes. "Come with me now, and we can put all this behind us. You can start over."

Geneviève had had enough and switched to English. "No. I will not go with you. I am staying here because I love him." An immediate flush rushed up her face and coursed through her body. She hadn't meant to say that, but somewhere inside she knew *Grand-mère* wouldn't like it.

Grand-mère glared. "You can't possibly—"

Henny took a step forward. "You heard my daughter, Cora. If you choose to be civil, you may stay, but if not, please leave."

"You'll regret this Anne." *Grand-mère* shifted her glare to Geneviève. "Your *grand-père* will arrive tomorrow. We'll see what he has to say about all this." She turned and strode to the door. "You have not seen the last of me." She left, without so much as a footstep heard.

Geneviève had never seen anyone oppose *Grand-mère* the way Henny had. Never until now.

Pierre hurried after *Grand-mère*. "I will try to find out what she might do."

Geneviève watched him go. Part of her wanted to go as well. Run back to her previous life. However, she knew she could never be happy there again. She *had* changed.

Another part of her warred with wanting to stay and not wanting to face Henny and the deputy. Henny was obviously pleased she had defied *Grand-mère*. Why had something inside her wanted to hurt her grandmother?

Deputy Montana no doubt was embarrassed by Geneviève's declaration. He'd made no indication if he felt anything similar.

True, he had kissed her, but she sensed that had been due to the intense situation they had found themselves in. Perhaps she, too, was still feeling that intensity and that was the reason why she'd made the pronouncement. She did care for him a great deal, but were her feelings strong enough for that kind of profession of ardor?

Not knowing what to do, she slumped into the nearby chair.

Henny wrapped her arm around Geneviève's shoulders and assisted her to her feet. "You're exhausted. Let's get you settled upstairs."

Felicity stood as well. "Do you need any help?"

"I think we'll be fine. I'll holler if we need your assistance."

Geneviève allowed Henny to act as her *mère* for the moment. She needed her *mère*—a *mère*.

Montana spoke to his sister as he struggled to stand. "Let's go home." He needed to get out of here.

His twin rushed to his side. "Do you think you should? I'm sure Aunt Henny will let you stay here."

"I don't want to." The pain in his chest had become unbearable. He couldn't take any more fussing over him. He staggered toward the door. "Are you coming?"

She hurried after him. "Shouldn't we at least wait until Aunt Henny comes down to say good bye?"

That would be polite, but his head—and heart—hurt too much to adhere to social niceties. "You wait. I'm leaving." He gripped the doorknob and paused a moment to get his balance.

Felicity ducked under his arm and helped him outside. "You're going to kill yourself if you try to go alone."

She was probably right, but he couldn't stay.

She helped him out to Cletus. "I'll take the reins." She left him leaning against the fence and swung into the saddle.

It took all his concentration and effort to climb up behind her.

Cletus plodded into motion, causing Montana to rock back and forth. Thankfully, Felicity was guiding the horse so he could concentrate on not falling off.

Montana's heart had leapt at Miss Marseille's declaration of love. Just as quickly, reality settled in to dash his hope in an instant. She had said what she had to say to assuage her grandmother without regard for his feelings. Feelings he'd thought he had well under control. Apparently not. Removing himself from her vicinity had been his only option.

At his cabin, Felicity left him at the front and took care of Cletus. When she came inside, Montana was seated at the table. He'd wanted to lie down on his sleeping mat, but the table had been closer.

"Are we going to talk about it?"

"Nope." He pushed away from the table in preparation to go to his sleeping mat in the corner.

"We are going to have to talk about this eventually."

"No, we aren't." His relationship with Miss Marseille was none of her business.

"You can't simply ignore a declaration of love."

"There was no declaration. She only said it to push her grandmother out the door. It meant nothing. I mean nothing to her. I've known that from the beginning. I have never been anything more than a distraction for her."

"I've seen the way she looks at you and how happy she gets when she anticipates seeing you. You mean a lot to her. She has real feelings for you."

He doubted that. She was merely a good actress. "I'm turning in."

Felicity looped his arm over her shoulders to assist him. "How do you feel about the lovely French lady?"

He removed his arm from his twin. "It doesn't matter."

"It does matter." She remained at his side as he crossed the room.

He wished she'd leave him be.

"You love her too. You need to tell her."

He would do no such thing. He didn't even know if he *did* love her. He hadn't allowed himself to entertain such a thought. He collapsed onto his makeshift bed of folded blankets on the floor. "Let me sleep."

"Aren't you even going to take off your boots?"

"Nope." He draped an arm over his eyes.

"All right. We'll talk about this in the morning."

No, they wouldn't. At least he wouldn't.

The kisses he'd shared with Miss Marseille drifted to and fro through his mind. He wished he could erase them from his memory. They would haunt him for a very long time. Perhaps her grandmother would succeed in taking her away, and he could begin forgetting about her.

How did one forget half of their heart?

Geneviève glanced around the small room with a pink patchwork quilt on a double-sized bed.

Henny pointed to various things as she told Geneviève what all was available to her. Assorted compact pieces of furniture lined the room—writing desk, bureau, washstand, and wardrobe. No piece was very significant, yet they all suited the charming room quite well. "If you need anything, I'm right downstairs."

"Nothing has changed between us."

"If you say so." Henny edged toward the door.

"What do you mean by that?"

"You're in my home, aren't you?" She gave a nod and left.

Home. This did feel like a home. But it wasn't *her* home. But could it be?

Though the room was small, it was welcoming like the lady who owned it. Geneviève ran her hand over the quilt. Had Henny's hands stitched this?

Did her being here somehow change things? Geneviève didn't see how.

That woman had still abandoned her family by not going after them and fighting for them. How could a mother do that? What kind of mother could live a happy life without her husband and children?

True, *Grand-mère* and *Grand-père* had taken them all far, far away from her. Still, hadn't there been anything she could have done? If she was innocent, then she wouldn't have actually been put in jail, would she? Though Geneviève wanted to embrace the truth of her *mère's* situation so long ago, it would mean believing the worst about the people who had loved her, her whole life.

A small place deep inside Geneviève ached to have all those missing years back with this woman—with her mother. To be raised by this generous, welcoming woman. How would she be different if she had? Would she be happier? Would her stomach not have been the tangle of knots it had always been growing up?

And what about Deputy Montana? What she had insinuated about him. No. She had insinuated nothing. She had boldly declared her love for him—had defied *Grand-mère.*

She could easily take it all back and ask *Grand-mère's* forgiveness and have her life return to the way it had been before she'd come to Kamola.

A little voice inside told her she'd wanted to come— not to retrieve her brother but to find out about this woman who knew about her *mère.* Who had turned out to *be* her *mère.* A *mère* Geneviève had longed for her whole life. Had dreamed of meeting her whole life. Had imagined her loving Geneviève unconditionally.

A door closed downstairs, and footsteps ascended the stairs before Pierre knocked and entered. He'd gone to the hotel and returned with her luggage.

She changed into her night dress and slipped between the sheets of the bed. Tomorrow, she needed to figure out exactly how deep her feelings went for the deputy—if her feelings for him were real at all. *Grand-mère* had said Geneviève deserved better than Deputy Montana, but it was the other way around. He deserved better than her. Better than a person afraid to make her own decisions. Better than someone who used him to get out of a difficult situation with a demanding person.

Regardless, through all this, she loved her grandmother. She truly did. The woman had always been there for her. She sincerely loved Geneviève and wanted the best for her. Until now, Geneviève believed her grandmother's choices were most prudent. Find her the right husband to elevate Geneviève in polite society. But was that Geneviève's aspiration? She desired love. She longed for her declaration about the deputy to be true.

How could she ever know if it was genuine or not?

Twenty-Six

THE FOLLOWING MORNING, GENEVIÈVE WOKE TO bright light peeking in through the cracks around the draperies. She had overslept. Though bone tired last night, she had tossed and turned for hours but had devised no solutions for her dilemmas.

First of all, she was under her *mère's* roof. She never would have fathomed such a thing. Staying here had seemed like a good idea, and Pierre had brought her luggage from the hotel. She didn't know what to do. She couldn't hide in this room all day, yet she was reluctant to face Henny.

She squared her shoulders. She was a Marseille, she could face even the most difficult of people. *Grand-mère* had trained her to do so, and Geneviève had faced people far more trying than Henny. But she wasn't a Marseille, not truly. She had been born a Seymour. Two families from the same tree.

Then there was Deputy Montana. She hadn't worked out how deep her feelings for him truly were. Had he merely been a distraction from learning about her *mère?* She hoped not.

Finally, her rude outburst toward *Grand-mère*. She must apologize for the way she'd behaved. But was she truly sorry? It was as though something inside her was trying to break free of her rigid past. Was she free? What should she do with her freedom? She didn't feel free hiding away up here. Time to face the woman.

Did Henny deserve her forgiveness? Geneviève's heart wanted Henny to be a *mère* to her. Yearned for all those stolen years with this woman.

If she hadn't wished to have Geneviève or a family, Geneviève might not be able to handle that. Then all her rash decisions of the past couple of months would be for naught. *Grand-mère* would eagerly take her back if it meant she was chosen over Henny. *Grand-mère* would win. Her brother seemed convinced Henny longed to be their *mère*, had always desired to be their *mère*. Pierre had memories of her from his childhood, faded but there. Geneviève didn't have even one to help her. The part of her heart reserved for her *mère* was void.

Time to put something there, good or bad.

The only dress she could manage by herself was one of the outfits Felicity had directed her to purchase for her outings with the deputy. She struggled to get her corset cinched with the leather burns on her palms but did the best she could. Her hands weren't nearly as sensitive as yesterday. Fortunately, the blue gingham taffeta dress had a looser fit than her designer made gowns. Recalling the fishing trip, she smiled and smoothed her hands down the skirt.

Having put off this encounter as long as possible, she exited the room and hobbled downstairs on her injured feet. If she'd slept this late in Paris, *Grand-mère* would have sent up a breakfast tray.

She entered the parlor, but no one was there. Nor was anyone in the small dining room. Voices filtered in from the kitchen. She stepped to the doorway.

Henny sat at the worktable with Mr. Hammond. They both stood, and Henny spoke. "You're awake. I have biscuits and jam. I can scramble a couple of eggs and fry some potatoes if you would like."

How had she learned to do all that if she was raised in society as Geneviève had been?

"A biscuit will be fine." Geneviève wasn't all that hungry. Her stomach had knotted itself into a ball.

Mr. Hammond dipped his head. "It's a pleasure to see you again. I'll take my leave so you two ladies can chat."

Though Geneviève knew Mr. Hammond was on Henny's side, she liked him. "It is nice to see you again. Please do not leave on my account." She would prefer to have another person here. Less likely all the family's dirty laundry would be aired.

"Thank you for the offer, but I must go." He turned to Henny. "I'll see you later." He ducked out the kitchen door rather than the front door.

Was everyone in Kamola so casual, friendly, and accommodating?

Henny gestured to a chair and spoke in a light cheery voice. "Have a seat. Your feet must still hurt."

She lowered herself into the offered chair.

Henny placed a plate with a biscuit and a pot of jam in front of her. "Do you prefer coffee or tea?"

"Whichever you have will be fine."

Henny poured her a cup of coffee.

Geneviève stirred sugar into the cup. "Where is Pierre?"

"At the normal school. He has classes until this afternoon—or rather later this afternoon."

She knew that but was grasping at things to say. "Do you prefer Henny or Anne?" She spread preserves on her biscuit.

When she hesitated, Geneviève prayed the woman didn't ask her to call her *Mère.*

"Henny is fine. I haven't been Anne for a long time." She took a sip of her own coffee. "And you prefer Geneviève over Daisy?" A hopefulness in her voice revealed her preference.

Even so, it was kind of her to ask. "As you have been Henny, I have always been Geneviève." She wasn't ready to erase all her years with her grandparents and be completely this woman's daughter.

"I will do my best to remember, but I can't promise not to slip now and then."

"*Merci.*"

"Please know, you are welcome to stay here as long as you want."

Henny appeared to be as nervous as Geneviève.

"*Merci.*" What else should she talk about? She took a bite and chewed slowly.

"I'm sure you have questions for me. I'll answer any you have."

Did Geneviève want the answers? Could she believe what this woman told her?

"Wait here. I'll be right back." Henny left and returned a moment later. She laid a photograph on the table. "This is you at two months and three days. You had been fussy the days before, but on this day, you were happy. It was almost as though you knew something special was going to happen."

Geneviève took the likeness and fingered it. She had always enjoyed having her photograph taken or portrait painted.

"Here is one of you and Winston on that same day. He was four and three months."

Geneviève received that one as well. Her eyes watered. By the loving care Henny took in keeping these photographs, Geneviève knew this woman had wanted her, her brother, and *Père*. A third image came her way.

"Your father and I on our wedding day. We snuck away and eloped."

She blinked to clear her vision. *Père* looked so young, and the bride next to him was obviously the woman at the table with her. "Why elope? Did you not want a large wedding?"

"I didn't need all the fuss as long as I had your father. We were so in love."

"I still do not understand why you married in secret."

Henny offered a small smile that harbored sadness. "Your grandparents didn't approve of me. They wanted someone better for their son."

Grand-mère wanted someone better than the deputy for Geneviève. "Why did they think you were not good enough?" Had they known something terrible about her character?

"Your grandparents came from old money, inherited down through many generations. My parents came from new money. My father earned every penny of his wealth."

Geneviève had heard her grandparents speak disparagingly of people who didn't have the right pedigree. "Is that the only reason? Money?"

"That is enough for some people."

That seemed sad to value a person by the amount of money they had and how they acquired it. Was Geneviève any better than Deputy Montana and his sister because her money came down through generations? Or for that matter, Henny? Someone back through time had to have earned it or acquired it in some way. "I do not believe money determines the value of a person."

"I'm glad to hear you say that. Your father said nearly those same words to me."

Geneviève was pleased to hear she was like her *père*. "I do not know what I am going to do. Stay here"—with a wave of her hand, she indicated the boarding house—"or return to the hotel."

"Then you've decided not to return to the Kesners'?" A hopefulness danced in Henny's words.

"I do not think so." She didn't want her former life with her grandparents making all her decisions and dictating her life.

An eagerness lit the older woman's eyes and bubbled in her voice. "Do you plan to remain in Kamola instead of heading back East or to France?"

She wasn't sure. She hadn't decided not to return home to either Virginia or Europe. Likewise, she hadn't decided to stay, but she knew she didn't really want to leave. "I have not made up my mind."

"Please know that you always have a place here."

Geneviève was glad to know that. "I think I might like to stay here for a little while." She wanted to get to know Henny—the *mère* who had been stolen from her. The woman who had tenderly ministered to her wounds.

Now that she had that settled, Geneviève needed to figure out how she truly felt about Deputy Montana. "How did you know for sure you loved my *père*?"

"It's not something you can quantify. There isn't any list to check off to know without a doubt. It's something you know deep inside. It's wanting to spend time with that person. Thinking about that person when you're not with them. It's gladly being willing to sacrifice things you never would have imagined before for that person."

"Is that how you feel about Mr. Hammond?" She nibbled at her biscuit.

"I've tried not to, but yes, I do. He makes me very happy." Henny took a sip of her coffee. "This is about a handsome deputy, isn't it? And what you said?"

Geneviève swallowed. "I did not think about the words before they came out. A part of me believes them to be true."

"Yet another part of you doesn't?"

"It is as if I want it to be true but am afraid it is not. Do you think he will come over today?" She both hoped he would and wouldn't.

"He might, but I hope he doesn't. Not because of anything you said or did. He needs to rest so he can recover. He had quite a wallop on his head. I had thought he would have stayed here last night—I was planning on it—but when I came downstairs, he and Felicity had gone home." Henny shrugged.

"I do not know why I said it. If I was going to say those words, I want them to be special. Not words thrown in anger at *Grand-mère*."

"You aren't the only one who has said things you regret where your grandparents are concerned." Henny put her cup to her lips.

"But you were so calm last night. I felt as though you meant it when you told her she could stay if she would be nice."

"I did mean it."

"How? When she and *Grand-père* took us away from you."

"I have had many years of practice quelling my anger, asking God's forgiveness, and forgiving your grandparents. It didn't come easy."

Geneviève leaned forward. "But you did it? Forgave them?"

"Some days I have, and others not so much. I try to think about what I have and not what I lost."

Strangely, Geneviève didn't truly cast blame on her grandparents. She loved them and knew they wanted the best for her, but it was time for her to determine what was best. "If you had known they would take us away, would you have still married *Père*?"

"I would. We were very much in love, and we had you and your brother."

That warmed her heart. "But how were you so sure?"

"I just knew"—Henny tapped her chest—"in here."

That didn't help Geneviève know for herself. "I am a mess. I cannot even make simple decisions or know how I feel. What kind of person does not know their own feelings?"

"Sometimes you need to simply choose and hope it is right. Given time, you will know."

Simply choose. She could do that, couldn't she?

Two days later on Friday, Geneviève sat at the kitchen worktable, spreading the icing on the spice cake she'd helped Henny make. Every time she managed to get one place smooth, it caused a blemish in another. This needed to be perfect. Henny was introducing Geneviève to all her quilting friends.

She had remained at Henny's partly because she wanted to get to know this woman and it was comfortable here. Also partly because if she stepped beyond Henny's property, her grandparents would snatch her away and likely whisk her off to Europe again. She loved her grandparents and loved Europe, but she also liked making her own decisions, having made the decision to stay for the time being. If she left Kamola, she wanted it to be her choice alone.

Henny entered. "The ladies are all here. I'm eager for you to meet them."

Geneviève's insides tightened, and she put her hand on her midsection. What if these ladies didn't approve of her? "I am not finished frosting the cake."

"You appear done to me."

"No. I cannot get this to be smooth." She swiped at the troublesome area.

Henny cupped her hands around Geneviève's which held the frosting spatula. "It looks splendid. The ladies will love it."

"I cannot get this part to be level. It is not perfect."

"It doesn't need to be perfect." Henny removed the utensil from Geneviève's hand and set it aside. "It will taste the same whether the frosting is flawless or not."

Geneviève stood and ran her hands down her dress. "I should not have been sitting. I have wrinkled my dress."

"Your dress is fine. There are hardly any wrinkles, and the few that are there aren't even noticeable. Come."

Geneviève took a deep breath to quell the bees bouncing off the insides of her stomach. She did not want to meet all these people, but it meant so much to Henny, and she found she wanted to do this small thing to please...her *mère*. She straightened her spine and squared her shoulders. "I am ready."

"You look as though you are going into battle. We are merely a gathering of ladies who enjoy sewing and talking."

She made it sound so simple. Geneviève had been taught that every single encounter with people was of the utmost importance. What if one of these ladies was the sister or wife of someone important? Or what if one of them knew someone who would report to the Kesners and in turn her grandparents on her behavior? She must be on her guard.

Geneviève followed Henny from the kitchen into the parlor on the other side of the informal dining room. Eleven strangers sat in a circle and one familiar face.

Felicity lifted her hand in a partial wave.

Geneviève gave her a nod of acknowledgement in return.

Henny stood beside the gathering. "You all remember that my son is staying with me."

"Is this his wife?" one of the older women asked.

A younger lady moaned out an "Oh."

Another spoke in a disappointed tone. "He's married?"

Henny held up a hand to quiet the ladies. "Not his wife, but his sister. I am pleased to present my daughter, Geneviève Marseille."

It seemed a little peculiar to have her *mère* call her that. Though it was her name, it wasn't the birth name this woman had given her.

Several of the ladies jumped to their feet, very unladylike, but friendly and full of smiles. "We are so happy to meet you." A couple of them took Geneviève's hands. Like Deputy Montana and Felicity, they were more casual but full of warmth.

One of the matrons clapped her hands. "Ladies, restrain yourselves. Sit down and give the poor girl room to breathe."

With apologies, everyone reseated themselves.

Then Henny went around the circle introducing each of her friends.

Geneviève employed one of the memory devices *Grand-mère* had taught her. Nothing was as grievous as not remembering a person's name.

"You already know Felicity." Henny then indicated a woman similar to her own age. "This is Agnes. She is the first person I met when I arrived in town. I don't know what I would have done without her friendship."

Geneviève chose a word which started with the same letter as the woman's name and pictured that letter framing her face. *Affable Agnes.*

How wonderful it would be to have a friend so long. Geneviève's longest friend would be Silvie, her lady's maid.

Then came *Nice Nicole* who greeted her in French, *Inspiring Isabelle* who had given her a ride when she had fled from the Kesners', *Friendly Franny* whom Geneviève had met at the mercantile, *Lovely Lily*, and a handful of others ranging from Geneviève's age to Henny's.

"*Enchanté.* Pleased to make the acquaintance of you all."

Henny guided Geneviève over to the settee, and the pair of them sat there.

The ladies chattered easily with one another and even included Geneviève in their conversations. Sometimes in this type of situation, the visitor could easily be left out for lack of knowing the others or the relevant topics of the area. But these ladies went out of their way to include her and inquired about her life abroad.

Their kindness reflected well on their hostess, Geneviève's *mère*. Henny was worth getting to know, and not merely a means to avoid her grandparents.

Twenty-Seven

THE NEXT DAY ON SATURDAY, MONTANA sat behind the desk at the sheriff's office, his least favorite part of the job. His first day at work since his injury. Sheriff Rix hadn't been convinced he was ready for duty yet, so he had stuck Montana in the office, sorting through old wanted posters and doing other menial paperwork. Montana's head still ached, but he'd been restless sitting around his cabin. This wasn't much better.

He stood and poured himself a fourth cup of coffee for the day. He took a swig and grimaced. The stuff tasted like dirt. Cord had done him no favors by having the pot already brewed. He walked to the window to stretch his legs.

Sammy stepped off the boardwalk in front and helped Miss Marseille out of Aunt Henny's buggy. Aunt Henny said something, nodded, and Miss Marseille nodded as well. Aunt Henny drove off.

"No, not today." Montana wasn't ready to face Miss Marseille yet. He deposited his mug on the desk as he skirted around it and slipped out the rear door.

Sammy opened the front one. "He's right in here, miss."

Montana eased the rear door closed as quietly as he could, but their voices still drifted to his ears.

"Well, he was in here a little bit ago." Deputy Sammy paused. "His coffee is still hot. I'm sure he'll be back soon. Have a seat."

No, Sammy. Don't invite her in. Send her away. Montana never expected her to come to the sheriff's office after everything that happened. His heart couldn't take seeing her, so he slunk away and didn't stop until he was well into the trees outside of town. He was a no-good coward and needed more time for his attraction to simmer down.

"What's the trouble?" Sheriff Rix said in a hushed voice.

Montana spun around. "What are you doing here?"

"I saw you hurrying off. I figured there was trouble. I came to lend a hand."

Montana slumped his shoulders. "No trouble." At least not the kind the sheriff was expecting. Montana's trouble came in a pretty little package with a French accent. "I just...I needed to get away."

Sheriff Rix straightened. "Away from what?"

Montana rubbed the nape of his neck.

"Or should I say who?"

"It's nothing." Nothing Montana couldn't handle with a few weeks or months of avoiding a certain lovely lady.

"Then I'll walk back to the office with you."

"You go. I'll be along in a bit." He was sure Miss Marseille would still be there.

"This is about the French lady, isn't it?"

"She came to the office. I'm not ready to face her." He doubted he would ever be ready.

The sheriff cocked an eyebrow. "Did you two have a fight?"

"Not exactly." Montana kicked at a clump of dirt.

"Then what, exactly?"

"You're not going to let this go, are you?"

The sheriff shook his head and folded his arms. "You obviously aren't fit for duty if a lady has you running scared."

Montana took a deep breath. "That day, after I got injured but before we walked back to town, we waited in a cleft for the hail to pass and the rain to slow. I kissed her. My head hurt so bad, and she was scared and babbling. I couldn't think of another way to get her to stop talking."

"I see. You think she's angry with you for that."

"No."

"Then you wish you'd never kissed her?"

"No. Yes. No." Montana shook his head, which sent the trees spinning. He closed his eyes for a moment to stop the motion. "It wasn't fair to her. Then when we were at

Aunt Henny's and her grandmother came, Miss Marseille said something. Something she didn't mean. She likely only said it because I kissed her. But now, I know I'll never be able to get her out of my head."

"So then let me get this straight. You kissed her, and you are sort of glad you did, but now you don't want to see her. Is that about right?"

Montana nodded.

"She must have said something pretty nasty for you to avoid her like this."

He could have handled that. "Not at all. She said she loved me."

The sheriff shook his head. "Then what are you worried about?"

"She didn't mean it."

Sheriff Rix rubbed a hand across his mouth and chin. "But you want her to mean it, and you don't want to hear that she didn't mean it."

"Exactly. Not until I get my feelings straightened out."

"They seem straight enough to me. You're sweet on her and she on you."

Oh, if it were only so. "But she's not. She only said she loved me to get her grandmother to leave."

"But you obviously love her, so why not tell her so?"

"Love? I don't know if my feelings go that far." But Montana did know.

"You're a fool."

Montana already knew that.

Sheriff Rix looked him square in the face. "It's obvious to everyone else that you love her." He poked Montana in the forehead. "You better accept that in here and fast, or you'll lose her."

"I know. That's why I left. I've been trying to sort out my feelings for the past two days." He was as messed up as the characters from that Shakespeare play.

"And?"

"They keep circling around to what her grandmother said."

"Which was what?"

"That I'm not good enough for her. I don't want to ruin her life."

The sheriff shook his head. "I don't reckon it matters so much what the grandmother thinks one way or the other. The only one who matters is Miss Marseille."

Montana knew that in his head, but his heart wasn't willing to risk it.

"Go home, rest, and sort things out. Take another couple of days if you need to."

"I'm going crazy there. Felicity keeps after me about Miss Marseille and expects me to have all the answers. She gives me that look like I drowned her cat."

Sheriff Rix nodded. "I know that look."

"I think what I need to do is scrub Miss Marseille from my head. Think on other things and pretend I never met her. Return to that day she stepped off the train and picture everything differently. Without her in it." He'd been a fool to escort her to the hotel. Carrying her across the platform had been bad enough, and his involvement with her should have ended there.

Sheriff Rix chuckled. "Good luck with that. Once a woman sashays into a man's brain, I don't know of anything which can dislodge her."

"She'll eventually leave Kamola. I'm sure her grandmother will make her." That was why Montana couldn't allow his feelings for her to get any more out of control.

The sheriff gripped Montana's shoulder. "If she has any of Aunt Henny in her, she'll stick around to get to know her mother. Besides, even if she does leave, that won't get her out of your head or your heart."

Montana was afraid of that, but he had to try.

After depositing her daughter at the sheriff's office, Henny drove to *Mademoiselle* Dumont's dressmaker shop, parked, and climbed out of her buggy. The French woman would be the best choice to clean and repair Daisy's shoes properly. She tucked the shoes into the crook of one arm.

As she reached for the storefront's door, it opened. Cora walked out and halted. "You? What are *you* doing here? You obviously don't patronize this store."

Henny wanted nothing more than to walk away. But what would that accomplish? "I'm having Celeste repair a pair of satin shoes."

"Geneviève's slippers?" Cora narrowed her eyes at Henny. "You are poisoning her against me. You hate me that much?"

Henny had told her daughter she had forgiven this woman, but times such as this made it hard to remember that. "Geneviève is an adult and can make her own decisions."

"She's a child. She doesn't know what's best."

"She's hardly a child. She's twenty-three. The same age I was when I had my son."

"My point. You were hardly in a position to care for two small children by yourself and refused to have a nanny."

"Winston and I were doing quite well until you and your husband took him away. We were happy."

Cora gave a haughty laugh. "One should never marry beneath their station, nor should one reach higher than their initial position in society."

Unbelievable. The ongoing conflict of old money verses new money. Henny stamped her foot. "Enough, Cora."

The woman's demeanor shifted to something akin to fear. "You've turned my grandchildren against me."

Henny refused to cave to this woman's emotional ploy. "I did nothing of the sort. You did that all yourself."

"Tell them you aren't really their mother. Geneviève will believe you." Cora's eyes swam with unshed tears. "I want them back. I love them."

So many retorts came to Henny's mind, but she bit her tongue. The Lord would not be pleased if she lashed out. *Turn the other cheek, Henny.* "I love them too. I *am* their mother."

"They don't even know you."

"They're getting to know me."

"I want my granddaughter back." Something changed in Cora's countenance. "The daughter I never had. At least give me that."

Surprisingly, Henny didn't hate this woman. She felt sorry for her. "All I wanted from you was a mother.

Someone to look up to. Someone to be kind and care about me. I had no one but Winston and my children. I could have been a daughter to you."

The woman's distress returned to condescending. "Don't be vulgar."

"I used to want your love. Then I feared you. Now I only feel sympathy for you."

"Pity is for the weak." Cora thinned her lips. "Talk to Geneviève, or I'll take the evidence to the authorities."

Henny was fairly sure Daisy hadn't returned the evidence to her grandparents or they would have used it against Henny already. She shook her head. "I'm through being afraid of you." She headed for the shop's door.

Cora called after her. "My grandchildren love me."

Henny wouldn't begrudge the woman that and swiveled around. "This doesn't have to be either or. They can love all of us."

"Chevalier will never tolerate that." Meaning her own husband.

"My children have minds of their own and will do as they please. Good day, Cora." Henny hurried inside before she said what she really thought of this woman. God loved her in-laws too. Henny had to keep reminding herself of that.

A couple of days later, Geneviève stopped her brother before he left the boarding house for the normal school. "I do not understand. Why is Deputy Montana avoiding me?"

"I told you not to trifle with the man's affections. What did you expect?"

What had she expected? At the time, she hadn't thought much about it and had no expectations. But now she expected him to at least let her talk to him, to explain what she'd said. To explain she was trying to figure out how she truly felt. "Would you speak to him on my behalf?"

Pierre held up his hands, palms out. "I don't think that will make a difference. I doubt he will speak to me either."

"Please try."

"What do you want me to say to him? That you are not sure of your feelings, but you want to know his?"

"*Oui.*"

Pierre shook his head. "No. Figure out *your* heart first, then *you* need to talk to him yourself. Anything I say—no matter how true—will hold no meaning. I must get to work." He kissed her on the cheek and left.

Her brother was right, but she wanted to see Deputy Montana. If she could speak to him in person, she could ascertain how she felt about him. Or at least she hoped so. How else could she sort this all out?

If her brother wouldn't help her and the deputy wouldn't see her, how was she supposed to make sense of it all? She needed to figure out a way to get him to grant her an audience.

The answer came later that day with a knock on the door. Henny ushered Felicity into the parlor.

Geneviève brightened and rose from the settee. "I am so pleased to see you."

Felicity stood rigid. "This is not a social call of pleasantries."

That snuffed the joy out of Geneviève. "What is wrong? Your brother is all right, yes?" What if he had relapsed from his injury?

"He's physically fine."

Henny stepped back. "I'll give you ladies some privacy."

Felicity lifted a hand. "That is not necessary."

Henny appeared uncomfortable but stayed. "How about I pour us all a nice cup of tea?"

"Thank you, but I won't be here that long."

Geneviève's stomach tightened. Something was definitely awry.

Felicity squared her shoulders. "Miss Marseille—"

"It is Geneviève." Why was her friend acting this way?

"*Miss Marseille,* I'm very disappointed in you for thinking my brother isn't good enough. You won't find a better man. I thought you were different."

Her heart sank at the assumed accusation. "I do not think he is not good enough. It is he who deserves better than me." Was this why the deputy wouldn't talk to her, because he believed *Grand-mère's* words too?

"Then why won't you talk to my brother?"

This was all turned around. "I have tried, but he will not see me."

Felicity's eyebrows twitched. "You have? He said he hadn't spoken to you."

"That is correct. I have tried, but he is either gone or is rushing out."

Felicity's posture relaxed. "My stubborn pigheaded brother. Do you still want to talk to him?"

"*Oui*, very much."

"You come by the sheriff's office tomorrow, and I'll see to it you get your chance to speak to him."

Geneviève's hope lifted, and she hugged Felicity. "*Merci.*"

Twenty-Eight

ON TUESDAY AFTERNOON, MONTANA STROLLED AROUND the back of the sheriff's office. He grabbed his cup from the stump and poured himself some coffee from the pot on the small pit out there. It had become too hot for a fire inside. He entered through the rear door. Deputy Cord sat behind the desk. Felicity stood by the cold, wood stove.

The hair at the nape of Montana's neck prickled. What were these two up to? "What's going on here?"

Felicity crossed to the desk and sat on the front edge. "Can't I visit my brother at work?"

Cord propped his feet on the desk with a clunk. "Your sister thought you needed checking on since your clonk on the head. I told her your head was too hard to have sustained any permanent damage. Besides, what's in there to hurt?" He tapped his own skull.

Montana didn't buy that. "What's really—?"

Felicity squealed. "A snake! Montana get it." She hopped off the desk and pointed at the first cell.

Montana turned to his twin. "Since when are you afraid of snakes, Felicity?"

"I'm not, but the poor thing could get trapped in here and die."

"I doubt that. If you're so worried about it, then you get it."

Felicity planted one hand on her hip. "Do you really want me crawling around on the floor in my skirt with him watching?" She thumbed toward Deputy Cord.

Cord, still sitting in the chair with his feet on the desk, tucked his hands behind his head. "I'd like to see that."

Montana huffed out a breath. "I'll find it." He hesitated a moment before entering the cell. "Where exactly did you see it?"

"Under the far end of the cot, next to the wall."

He moved in that direction and bent on one knee.

A moment later, the cell door clanked shut and the key jangled in the lock.

Montana righted himself and lunged for the door.

Felicity yanked the shard of metal from the lock and jumped away, but not before he reached through the bars and snagged her wrist. She gasped.

"Give me those, Felicity." He pulled her toward him. He would be able to wrestle them from her even through the bars.

She giggled and tossed the key ring toward the desk. It landed on the surface near the edge and skittered off, clattering to the floor.

He released her. "Why are you doing this?"

She faced him and folded her arms. "I'm tired of your moping and whining."

He should have known there wasn't any snake. "Cord, let me out."

The other deputy chuckled. "Moping and whining?"

Montana glared at him. "You keep quiet...unless you want to free me."

Felicity tucked her hands behind her. "There is a sweet young lady who has been trying to speak with you, but you keep disappearing."

He wasn't ready to see Miss Marseille. To talk to her. To hear that her words were meaningless. "I'll talk to her later. I've been busy."

"Well, you're not busy now. You have nothing to do and nowhere to go."

This was ridiculous. They wouldn't really leave him in here. "You've had your fun. Now release me."

"Brother dear, the fun hasn't even begun."

"I'll speak with her. I promise. Now, release me." He would say anything to get out of there.

His twin put on the sweet and innocent face she used a moment before she stole his cookie. "Oh, I know you will. Miss Marseille will be here shortly."

"No." Montana shook his head. He was being trapped so Miss Marseille could come. He wasn't ready to face her. The more he tried to tame his feelings for her, the stronger they seemed to get. His only solution was to wait until she left town. "Cord, let me out of here. You know this isn't right. Sheriff wouldn't like you doing this."

Cord pulled his mouth to one side. "What Sheriff Rix said was that under no circumstances was *I* to lock you in a cell. He didn't say anything about stopping someone else from doing so. And he didn't say I was to release you if you found yourself in this situation. So I'm a little fuzzy on the matter." He swung his feet to the floor and stood. "I'll go ask him." After retrieving the keys from the floor and pocketing them, he poked out his elbow to Felicity. "Would you fancy a walk with me?"

Felicity looped her arm with his. "That sounds lovely."

"Cord, when I get out of here, I'm going to repay this favor."

The pair strolled through the doorway.

Montana shook the bars, which clattered. "You can't leave me in here."

Felicity waved before closing the door.

"Cord! Felicity! You both will be sorry for this!" He rattled the bars again. Of course, there wasn't any way out of the cell. A jail was designed to keep the trapped in. Maybe Miss Marseille wouldn't show.

Bees once again swarmed in Geneviève's stomach as she approached the sheriff's office. With a calming breath, she entered, but no one was there. The chair behind the desk sat empty. Disappointing to have missed Deputy Montana *again*. Felicity had assured her he would be here. It hurt that he wouldn't at least see her. She turned to leave and caught sight of something—or rather someone in the near cell.

A prisoner—no—Deputy Montana stood as still as a statue at the *Louvre*, leaning against the stone wall. The iron door was latched closed. He watched her yet said nothing, following her with his gaze.

She took a step toward the bars. "What are you doing in there?"

He had his hands wedged deep inside his trouser pockets. "Apparently waiting for you."

"Why in there?"

He remained against the wall. "Felicity and Cord thought this would be a good place for me to pass the time until your arrival."

"So, he locked you in there for no reason?" She had to admit this was effective.

"Actually, it was Felicity."

Why would his sister do that? "Where is the key? I will let you out."

"Cord took it with him."

"I will go find them and tell him to release you from this cage." She turned to the exit.

"Wait. Don't." He pushed away from the wall.

She studied him. "Why?"

"I can save you a lot of trouble. I know why you're here."

Had Felicity told him?

He went on. "I know what you said at Aunt Henny's was to irritate your grandmother."

That was true. Partly.

"Your words meant nothing. I understand. Don't worry about it."

That was *not* true. She moved all the way over to the cage. "I did say my words in retaliation to my *grand-mère*, and they surprised me."

He held up his hand. "Please stop. Just go."

"No. I will not." She was glad now he was behind bars so he couldn't walk away from her. "When I told *Grand-mère* I loved you, the words came from someplace deep inside. I did not know I was going to say them. I did not know if they were true. I have spent this past week trying to figure out why I said them. I did not say them to hurt you. But my heart knew. It had been wanting to say them, but my upbringing kept my heart silent, my feelings squashed. I was raised to believe love did not matter. That if I married for love, I would be doomed to an unhappy miserable life. I would either be heartbroken or be a spinster alone. It was *Grand-mère's* duty to make a good match for me, and I needed to be content with it and make the best of my circumstances. Be a dutiful wife to further my husband's endeavors. After spending time with you and coming to care about you a great deal, I know I could never be happy with such a life. I would rather spend the rest of my life a spinster with a broken heart, than to never have loved at all."

"Are you saying you *do* love me?"

"I am. I did not know it until I came in here and thought you were gone again. My heart ached to see you. I thought I loved you before coming, but not until I saw you did I know for sure." At least she thought she was sure.

He gazed at her without saying anything.

Oh, dear. Perhaps he didn't feel the same. "Please say something."

"I—I don't know what to say."

"You have two choices. Either tell me you love me too, or tell me you do not love me."

He shook his head. "It's not that simple."

"It is. You either love me or you do not."

"It would never work out between us. We come from different worlds. I would never ask you to stoop to this level to live in my world, and I would never fit in yours."

That sounded an awful lot like he loved her. "Tell me. Do you love me or not?"

"I do, but—"

"But nothing. We will make our own world where we both fit."

"That's an idealistic dream. Life doesn't work that way."

"I want to hear you say it."

"What? That a world where we both fit doesn't exist? That such a place never will?"

"No. That you love me."

"Why? It won't do any good. It won't change anything."

"I still want to hear you say it. I *need* to hear you say it."

He gazed at her a long moment before his lips moved, and his words came out with a husky catch to them. "I love you."

Her heart danced at his declaration. "Are you willing to give up on that love?"

He heaved a sigh. "We don't have a choice."

"*I* have a choice even if you cannot see one. I guess I will have to find the world we both fit in without your help."

He squinted at her. "You truly believe things could work out for us, don't you?"

"I have to. Anything else is too devastating."

He stepped closer, reached through the bars, and took her hands. "If you are so determined, I'm willing to give it a try. I still find it hard to believe someone of your status would actually consider someone like me as worthy of you."

"You have it wrong. It is I who am unworthy of you. You are a good person. You always seek to do what is right. I have always been self-serving and selfish. Seeking to find who will elevate me in social standing and wealth. It is you who have elevated me in a far more meaningful way. I have seen the love of God through you. You have shown me a different way to live my life, a different way of thinking. I never realized I was unhappy. Not really unhappy, but not happy. How could I not know that?"

"It was all you knew. I don't know if you would be happy in the long run living a different kind of life. You would miss your old way of living and your fancy things."

Would she? There were many good things about it. "I want to try. Are you willing to try?"

"If it doesn't work? Will you run back to your former life and leave me behind?"

She didn't like that idea and hadn't thought about such a future not working out. *Oh, dear.* "I would need to be sure, would I not?"

He nodded.

She hated having doubts. She didn't want to. She loved him and wanted to be sure of the way forward. "How can I be sure of anything?"

He shrugged. "I don't know."

Confusion bubble up inside her. She tried to tamp it down. "Are you sure?"

"Of what? That I love you?"

She nodded.

"I'm sure."

She envied his confidence. "Do you think we could make it as a couple?"

"Not if your grandmother has anything to say about it."

She didn't want to think about *Grand-mère* right now. "What if she did not? What if I could do anything I wanted?"

"I can't provide you with anything close to the kind of life you're used to."

What he didn't know was he didn't have to. She had money from her *père*, or rather her *mère*. Should she tell him? Could she only be happy with him because she had her money? If that were the case, did she even love him at all? Her eyes teared. "My heart says, 'I love you,' but my head asks, 'Are you sure?'. It taunts me."

He caressed a stray tear away. "Don't cry."

"I cannot help it. I do not know how to make this decision." She pulled away and ran out the door.

She was pitiful and didn't deserve someone like the deputy. That twisted her heart.

Twenty-Nine

THE SHERIFF'S OFFICE DOOR YAWNED OPEN after Miss Marseille's hasty departure. This had been what Montana had been trying to prevent by avoiding her. Montana wanted to call after her, wanted her to return, wanted to hold her in his arms, but it was best she was gone. He wished he hadn't had to hurt her. He'd been surprised she had been so hurt.

He turned and kicked the metal frame of the cot. Pain shot through his foot and up his leg. He deserved far worse. Gripping the cell bars, he gave them a shake. He longed to go after her even though he knew he shouldn't.

Just let this all drift into the past. Then she could live as she eventually would without him, the life she was born to live.

He slumped down onto the edge of the cot and raked his hands into his hair, fisting them.

"Lord, comfort Miss Marseille. Ease the pain she's feeling. Show her this is best." He heaved a sigh. "Why does my gut tell me this is not best for me? Distract me from my selfish thoughts. Return her to the world she came from and bring her someone who can make her happy. Someone whom she can truly love and who will love her and treat her as she deserves to be treated."

He leaned against the adjoining cell's bars. His heart ached. He never knew he could feel this way. He hadn't given courting—or matters of the heart—much thought. He had wondered occasionally if a wife and family might ever be in his future. Being a deputy, he figured not.

These bars weren't the only cage holding him captive. His heart would be imprisoned forever, and Miss Marseille held the only key.

Heavy boot steps clomped on the boardwalk outside. A man's footsteps. Cord? Finally.

Sheriff Rix sauntered in. He did a double take then shook his head. "I warned Cord."

"It wasn't his fault...well, only partially. He didn't technically do this to me. My sister did, but he didn't do anything to stop her."

"I'll get the keys and let you out." He slid open the drawer.

"Cord took 'em."

The sheriff shook his head again. After sitting in the chair, he pulled the drawer open farther and reached his hand in palm up as though he were fishing something off the underside of the desktop. "Don't tell anyone about this. Except Cord. He already knows." He retrieved his hand and a solitary cell key. "It's for emergencies."

"You told Cord about this secret key but no one else?"

"Cord only knows because he got himself into a bit of a pickle. We had a train robber locked in there, and his friends came to fetch him. They put him in the cell and tossed the keys out the back door."

Montana chuckled. "I'll have to give him a hard time about that."

"The least he deserves for allowing this." Rix stood and crossed to the cell. "What did you do to make your sister mad enough to stick you behind bars?"

Montana rubbed his neck. "I was trying to avoid talking to Miss Marseille."

Sheriff Rix froze with the key an inch from the cell door. "Still?"

"I spoke to her a little while ago, the reason I'm in here. I had no choice. I made her understand she's better off without me. She deserves better."

His boss withdrew his hand and the key with it. "You did what? I've seen you when you were going to meet her. She is good for you. You're not generally a brooding-type person, but you've been happier since she's been in town."

Montana had noticed the difference in himself as well. "I can't do that to her."

"Do what?"

"Pull her down to my level. Her grandparents would never approve of me. I can't provide for her in the way she's used to." Montana pointed to the lock. "Are you going to release me?"

The sheriff palmed the hunk of metal, sat in the chair, and propped his feet on the desk. "I always took you for a smart man. I was given to understand she said she loves you. Now you're telling me you turned her away? Cooling your heels in jail might be exactly what you need."

"Sheriff Rix, you can't leave me in here."

"I say I can. We put drunks in there to sober up. I think you are drunk on self-righteousness." He stood. "I need to find Cord to see what he has to say about your incarceration." He crossed to the door. "I'll check on you later. You think on what you've done. Hopefully, you'll come to your senses." He pocketed the spare key and left.

Montana slumped onto the cot again. Wanting what was best for Miss Marseille *was* the right thing to do. Wasn't it?

"Lord, why can't they all see that?"

Choose ye this day whom ye will serve.

What? He knew that was part of the verse from the book of Joshua, chapter twenty-four, verse fifteen. He looked heavenward. "What does that have to do with me being right and wanting the best for Miss Marseille?"

Pride goeth before destruction and a haughty spirit before a fall.

"Again, what does that have to do with me being...?" He didn't finish his question. He didn't dare. He was being prideful in thinking he knew what was best for the pretty French lady.

"Forgive me, Lord."

It wasn't his to decide what was best for her. He could only decide what was best for himself. But what was that? Or rather who?

A beautiful lady with a lilting French accent.

Henny heard the front screen quietly open. She was anxious to find out how Daisy's encounter with the deputy went and hurried to the foyer.

Her daughter faced the screen as she eased it shut, apparently trying to not make any noise. When Daisy—no Geneviève—turned and saw Henny, she startled, sucking in a breath. Tear streaks marred each of her cheeks.

Henny went to her daughter's side and hooked her arm around her shoulders. "What's the matter? Doesn't the deputy return your affections?"

"He does, but I do not know if I do."

"I don't understand." Henny was grateful her daughter didn't brush her away. "Come sit down." She guided her to the settee in the parlor.

Dai—Geneviève sniffled. "How can I know if I am truly in love? How do I know if what I feel is strong enough to last?"

"Emotions ebb and flow, up and down. Flighty at best. You must decide *here*." She touched her head. "And determine to make it work no matter what trials or hardships come your way."

The girl was silent for a moment. "*Père* didn't do that with you, did he?"

"Don't be too hard on him. He tried, but your grandparents wore him down. They have wills made of iron." Henny stood. "Wait here. I have something I want you to read." She went to her room and retrieved her late husband's letter. She sat and handed it to her daughter. "Your brother gave me this letter your father wrote to me shortly before he died."

Geneviève read with tear-filled eyes. When she finished, she handed it back. "If *Père* couldn't withstand their wills, how can I? They know what is best."

Henny didn't want to disparage Cora or the senior most Winston to the young woman. They had raised her. "They believe with all their hearts that the things they want for you and everyone else are best. I think their actions serve *themselves* best. You must decide your own way." She wished she'd been stronger in her younger years to resist her in-laws, or at least, to have had someone she could depend on. With no family of her own left, she thought the people she could count on were Winston's family. She had been wrong.

"When I went to the sheriff's office, his sister and one of the other deputies had locked Deputy Montana in a cell so he could not avoid me. When I saw him, my heart leapt. I was sure in that moment I truly loved him."

"But now you aren't sure."

"He said he could not provide for me in the way I am used to. My thought was that it did not matter because *I* have the money *Père* left me. Your money. How can I think I truly love him if I know I do not have to live as a pauper?"

Henny understood. Men didn't care for their wives to have more wealth than themselves. "I think this is something you and he need to discuss. Perhaps, you can each share in paying for what you need."

"What do you mean?"

"Maybe you could purchase a modest home for the two of you and hire someone who would work as both a housekeeper and cook. Montana could pay for the daily living expenses such as food, livestock and the keeping of them, as well as other such provisions."

"Do you think he would be happy with such an arrangement?"

"You won't know if you don't ask."

"What if I give him all my money so it is his?"

Bad idea. "I don't think that simply because you are a woman you should have to turn over all your assets to a man." Henny wished she'd had a choice. "You are an intelligent young lady who is capable of making financial decisions of your own. Every decision you make might not be a good one, but that's how you learn."

Geneviève didn't want to relinquish her inheritance, but she also didn't want to lose the deputy. "Perhaps I will give it back to you."

"I don't want your money. Your father gave that to you."

"Because it was *yours* to begin with." It hadn't been right for Henny to lose control of all her wealth. "You are the rightful owner."

"I have the portion he bequeathed to me. That's plenty for me to live on. The life I lead doesn't require the amount of funds my former one did."

"You were raised in privilege, how did you cope without the affluence and having others doing everything for you? How did you learn to cook?"

Henny chuffed a laugh. "I confess those early days and years were hard. I had a couple of generous ladies who took pity on me and taught me to cook a few simple meals. I learned to clean and sew more than a fancy—useless—bit of needlepoint."

"Do you think I could learn to do those things?" Geneviève couldn't imagine acquiring so many new skills and preparing a meal worth eating.

"Of course you can. You are more capable than you realize."

"Deputy Montana said something similar to me when he was injured."

"He's right. I think we are all more capable than we give ourselves credit for. We rise to the expectations others have for us. If they expect little, we are capable of little. However, in dire circumstances, we can do more than we ever thought possible. I never would have imagined I could live in the Wild West and support myself." Henny held out her hands. "Yet here I am, doing precisely that. I wouldn't change it. I'm a better person for my experiences."

"I want to be a better person."

"Acknowledging that is the first and most important step." Henny shifted to more fully face Geneviève. "Close your eyes and picture yourself in the most lavish house you can imagine with expensive things around you."

How was this going to help? She closed her eyes anyway. "Are my grandparents there?"

"No, only you and how many ever servants you want. Everything is perfect. There is only one thing. Deputy Montana is not in this world. How do you feel living in this place?"

Geneviève liked her pretty things. They didn't necessarily make her happy, but they gave her a level of comfort, like all was well. But it wasn't. She longed for more. "I am happy but not content. Why can Deputy Montana not be there?"

"Because he can't in that scenario. Now, picture yourself living in a home like the one Deputy Montana lives in. You have no servants, but you have the deputy at your side. How does this place make you feel?"

Geneviève pictured herself in the deputy's cabin with a crackling fire in the hearth. She wore one of her fanciest dresses with puffy sleeves. No, that wasn't right. She changed the dress to the one she wore fishing. Much better. Deputy Montana smiled at her from across the room. Her mouth pulled into a smile too, and she warmed all over. "Happy *and* content. More than happy." She popped her eyes open. "How can that be?"

"Sometimes, matters of the heart can't be explained."

"Would you teach me to do what you do, manage a house and cook?"

"I would love to." Henny's eyes glistened.

Geneviève finally felt a connection to this woman, to her *mère.*

Thirty

GENEVIÈVE SAT IN THE DAISY GARDEN in the backyard at the boarding house. Many of the flowers had bloomed. Her *mère hadn't* abandoned her nor forgotten her. Quite the opposite. She had planted a garden of flowers in her honor to remember her and keep her close. And to honor and keep Pierre and *Père* close.

Geneviève didn't feel like a Daisy, but she was also feeling less like a Geneviève in light of her real history. Even with all her grandparents' underhanded deeds, she didn't want to lose them. She still loved them.

Henny had all manner of daisies, white, yellow, orange, red, pink, and purple, a colorful array of life that provided memories for Henny. If Geneviève loved her, was she betraying her grandparents? Now that she had gotten to know this woman whom she had resisted meeting, she could picture her life with Henny—*Mère*—in it, at least in a small way. Trying to think of her as *mère* was strange. It didn't quite feel right. Nor did it feel wrong. One part of her longed to embrace the idea of having a *mère* who was alive and wanted her. Another part wished to return to her simpler life before *Père* died. She missed him dearly, but she refused to revert to the way things had been with her grandparents. *Père* was gone, and he had wanted her to get to know her *mère*.

The kitchen screen door creaked. Deputy Montana descended the porch steps.

She wanted to run to him but stayed put after he had turned her away at the jail.

He hung his head. "I want to apologize for my actions and the things I said. For not encouraging you. I was a fool."

Geneviève stepped forward. "You were right. My grandparents will never accept you in my life. I need to get to a point where I am strong enough to stand up to them. I am sorry to not be strong enough yet, but Henny...Anne Henderson...my *mère* will stand with me to be strong. I do not want to lose my grandparents' love or company, but if they do not accept you, then they are the ones making the choice to break ties and not me."

His smile grew. "Does that mean you'll give me another chance to make things work with you?"

"I want to, but I was trying to figure out if I am strong enough to do so."

"You mean because I can't provide for you to the level you are used to?"

"*Oui* and no." She sent up a silent prayer that he could accept her decision. "Do I love you enough to give up all my fancy things and way of life? I do not know because my thought was that I did not have to because I have my inheritance *Père* left me, so I do not need to depend on my grandparents. However, if I did not have that money, would I be strong enough to live a life with you without all the comforts I am used to? I do not know, because I do have money. So I thought to give it all away."

"You shouldn't have to do that. It's yours."

"I came to the conclusion that I am a woman of means. If you, being a man, do not like me having more money than you, then I do not know if we will suit. Will my finances be a problem for you?" She prayed not. She longed for him to say her wealth didn't matter to him.

He rubbed his neck. "Then, what would you need me for?"

"Because I love you."

"I'm not sure how I feel about you not needing me to provide for you and the family we will hopefully have. Will you give me time to think on this?"

"Of course." She understood this went against the normal way of things. It was hard to change a person's thinking to something the complete opposite in an instant. She hadn't fully adjusted to having a *mère* who was alive.

He straightened and shook his head. "No. I don't need time to think about it. I love you and want to spend my life with you. Together we will figure out how to make this work and, as you said, create a world we both fit into."

She couldn't believe it. Her insides fluttered with excitement. "Truly?" She held her breath.

"Yes. Are you willing to figure out life together with me?" He held out his hand.

She put hers in his. *"Oui.* I love you."

"I like the way you say that." He pulled her close and lowered his lips to hers.

She wrapped her arms around his neck and held on, returning his kiss. A tingle rippled throughout her. She never wanted him to let her go.

After a moment, she did release him. "I have a question."

He kept his hands locked at the small of her back. "Anything."

"If Montana is not your Christian name, what is?"

He moaned. "Not the question I expected. How about I kiss you again instead?" He leaned closer.

She put a hand between their mouths to stop him. "What question did you expect?"

He shrugged a shoulder. "I don't know, but not that."

"Are you not going to tell me?"

He took a deep breath. "If I tell you, do I have permission to use your first name?"

"Oui."

"I supposed you will find out eventually anyway." He hesitated a long moment, and she thought he might not tell her. He heaved a sigh. "Francis."

"That is a good name." Why had he been so reluctant to tell her? "Like King Francis the first and second of France in the 1500s."

"Kings? You are the first person to not laugh at my name."

"It is a noble name. You should be proud of it."

"It's not noble around these parts, so I would appreciate it if you never use it. The other deputies would ceaselessly mock me."

That seemed silly, but she didn't want to bring harm to him. "Then what shall I call you now?"

"Montana will do fine."

"Very well. I will call you Montana." She gave him a coy smile. "For now." She would find a suitable pet name for him. One that wouldn't induce mocking from others.

"For now? What's that supposed to mean?"

She would keep him guessing at the present. Rising up onto her tiptoes, she kissed him again.

The following day, Geneviève took Montana's hand as she stepped out of Henny's buggy in front of the Kesners' house. Her insides tightened. She wore the best dress she had with her which was appropriate for this meeting. Pierre assisted Henny.

Geneviève was grateful to not be alone. Though a stronger person than when she had first arrived, she feared she might buckle under her grandparents' pressure as *Père* had. She knew she needed to confront her grandparents before she could begin a life with the man she loved. That he had agreed to accompany her told her how much he did love her.

Montana offered his arm to her. When she took it, he patted her hand. "You are going to do great. You are strong and capable."

"*Merci.*" How silly it had been of her to think that accepting a gentleman's offered help was some grievous breach of etiquette or would sully her reputation.

Pierre lifted the brass door knocker and clacked it several times.

The butler answered and let them inside.

Geneviève gulped in a breath as she entered. Her grandparents would not be pleased with her decision. Hopefully when they realized she was determined, they would see reason and accept she wasn't under their control any longer.

The butler left them in the foyer and disappeared through one of the many doors off the entry.

She hadn't seen *Grand-père* in almost three months. She both looked forward to seeing him and worried over his reaction to her independent actions of late.

When far more time than was appropriate passed, *Grand-père* and *Grand-mère* entered the foyer.

Longing to go to him, Geneviève took a step forward but stopped herself when she didn't see the welcoming sparkle in his eyes.

Grand-père leveled his gaze on Geneviève and her brother. "Pierre. Geneviève. I'm glad to see you being reasonable." He shifted his attention to Montana. "Thank you for escorting them. You may go."

Montana looked to Geneviève then Henny. Did he realize *Grand-père* had dismissed him?

Geneviève swallowed hard. "I have come to retrieve the rest of my belongings."

Grand-père's expression turned from neutral to irritated. "Whose money paid for them?"

"Um." Her words lodged in her throat, choked out by his tone and countenance. "Uh."

"Don't sputter like a commoner. You sound ill-bred."

Grand-mère, a step behind her husband, remained silent, though she appeared to want to speak.

Montana wrapped his hand around Geneviève's.

She drew strength from him and garnered the courage to speak. "Your money, *Grand-père,* but what would you do with a closet full of lady's gowns?" She regarded her lady's maid down the hallway with a couple of other servants lingering there. "Silvie, please pack the remainder of my belongings." She managed to keep her voice from shaking. She had never stood up to her grandfather like this.

Grand-père spoke in an even tone. "Don't you dare, Miss Dubois, or you will be out on the street."

Henny took Geneviève's other hand. "I'll help you pack your things."

Geneviève had all these people on her side—her *mère*, her *frère*, and Montana, even Felicity if she were here. She had always felt alone before. She didn't now. She straightened her shoulders. "Silvie, if you would like to come with me, I will hire you to continue to be my lady's maid."

Grand-père narrowed his eyes. "Geneviève, don't be ridiculous. Come to your senses."

She had. Maybe for the first time in her life.

Pierre leaned a little forward. "We have come to our senses. We are going to remain in Kamola to get to know our *mère*."

"I am disappointed in you, Pierre."

"As I am in you. Have you no shame for all the things you've done?"

"I've done nothing wrong." *Grand-père* pointed at Henny. "She's the one you should be concerned about."

"You've done nothing wrong? We still have those incriminating documents. We would hate to use them but will if you try to do anything to harm our *mère*."

Geneviève didn't like to hear them fighting. "Please stop. Why can we not all get along?" She held out her hand to include her grandparents, her *mère*, and Montana.

Grand-père scoffed. "Don't be naïve. One cannot have two masters. You will revere one and loathe the other. You have always been weak-willed."

Her grandfather's words stung, and tears burned her eyes. She had hoped he would take pride in her self-reliance.

The young Mr. Kesner stepped into the entry with his *grand-mère* and addressed Geneviève's grandparents. "You have outstayed your welcome. Please pack your things and depart."

Grand-père leveled his gaze on the young man who didn't flinch. "You don't have the authority."

Madame Kesner lifted her chin. "He does." She glanced down the hall where servants waited. "Hazel, help *Madame* Marseille's maid pack. Rogers, assist *Monsieur* Marseille's valet."

"You'll regret crossing me, *Madame* Kesner."

The old woman smiled serenely. "I'm too old to care."

"Your grandson may think differently when he is seeking favors from people of power and influence."

Lamar squared his shoulders. "I doubt that."

Grand-père narrowed his eyes at Geneviève and her brother. "Neither of you will see one penny of my money while you are associating with that woman."

Geneviève straightened her shoulders. "We do not need it. We have our inheritance from...our *mère*. Even if

I did not, I still want to get to know her. No amount of wealth can keep me from learning about her, but I want the two of you in my life as well."

"That's not possible."

Grand-mère took hold of her husband's arm. "Please, Chevalier. We'll lose our grandchildren like we lost our son."

He pulled from her grasp. "We got him back. Our grandchildren will come crawling back too. This is what you get for overindulging them. I told you to keep tighter reins on them. You should have married her off years ago."

Geneviève realized for the first time, *Grand-mère* might have been as trapped as she had been. Were her grandmother's actions and attitudes nothing more than a false vibrato of her husband's? Had she merely been following his orders and wishes? Geneviève focused her attention on *Madame* Kesner. "Would it be all right if I return later for my things?"

"Any time you would like, my dear."

"*Merci.*" She turned toward her companions. "We shall leave."

None of them countered her, and they eagerly moved out the door.

At the bottom of the veranda steps, Montana faced her. "You were splendid in there."

She wrapped her arms around him, not caring if it was inappropriate. "Thank you for being here with me."

"I wouldn't be anywhere else." He kissed her, right there in the Kesners' drive with her *frère* and *mère* watching.

Geneviève was exactly where she wanted to be—in Deputy Montana's arms. She had made the right decision. She would miss her grandparents and prayed they had a change of heart, but she wouldn't regret her choice.

Epilogue

ONE WEEK LATER ON HER SON'S arm, Henny waited around the side of her house. She wore her best Sunday dress. She could hardly believe what she was about to do. A June bride at her age.

Winston patted her hand. "He is a fine man. I think you have made a good choice."

She couldn't believe how much her son's approval meant to her.

"I am still contemplating legally changing my name back to my birth name of Winston Seymour."

"Please don't think you have to do that on my account. Both Winston and Pierre are a part of you, just as Anne and Henny are both a part of me." Her daughter still hadn't accepted her birth name, but Henny didn't mind as long as she was willing to have Henny in her life. Though she would call her daughter by whichever name she preferred, Henny would always think of the young woman as her little Daisy. Her daughter had been apprehensive about standing up with Henny, but she had agreed. She shifted her attention to her son again. "Please don't change your name in retaliation against your grandparents."

"Why not? They deserve more dire consequences than that for what they have done."

"It won't make anything better. They thought they were doing what was best for you. You don't want to spend your whole life harboring bitterness."

"Some days I do. I want them to hurt as much as they hurt *Père* and you. Other days, I want to completely forget about them."

Her poor son was struggling with finding out his mother was alive and his grandparents' treachery as much as her daughter was but in different ways. He wanted to have nothing to do with his grandparents. Whereas Daisy—Geneviève longed to return to them, even knowing the woman she had become would never be content in that environment any longer. Her grandparents would demand all of her or have nothing to do with her.

Henny prayed both her children could find some sort of peace with what their grandparents had done. Henny had come to terms with it as well as her own poor choices and actions a long time ago. She had to in order to live with herself and have a modicum of peace. She'd given it all over to the Lord and prayed daily for her children and husband.

Agnes Martin, her good friend from the quilting circle, and Geneviève came around the side of the building. Her friend smiled. "They're ready for you."

"Thank you." Henny was pleased her quilting circle ladies had gathered for her special day. They had eagerly helped her get ready.

"You are as beautiful a bride as any. I am so happy for you." Her friend blinked as though she were trying to quell her emotions. "The pair of you make a wonderful couple. It's about time the two of you got hitched."

"Thank you."

"I'll go take my seat." Agnes strolled away.

Geneviève smiled. "You do look lovely."

"Will you and Deputy Montana be next?"

"I hope so. He hinted as much."

"But he hasn't proposed yet?"

"Not formally. I cannot tell if he thinks he has by beating a bush around, or if he is waiting. But today is for you. I will see you by the clergyman." With a nod, she walked off.

The young man better get his horse in motion or someone else might try to steal his girl.

When Henny moved to follow, her son held her in place with a hand on her arm. "What is it?"

"Wait a moment longer." After a few seconds, he spoke. "I did not want her to hear. The deputy asked for my blessing to propose to Vivi."

"You told him yes, didn't you?"

He chuckled. "I did. He wanted to know if he should ask you as well. Also about asking our grandparents."

She hoped he didn't ask the grandparents. "What did you tell him?"

"That he did not need to ask you because you are not the male head of the family, but it would be nice if he did. I suspect he will ask you after the ceremony."

"Thank you. And your grandparents?"

"I told him not to ask them. They would only say no. If she wants their blessing, she can ask them, but they will never give it."

Henny knew that pain and could still feel its sting.

He patted her hand. "It is time for you to go to your beau."

She nodded and walked with him across the yard, toward her future.

As she passed between the groups of friends, she hesitated near Deputy Montana. "My answer is yes."

At first, the young man appeared confused, but then he understood. "Thank you."

Gazing at her soon-to-be husband, she continued to the front where her daughter and the preacher stood with him. She squeezed her daughter's hand. "Thank you."

Henny stood in her backyard by her daisies with the man she loved, the preacher, her children. and a host of friends. Some people thought they should marry in the church, but Henny wanted to be near her garden which had represented her family for so long. Saul understood and had gladly agreed.

It seemed as though she'd been waiting her whole life to begin living. First as a young girl anxious to grow up. Then as a young woman hoping to meet the man of her dreams and get married. Then when her parents died, she longed for the pain to go away. Winston had been a huge help in that area. Then yearnings for children to come and her in-laws to accept her. And lastly, anticipating the day her past would catch up to her and her in-laws would have her locked away.

Today was the day she was going to stop waiting and live her life with the man of her dreams.

Saul Hammond.

The preacher pronounced them husband and wife, giving Saul permission to kiss her. And kiss her he did. Henny was finally at peace and happy with her life on earth.

Author Note

The Débutante's Secret, the fourth in The Quilting Circle series, was a fun story to write. I enjoyed spending time in Kamola with Aunt Henny and the quilting circle ladies again. I love their friendship and how they stand by each other regardless of what one of them is going through. True friends are gifts from above.

Geneviève and Montana seem like an unlikely couple, but I think they complement each other and bring out the other's best. After having the stranger pop up in book three, I knew I needed to dig into Aunt Henny's past, explore her background, and find out who this man was. Geneviève and Montana's romance was the perfect story to do that in as well as delve into Aunt Henny's romance with Saul Hammond.

In writing this story, I knew the title was two-fold. Geneviève is a débutante who has secrets, but Aunt Henny is also with a skeleton or two in the closet. Did you guess that the title referred to both women?

In book five of The Quilting Circle series, I plan to tell Lamar Kesner's story. The poor man has had several lovely ladies within reach, but their hearts belonged to someone else. It's time for him to capture a special someone's heart.

I hope you enjoyed reading Geneviève and Montana's story as much as I did writing it.

Happy Reading!
Mary
☺

If you enjoyed *The Débutante's Secret*, or any of the Quilting Circle series books, I'd love it if you would consider posting a review on Amazon, Christianbook.com, Goodreads.com, BarnesandNoble.com, BookBub.com or anywhere else books are sold or reviewed. Reviews are a tremendous help to authors! Thank you for anything you can do.

I'd love to connect with you. Readers can find me at:

FaceBook: Mary Davis READERS Group–
www.facebook.com/groups/132969074007619/

Blog: marydavis1.blogspot.com

Subscribe to my Newsletter: marydavisbooks.us17.list-manage.com/subscribe?u=cbe8a2ec4ef27cfcf51813f02&id=82ad258f06

Amazon: www.amazon.com/Mary-Davis/e/B00JKRBJKE

Goodreads:
www.goodreads.com/author/show/8126829.Mary_Davis

BookBub:
www.bookbub.com/profile/mary-davis?list=author_books

Discussion Questions

1. What was your favorite quote/passage? Why did this stand out and how could you use it in your own life?

2. How well does the book's cover convey what the book is about? Do you think the back-cover copy did a good job of indicating what this book is about? If the book were being adapted into a movie, who would you want to see play Geneviève, Montana, Henny, and Saul?

3. Suffering myself from a generalized anxiety disorder with many facets to it, I decided to give Geneviève anxiety issues. She does her best to deal with it as well as her self-doubts. Can you relate to Geneviève? Do you struggle with or have anyone close to you who struggles with a mental health issue? What do you find helpful to cope with it?

4. Which character did you relate to the most, and what was it about them that you connected with? To what extent do they remind you of yourself or someone you know? Do you empathize with the characters? What fears do they each harbor?

5. Describe the dynamics between Geneviève and her brother, Geneviève and her grandparents, Geneviève and Montana, Geneviève and her mother, and Aunt Henny and each of the characters. How do the characters change, grow, or evolve throughout the course of the story?

6. What are the major conflicts in the story? What events in the story stand out for you as memorable? What main ideas—themes—does the author explore? Are they relevant in your life?

7. The stranger from book three is back, and he's watching Henny again, or so she thinks. She questions if she is imagining things or making too much of a fuss. She learns that the man is her long-lost son and that her daughter is also in town. Do you think Henny had any good choices all those years ago other than to flee? If she had stayed, she would have been locked up by her in-laws and still have lost her children. What might you have done in her place?

8. Did any parts of the book make you uncomfortable? If so, why did you feel that way? Did this lead to a new understanding or awareness of some aspect of your life you might not have thought about before? Has this novel changed you or broadened your perspective?

9. What do you think will be your lasting impression of the book and why? Did the issues that were raised touch or impact you in any way? Would you recommend it to a friend, and if so, why? Can you see yourself reading it again?

NOW, A SNEAK PEEK AT

THE LADY'S MISSION

THE QUILTING CIRCLE BOOK 5
COMING OCTOBER 5, 2022

One

Central Washington State, Summer 1894

LAMAR KESNER STOOD IN THE LARGE, barn-style double-doorway opening of his workshop in a pair of lightweight trousers from last year, with his shirt sleeves rolled to his elbows. Grandmama had retired both articles of clothing from social use as they were "old" and "out of date," but they were suited for tasks in his shop.

He lifted a narrow copper tube that went on the heating apparatus for his hot air balloon and peered through it. No blockage. Then the issue must be with some other part.

He favored spending his time in Kamola to any of the properties back East, with the fewer social obligations. He had reliable, loyal people managing Grandmama's holdings and reporting back to him. Staying here allowed him to partake in his hobby. Grandmama indulged him, because she knew it kept him here rather than elsewhere.

Grandmama could move back East, but she preferred to oversee the Washington State Normal School his grandfather had a hand in bringing to fruition before he passed two years ago. Grandpapa had also encouraged

Lamar's interests and had the outbuilding constructed for him. Together they had started this current endeavor, hot air ballooning. This was his third such balloon. High in the air, he felt as though he could get away from all the demands and expectations. It was a place no one could bother him.

One of the footmen approached. Mr. Derby cleared his throat before he spoke. "Your grandmother wishes an audience with you."

"Thank you. I'll come right in." He set the tubing on his work counter and headed toward the manor house. The distraction would give him a chance to contemplate what aspect of the device to address next.

As he entered, Rogers stood waiting. The valet scrutinized Lamar. Though the man's expression didn't change, Lamar knew the servant would have something to say about what he wore.

Lamar lifted a hand. "She'll have to take me as I am. I plan to return to my workshop post haste."

"Very well. She's in the parlor."

Lamar strolled along the hallway and into the room.

Grandmama sat in her usual place, a high wing-backed, stuffed chair with claw feet. The size and stature of it almost resembled a throne. Well, she was queen of her castle. "Lamar! Gracious, your attire. Hurry and change." She glanced toward the doorway. "Rogers?"

The valet appeared. He must have been around the corner out of sight. "Yes, ma'am?"

"See to it my grandson has something proper to wear."

"I have his suit out and ready." Rogers obviously knew something Lamar didn't.

Grandmama wiggled her fingers toward Lamar in a shooing fashion. "Go on. You can't greet our guests looking like that."

Guests? Guests his grandmother had conveniently forgotten to tell him about. "Grandmama, you didn't invite another marriage candidate, did you?"

She beamed a sweet smile. "Be nice. She could be the one."

That was doubtful. Another vapid socialite to contend with.

"When are you going to give up on this?"

"I'm not. Now go make yourself presentable." Grandmama's quest to locate him a suitable wife had grown tiresome.

She meant well, but he didn't need help in finding a wife. The Lord would bring the right woman into his life in His time.

Rogers led the way upstairs.

Lamar washed and dressed in the chosen suit before returning to the parlor. He joined his grandmother and stood by the fireplace mantel, too nettled with the prospect of another boring débutante to sit. He would rather be in his workshop. "Who is it this time?"

"A young lady from New York with impeccable breeding." Grandmama would choose nothing less. "I think you'll like this one."

Doubtful if she was anything like so many of the others. "Does she have a name?"

"Miss Cordelia Armstrong, and I hear she is a rare beauty."

Of course. Rare beauty or not, it would be rarer still if she was an interesting conversationalist or had the tiniest bit of intellect. Fashion and beauty were what most of them cared about. Like those things mattered to men. Maybe he was being unfair by setting his expectations too high.

Rogers poked his head into the parlor. "Carriage approaching, milady."

Every nerve in Lamar's body tightened. Time to be companionable.

Soon enough the front door opened and low voices filtered into the room.

Grandmama pinned him with a stern look and spoke softly so her words wouldn't carry outside the room. "Smile, Lamar. How can you ever catch a lady with a scowl? You don't want to scare her off."

Maybe he did, but he hadn't realized he'd been scowling. He flashed his best smile. "I will be ever the gentleman."

"That's better."

An impeccably dressed middle-aged man and woman entered with a younger lady lingering behind them.

Rogers announced them. "Mr. and Mrs. Armstrong and their daughter."

Lamar crossed the room and greeted them. "Welcome. I'm Lamar Kesner." Then he indicated his grandmother. "May I present Mrs. Henry Kesner?"

Mr. Armstrong dipped his head. "We are honored to be welcomed in your home."

Behind them stood their daughter with dark locks cascading over her shoulder. She appeared older than he'd anticipated. He'd assumed she would be around eighteen to twenty. This young woman was likely in her early to mid-twenties, only four or five years younger than himself. Why wasn't she married yet?

Lamar tried to assess what kind of person she was but wouldn't be able to tell until he interacted with her. Grandmama hadn't exaggerated her physical appeal. But was there anything more to her? Or did she hope to catch a husband by looks alone? "Who is this raven-haired beauty?" This was how the game was played.

"Our daughter Cordelia Armstrong."

The young lady gave a coquettish smile and lifted her hand to him.

He took her offered hand and bowed over it. "It is a pleasure to make your acquaintance."

She giggled.

Please, not a giggler. It grated on him when young ladies giggled for no apparent reason. Nerves he supposed.

She gazed up at him with that same starry-eyed expression he'd seen so many times before and fended off. Of course, she came from money, had the right breeding, and had no doubt been trained in the finest finishing schools money could buy. And she had the quality Grandmama thought he valued most—beauty—like the previous dozen proper young ladies she'd tried to foist on him.

Was there anything intriguing in Miss Armstrong's pretty little head with which he could hold even the briefest of conversations? All that social convention required of the woman he married was to behave appropriately for *his* station and to give him children, but he wanted more than a mother to his heirs. A woman with whom he could have decent conversations about things of the world. Someone who could form her own opinions.

He had met a few captivating ladies of breeding. He'd shown a passing fascination with Isabelle Atwood—now Dawson. She rode a bicycle and didn't let convention tell her how to behave. Then there was Nicole Waterby—now Keegan—who came to town in buckskins and could shoot as well as any man. Talk about unconventional. Last but not least, Geneviève Marseille—soon to be Gladwell. A French socialite who traveled halfway around the globe and discovered her American roots.

Three unique ladies who could have held his attention, but each of their hearts belonged to another. Three fortunate men. To have a woman like one of them give him their love would be wonderful, but maybe he wasn't destined to have love. If he couldn't have love, did he even want to bother with a wife?

Keeping her hand in his, he guided her to the settee in the parlor. "Please have a seat."

She did and continued to stare up at him.

Then giggled.

This was destined to be a long visit. Lamar resumed his stance at the fireplace. If he removed himself from the center of the people, maybe they would forget to include him in the conversation.

After an exchange of a few pleasantries, Grandmama directed a question to Miss Armstrong. "How do you like Kamola so far?"

"You have a quaint little town here, but I haven't seen much of it. Only from the train station to the Atwood Hotel and then here. I would love to see more of it."

"That's a wonderful idea." Grandmama smiled and shifted her attention to him. "Lamar, show Miss Armstrong Kamola. Drive her all around."

Mr. and Mrs. Armstrong nodded their approval, and Mr. Armstrong answered for his daughter. "Cordelia would be honored to have you escort her."

"Oh, I would." Miss Armstrong gazed at him expectantly, blinking.

Lamar was outnumbered. Apparently, the young woman's parents were as eager to make a match as Grandmama. *Trapped alone with the giggling girl in a buggy?* He would rather stay here where there were others to help carry a conversation. What acceptable excuse could he offer? "It would be my pleasure."

Grandmama addressed Rogers. "Have the stable hitch a conveyance. Preferably an open-air one. It's a pleasant summer day."

Perhaps Miss Armstrong was, in some way, unmarriageable. A simpleminded person?

All too soon, Lamar sat in the buggy next to the young lady. Hopefully, this wouldn't be as bad as he anticipated.

"Mr. Kesner, tell me *all* about your town."

He would rather not. "Please call me Lamar."

Her eyes widened. "Are you sure? That's not proper."

"I'm quite sure." If she conceded, it would give him a better idea of the kind of person she was.

She bit her bottom lip. "If you insist...*Lamar.*" She giggled.

Mercy. Time spent with this young woman was going to be tedious. At least she had agreed to use his first name.

She gave him a sly smile and spoke in a small, almost childlike voice. "I don't think my parents would approve, so I can only use your Christian name when it's just the two of us. It will be our little secret."

Very tedious. How could he convince Grandmama that Miss Armstrong was not a suitable candidate?

"Does that mean you will call me Cordelia?"

"If you'll allow me the privilege."

"I think I might like that."

That was a positive in her favor. "I am honored, Cordelia."

She giggled. "I've never had a gentleman use my first name before."

A part of Lamar inwardly cringed at her tittering, while another suddenly felt bad for thinking poorly of this lady. She was sweet. There were much worse socialites to have to spend the rest of his life with. She wouldn't be near the equal partner he hoped for, but she did seem to need someone to look after her. He would hate for some cad to take advantage of her. Was concern for her well-being enough to build a relationship on? Enough to entertain the idea of courting? No. He could easily see she would not make a suitable lifelong match for him. The question was, how to convince Grandmama of that.

Cordelia batted her eyelashes at him. "What do you like to do in your free time?"

Grandmama had cautioned him against discussing his hot air balloon hobby to potential marriage candidates. How could Lamar skirt her question? In his experience, women didn't like men to have frivolous vices. If this one became too much of a nuisance, he would show her exactly how frivolous he could be.

She whipped her head to the side. "Is that a college?"

That was a fast change in subjects and spared him from answering her previous question. "Washington State Normal School. They train teachers. Did you attend a college or university?" He could guess at her answer.

"Me? Oh, no. I did go to Mrs. Patterson's School for Girls and learned about proper behavior for a lady. Or at least they tried to teach me all of it. There was so much, I couldn't remember everything."

No interesting conversations happening on this buggy ride. "Have you ever wanted to go to college?"

She tilted her head toward him and hesitated a moment before answering. "Oh, I'm not smart enough for anything like that."

Apparently, nothing but silly lady musings going on in her head. Yet something in her eyes said, if given the chance she could do more.

She glanced away almost shyly then pointed. "Is that a dressmaker's establishment?"

He glanced at *Mademoiselle* Dumont's shop. "It is."

"May I go?"

"Wouldn't you rather go with your mother and my grandmother?"

She widened her doe-brown eyes on him and batted her lashes. "Please. You don't have to come in. You can go wherever you want and return later."

Grandmama would skin him alive if he abandoned their guest on an outing, but it would give him a break from this vapid débutante. "It would have to be another one of our little secrets."

"Oh, yes." She put her index finger to her rosy lips. "*Shhh*, our secret."

He redirected the carriage and parked in front of the establishment. He got out, rounded the vehicle, and helped her down with an offered hand.

Her voluminous dress or foot caught on something, and she tumbled into him. He clasped her in his arms. She fit nicely. Their gazes locked for a long moment. He was surprised to find he liked having her in his arms.

"Oops. I guess I'm clumsy today. Thank you for rescuing me."

He'd hardly rescued her, but he had kept her from a nasty spill. "Shall I escort you inside?"

She stepped from his embrace and placed a gloved hand on the front of his jacket. "You don't need to do that."

He resisted the urge to take hold of her hand. "How long do you think you'll be? Would an hour be enough? Or two?" He hoped two.

"I could look at clothes all day."

Of course, she could. What woman couldn't?

"Would three be all right?"

That would be wonderful. "I'll return in three hours."

She gave him an impish smile, spun with a flourish, and entered the dressmaker's.

He stared after her but caught himself. "Stop it, man. She's nothing but another silly socialite."

Though holding any kind of meaningful intelligent conversation with this woman would be out of the question, he found her mildly intriguing. Something in her twinkly brown gaze said there was more to this lady than what met the eye.

Or was that merely wishful hoping on his part?

A bell over the door of the dressmaker's shop jingled as Cordelia Armstrong entered. She had hoped for a silent arrival so she could depart in the same manner, unnoticed. That would not be the case.

A stylish woman of about thirty descended upon her position.

Cordelia glanced over her shoulder and wiggled her fingers at Lamar Kesner. She hoped he didn't plan to stand there for long, or worse, decide to come inside.

The woman stopped in front of her and spoke with a French accent. "Good afternoon. I am *Mademoiselle* Celeste Dumont. What may I help you with? I see by your dress that you have very good taste in fashion."

Cordelia's parents had seen to that. Nothing but the best. "I simply wanted to pop in and take a look around." She glanced out the window.

Though still watching her, Mr. Kesner—or rather Lamar—rounded his carriage and climbed aboard. He touched the brim of his hat and put the horse into motion.

Cordelia heaved a sigh of relief. She hadn't known how much longer she could keep up the feeble, meaningless conversation. It wasn't easy talking about worthless nonsense. She'd almost put her foot in it by mentioning the college. Fashion was always a good option, as it was expected of ladies and men shunned the topic.

She retrained her attention on *Mademoiselle* Dumont and continued her witless act. "I'm not planning to purchase anything today. I merely wanted to see what you have. Is that all right?"

"Of course. I have books with my original designs in the sitting area if you are interested in viewing them."

No, that would take too much time. "Thank you. I'll start here. You have so many beautiful things." She pointed to the rack of trims. "I just love lace. I don't think a gown can have too much."

"Any piece of fashion adornment can be overdone, but there are ways to manage it without it being tasteless."

Lamar Kesner had driven out of sight.

"Thank you for letting me look around. I'll bring my mother to help me choose something." Cordelia opened the door. "*Au revoir.*" She dashed out before the proprietress could delay her.

A glance both directions along the street assured her Mr. Kesner had indeed left.

www.ingramcontent.com/pod-product-compliance
Lightning Source LLC
Chambersburg PA
CBHW061610190726

48288CB00007B/2256